PRAISE FOR COURT STEVENS

"*We Were Kings* is the best kind of mystery novel—intelligent and bursting with heart. As Nyla untangled her family's secrets, the twists left me breathless."

—BRITTANY CAVALLARO,
NEW YORK TIMES BESTSELLING AUTHOR

"Bingeable. Atmospheric. A book that grabs hold and doesn't let go. As a lifelong fan of suspense novels, I found *We Were Kings* brilliantly fresh while also saturated with a classic feel. A Nancy Drew for modern audiences."

—CAROLINE GEORGE, AUTHOR OF *THE SUMMER WE FORGOT*

"The final reveal is surprising and chilling."

—*KIRKUS* FOR *THE JUNE BOYS*

"Stevens takes a good swing at resolving lost faith and trust while trying to rebuild the strengths and bonds of family and friends."

—*PUBLISHERS WEEKLY* FOR *THE JUNE BOYS*

"Tense and haunting, *The June Boys* is not only a terrifying story of the missing, but a heartbreaking, hopeful journey through the darkness. Beautifully written and sharply plotted, this is a story that lingers long after you turn the final page."

—MEGAN MIRANDA, *NEW YORK TIMES* BESTSELLING AUTHOR
OF *ALL THE MISSING GIRLS* AND *THE LAST HOUSE GUEST*

"Masterfully plotted with stunning twists and turns. Hang on tight, *The June Boys* is a fantastically crafted suspense that keeps you guessing until the last page!"

—RUTA SEPETYS, INTERNATIONAL BESTSELLING AUTHOR

"*The June Boys* by Court Stevens is a gripping suspense that hooked me from the first sentence. Fabulous characterization and a layered plot with tension that escalated with every page. Highly recommended!"

"I just finished *The June Boys*, and I loved it. The feeling of the intensity of friendship at that age, the tension of the chase to find Welder, all the twists to get to who it was—I was hooked and couldn't stop reading. I wanted to cry with Aulus every time I read his letters and felt that Thea was that friend everyone needs. Though flawed, she is devoted to her friends with a ferocity that I loved."

WE
WERE
KINGS

ALSO BY COURT STEVENS

The June Boys
Four Three Two One
Dress Codes for Small Towns
The Lies About Truth
The Blue-Haired Boy
Faking Normal

WE WERE KINGS

COURT STEVENS

THOMAS NELSON
Since 1798

We Were Kings

Interior design by Emily Ghattas

Published in Nashville, Tennessee, by Thomas Nelson. Thomas Nelson is a registered trademark of HarperCollins Christian Publishing, Inc.

Thomas Nelson titles may be purchased in bulk for educational, business, fundraising, or sales promotional use. For information, please email SpecialMarkets@ThomasNelson.com.

Publisher's Note: This novel is a work of fiction. Names, characters, places, and incidents are either products of the author's imagination or used fictitiously. All characters are fictional, and any similarity to people living or dead is purely coincidental.

Library of Congress Cataloging-in-Publication Data

Names: Stevens, Court, author.
Title: We were Kings / Court Stevens.
Description: Nashville, Tennessee : Thomas Nelson, [2022] | Summary: A twenty-year-old crime, an accelerated death penalty, and an elitist family cover-up forces eighteen-year-old Nyla to race against the death row clock to save her mother's best friend.
Identifiers: LCCN 2021032849 (print) | LCCN 2021032850 (ebook) | ISBN 9780785238485 (hardcover) | ISBN 9780785238478 (epub) | ISBN 9780785238492
Subjects: CYAC: Families--Fiction. | Secrets--Fiction. | Prisoners--Fiction. | Mothers and daughters--Fiction.
Classification: LCC PZ7.1.S74444 We 2022 (print) | LCC PZ7.1.S74444 (ebook) | DDC [Fic]--dc23
LC record available at https://lccn.loc.gov/2021032849
LC ebook record available at https://lccn.loc.gov/2021032850

Printed in the United States of America

22 23 24 25 26 LS

For Dorothy Stevens, my grandmother

Matthew 13:46

PART I

BEFORE

We're waiting to find out if Frankie will be executed. A strange day, to say the least. Frankie's a murderer *and* my mom's best friend. She's why we live in Kentucky, and why we live with Richard, and why the three of us—Mom, Richard, and me—are in the garage. This is where we will be until Jimmy the lawyer's call comes. The garage has the best cell reception and Mom's weight bench.

Mom heaves the sixth rep of two hundred and thirty pounds toward the rafters. Richard presses two fingers against the middle metal bar, totally focused on spotting her. I'm here because there's no way a sixty-nine-year-old man, even one in his condition, can lift that bar off her face if and when she drops it. Also because I have the newest iPad among the three of us and am in charge of social media. There's a chance Vox or the *Herald* or even someone local in the #OpposeADPA group will break the news before

Frankie's lawyer has a chance to get out of the courtroom and call. Word is there will be a verdict today.

Jimmy the lawyer has "high hopes" the appeal will be remanded back into the court and has told Mom not to worry. *"There wasn't enough evidence twenty years ago and there's not enough evidence now."* Plus, the judge is a Democrat who mostly opposes the Accelerated Death Penalty Act.

Mom exhales and shoves the weights upward. Again and again. She crosses ten reps—probably her personal best at this weight. Her face reddens, her veins thick and bulging; her dark hair is sweat-matted to her forehead. She strains words through gritted teeth, the bar at full extension. "If she'd been convicted at any other point in history . . ."

There's no response from Richard, only a brief glance at me. We know the refrain by heart. *"If she'd been convicted at any other point in history, she would not be facing lethal injection."* Or it's not likely she would. Kentucky had a moratorium on executions until recently. Criminals carrying death sentences tended to die of old age in the prison infirmary rather than with the whole country watching and in an uproar.

"Beth, take a rest," Richard urges.

Her elbows lock, the weights hovering in the air.

"We can't lose her," she whispers.

These same words seep from her nightmares. Mom and I share the upstairs Jack and Jill suite of Richard's house,

4

and even when both bathroom doors between us are closed, she wakes me up screaming. *"We can't lose her"* is as constant as a snore.

The nightmares started on June 20 when the Accelerated Death Penalty Act was signed into law. The ADPA promised to save taxpayers thousands of dollars by taking criminals charged with especially heinous and brutal crimes and fast-tracking their executions. No more long appeals taxing the system. No more paying for non-great American citizens to be fed, guarded, and educated indefinitely. Following June 20, inmates on death row had thirty days to present a final appeal and then another thirty days to live if and when the appeal process failed. Across the country, families of victims and inmates are waiting on life-and-death news.

Everyone is wound up. The ADPA is front and center in the media. There are marches, assemblies, opinion pieces. You name a type of campaign and it's happening everywhere, from the streets of New York City to the plains of Wyoming. I want to fast-forward the clock and find out what happens—even if it's bad news. Especially since I don't understand why Mom always says *we*.

"We can't lose her." "We need her." We. We. We.

There's no *we*. Frankie is her childhood best friend, not family, and Richard and I have never even darkened the doors of Floyd Penitentiary.

Mom's strange obsession with Frankie is probably most unfair to Richard. Imagine you're an old dude, feeding cats and working crosswords, and then this woman and her daughter show up at your door. It takes a certain type of hero to keep his word from twenty years ago—*"If you ever need help, I'll be here."* I'm not sure what led him to say that—they're aloof on their origin story—but at this point, I don't care. He's Richard and I love him.

The weights stay poised over her face. Teetering. "Let them drop, Mom," I say.

"You're supposed to be scrolling." Her words rush out with a staccato breath.

"And you're supposed to remember you're not a professional bodybuilder."

Her elbows bend slightly and Richard guides the bar toward the cradle. I think she's done, but her chest bucks upward and with a primal groan she lifts the weights again. Arms quivering, she counts under her breath.

I can't watch anymore so I do as she instructed. The news breaks first on social media. Richard sees me wince and reads my mind. The call comes seconds later. *Jimmy Norton (Attorney)* appears on the screen.

"Answer it," Mom says.

I leap out of my lawn chair, hit Accept on the phone, and hold it to her ear. Richard and I are frozen into our strange positions, each on either side of the barbell, the weights next to our faces as we bend to listen to Jimmy's three words: "Beth, I'm sorry."

The weights clatter to the ground.

CHAPTER 1

I know the story.

In June of 2000, Cora King, the eighteen-year-old daughter of Kentucky senator Rebecca King, went missing from her family's estate on Nockabout Island. Five months later, a local fisherman found what was left of Cora's body. The fish and the lake had stolen nearly everything from her. The medical examiner used her dental records for identification. The investigation centered on three individuals: Frankie Quick, the best friend; Ben Stack, the boyfriend; and Martin Jarvis, a previous boss / love interest who was later discovered to have died on the same day Cora disappeared. The case was automatically high profile.

Authorities landed on Frankie because she had a juvie record for assault (an assault on Martin Jarvis, no less). In the case of the *State v. Francis Quick*, there was no significant DNA evidence, no motive, no witness.

But it didn't matter.

Almost as fast as anyone could type the words *arrested*, *arraigned*, and *convicted*, Francis had a death sentence slapped on her. Everyone knew why: Cora was a senator's daughter.

That's the crux of the Wiki article plus added commentary from Mom.

I was eleven or twelve before I realized not everyone's mother had a best friend in prison. And not everyone's mother refused to travel over the weekend because she'd miss her Saturday visit to the penitentiary. And not everyone's mother funded a convicted felon's legal fees before she paid rent. Not even when I overheard one of the girls in my coding club tell another, "Her mom is friends with a murderer and my mom says I can't go over to her house to play," did it occur to me that Frankie's place in our life was an oddity.

By the time I turned thirteen, I'd done enough googling to consider myself an expert on the case, and that's when I sat Mom down during Richard's bowling night and said, "I get that Frankie probably didn't kill the King girl, and justice is a big deal, but, like, what's your part in this? Why the obsession?"

Mom reached across the table and twisted a lock of my hair around her finger and said, "She's my best friend."

"Yeah, but—"

"Nyla, we don't give up on people when bad things happen. We stick. And we stick when the rest of the world makes up the BS the world makes up. You'll understand when you're older and feel that way about your own friends."

"You're the only one who gets to have friends," I said.

It was an automatic response. A reflex. I didn't even say it with attitude.

I watched my truth register—our countless moves before landing on Richard's doorstep, all the clubs and programs I'd gotten a few weeks into and then had to withdraw from, the constant lunchroom dilemma of where to sit. All in the name of helping Frankie. There were so, so many.

"Oh, Ny, baby. I'm sorry. Someday you'll understand."

"When is someday?" I had asked.

She hadn't answered and I quit caring and did my best to accept that Frankie was the most important person in Mom's life, and that's the way it was.

CHAPTER 2

Mom is in bed. Richard's on the toilet. That leaves me to open the front door to the barrage of knocks.

Two women in heels, linen pants, and silky summer scarfs stand on the stoop. They're eager and hopeful in their perfect eyeliner and lash extensions. The square logo magnets on their cars identify two local news stations. One extends a microphone toward me; the other touches a button on the camera hiked over her dainty shoulder. "We're looking for Elizabeth King."

"I'm sorry, who?" I ask.

"This is the address of Elizabeth King, yes?" the blonde microphone girl asks.

"No," I say, not fully registering the question.

The camerawoman consults her notepad. "She goes by Wagner now. Beth Wagner."

I can't sync up truths and lies fast enough to convey

verbal responses or proper emotions. The instinct to yell, "Mom!" toward the upstairs bedroom is nearly overwhelming, but these women keep pounding me.

"Are you a member of the King family?"

"We'd love to interview Beth about the ADPA decision to execute Francis Quick for the murder of her sister, Cora."

"Is Beth home and available to speak to us?"

Her sister, Cora? Elizabeth King, not Wagner? Anger flares red to a bright blue and I almost slam the door. I gather my wits. "No comment." I step backward and collide with Richard. He reaches past me, grips the knob firmly, and gestures to the reporters that he will close the door whether they're in the way or not. They move. The blonde's voice comes through the crack. "We'll leave our cards in the mailbox."

Back against the door, I face Richard.

"Nyla," he says.

If I had any doubts about what the woman said, they crumbled with Richard's use of my name. From day one, Richard has called me Lion or the Lion King Kid. "It's Ny-la, not Nala," I'd respond, mildly annoyed, until the verbal routine grew into our unique, quasi-grandfather love language.

This is a different tone, far more fearful.

"Richard," I say.

He stands, head bowed, no longer the man who strongarmed the door closed. He feels the singular question: *Is*

Mom Cora's sister? And perhaps he feels the follow-up: *Did you know?*

He wears a gentleman's cap and a bathrobe over swimming trunks he claims are more comfortable than anything else he owns. Patchy gray hairs poke from the top of the terry cloth, and wrinkled skin gathers prune-like around his collarbone. He won't meet my eyes.

Which I interpret as *Yes, she is* and *Yes, I did.*

"Gotcha," I say.

Richard is many things. A retired social worker, a Vietnam vet, a man who walks his cat on a leash. His house, our house, is pink on the street-facing side, the garage another glaring shade pinker; the orchidaceous paint job is a leftover gift from his ex-wife. He is enigmatic, kind, and probably my favorite person in the world. That he was capable of keeping this secret makes angry tears well up, but when he hugs me, I let him. His is the lie of a puppet, and I'd rather ream the puppeteer.

"Mom!" I raise my voice, hoping to rouse her. No response. I yell again at the top of the steps and again when I'm standing in front of her bedroom door. Nothing. I don't waste time knocking; I pry my way inside.

Upturned plastic crates and their contents cover the carpet. Stuff is everywhere, a messy nest for the mouse curled into the middle of the bed. The condition of the room gives me pause. Mom is a minimalist and compartmentalist by nature. Before the ADPA, much of her life stayed wedged into labeled twelve-by-twelve crates. "Mom," I say again.

A groggy voice comes from beneath the covers. "I'm sleeping."

I rip layer by layer away until she is exposed.

I catch myself staring at her form. The woman before me is embarrassingly fit. These muscles are the rewards of protein shakes and wrist and ankle weights and a home gym makeover. I overheard a landlord call our last rental termination "The end of the Elizabeastan Era." Lying here like this—pitiful and small and unwashed—is the ultimate antithesis of my mother.

She shields her eyes against the light. "Where's Richard? What time is it?"

She means, *What day is it?*

Three days have passed since we got the news about Frankie and she hasn't been out of the room except to pee. All food has been refused. Richard and I think she is drinking from the bathroom faucet. At all hours of the night, she rifles through things and listens to newsreels and videos about outcomes in the death penalty cases across the country.

Behind me, Richard climbs the steps in his careful one-step-at-a-time cadence. I am not sure whose side he will take when he reaches the top.

"Mom, you need to sit up and talk to me." I smooth the skin on my forehead with the palm of my hand, all of a sudden unsure if she can handle my anger atop her grief.

"Why?" she asks, pulling several layers of covers back over her body.

She's sinking into herself and I'm tempted to let her. But the size of the lie drives me mercilessly forward. I tear the covers away and toss them onto the floor. Suddenly she's on her knees and reaching for the covers like a teenager in a pillow fight. "I asked you to leave me alone for a few days. *Bless.*" Her knuckles grow white as she clenches the fabric. "And I never ask either of you for anything. *Bless.*" I reach for the sheet and end up on the floor; she's back on the bed under her pile of cotton with only two eyes and wild, oily hair visible, like she's Oscar in his garbage can. "Why is that hard? *Bless.*"

Bless is the F-word of her curses.

I force myself to stand.

I curl my fingernails into the skin of my palms until the skin breaks.

I speak in a measured, calculated voice. "There are reporters at the door asking for Elizabeth King. Should I tell them you'll be down now, or do you need a few more weeks to wallow in your lies?"

CHAPTER 3

W hat comes out of Mom's mouth can't be classified as a scream, cry, or yell. There's not a word that's guttural enough to convey the sound she makes, but there is one to describe her afterward: *unhinged*. Crates take flight. Drywall is damaged. Feathers are ripped from her pillows. She fights an opponent Richard and I can't see. I watch momentarily but I'm suffocated by her emotions.

Closing the door, I retreat to the kitchen. I need to get out of the house and think. Richard grips my forearm as I nick the keys to his car. "Get angry, not stupid, please? I can't fix this if you kill yourself driving like an idiot."

I nod and leave the house.

The street is empty and there's a full tank of gas in the Honda. I don't know where I should go, but I can't stay here. Not when I'm this angry. I'll hurt her rather than help me. I have a smidge of information and I need buckets and buckets of truth.

Windows down, moonroof open, a summer breeze tosses my hair around the edges of my shoulders as I exit the neighborhood. I need to drive at very illegal speeds, but my promise to Richard tempers my lead foot. I take the parkway ramp, knowing it'll be empty. As I drive, I can feel all my involuntary organs begging for attention. My lungs are tight. When I swallow, the taste is thick and bitter. Everything tingles during little aftershocks. I pound my fist against the wheel and on the second strike there's a stabbing pain in my finger.

I pull the Honda across the rumble strip and park on the shoulder to assess the pain. The finger's probably not broken, but the punch shattered my mother's sapphire and diamond ring. Part of the setting landed on the back seat; another is stuck in the carpet by the rear lift door. Two tiny diamonds are missing, their prongs bent. The white gold band is split where it was once sized.

We have been ejected from apartments, eaten beans and rice for weeks, and hawked nearly everything of value at one time or other over the years—but the ring and its matching earrings have never been on the chopping block. The earrings were from her father; the ring, a birthday gift from her granny.

I hold the remaining pieces in my palm.

I love the ring.

I loved what I thought it meant to my mother and that it was something she passed down to me.

That's when I cry.

CHAPTER 4

I don't feel better when I stop crying; I merely run out of tears.

I want a rationale for why she lied.

The trouble with liars: *their* word can't set the story straight. Richard has been in our lives for four years. I need someone from twenty years ago, but we have no twenty-year friends, other than Frankie, and I'm not keen on being toe to toe with a felon. Even if I got up the guts to ask her questions, I am fairly sure Floyd has set visiting hours, and who knows what Frankie's new ADPA timeline did to her privileges. There could be more leniency, could be less.

My foot is heavier than the advised maximum speed and I blare Kelis (at a decibel that will likely result in a visit to an audiologist someday) and search for an answer. At ninety-five miles per hour I think not of a solution but of a possibility.

Mom didn't keep a person over the last twenty years. She kept an object. Her granny's ring. Not Beth Wagner's granny. Elizabeth King's granny. For once, being versed in Frankie's story helps me. Cassandra King. She's my starting place.

I type Nockabout into the GPS app. An address for *The Center, 414 Circle Dr., Nockabout Island, KY* pops up. I set the destination while the app adds a note about varying ferry schedules. I'll handle the ferry problem when I get there.

Waze routes should carry me through the small town of Columbia, which I discover is only forty-eight miles away. Nockabout's another twenty from there. Mom ran away from home, but she didn't run far. The Pilot is old enough there's no auxiliary cable. Worn out on rage-y music, I opt for the radio. Scan lands me near the lower 80s of the FM dial and a talk radio broadcast.

The DJ says, "Well, unless new evidence is found. Which, in the case of Francis Quick, would be unusual. This case isn't cold, people, it's frozen in twenty years of captivity and an assumption that the justice system is flawless. But what if the system failed Francis Quick? Isn't that a question worth asking before the ADPA saves us all a buck? Certainly a question I would want asked if it were me in the hot seat. And, friends, it could have been. I'm a Lone Valley boy myself. I worked summers at the Green River Marina, took a tour of the Center like every other high schooler in the county, and I knew the Kings. Not well. But well enough. I never believed Francis Quick beat up Martin Jarvis, and I certainly don't believe she killed Cora King."

The minute I have enough signal to Google, I pull off the highway for a refresher on Nockabout. After minimal searches, I learn how to place Nockabout Island on the Kentucky map by locating the townlet of Lone Valley, nestled directly against the southern edge of Green River State Park, and then finding the speck of land parallel to Lone Valley's snaking shoreline. The lake stretches out like an elongated Chinese dragon, and Lone Valley sits midway along the underbelly. Google says it's home to 531 people.

An out-of-commission railroad bridge comes up in Google images when you enter Nockabout Island or Lone Valley, and every article that mentions the townlet or the island ends up as a story about Cora King or its well-respected methamphetamine recovery clinic called the Center (where I'm routing to) or a mine that shut down in the fifties. Some local personality had quipped, "We're known for murderers, miners, and addicts." According to the Wiki page, the mine is the wealth behind the King family.

The King family.

My family.

What led to Mom's excision? Is this the road she left on? Did she steal a car, drain her bank account, tell off her father, get kicked out? In my anger at being lied to, I've almost lost the primary thread of the story.

Her sister was murdered.

I don't have any siblings or dear friends. I lived elementary and middle school between clumps of fellow students, and then in high school I migrated between special interest clumps and proximity clumps—girls I ran with, kids in that one youth group, a guy three doors down from an old apartment, seniors who don't have their own cars and ride the bus. None of them felt worth keeping after I graduated; they were barely even worth Instagram selfies.

Mom's the closest thing to a best friend I've ever had. And yeah, I'm second to Frankie, but being second to someone who's never around isn't all bad. I never watch Mom choose Frankie over me. There are none of those high-stakes movie scenarios where Mom can save only one of us. Until this morning, being threatened by Frankie was a little bit like being threatened by Ozzy Osbourne. You know it's creepy, but creepy's not all up in your space.

Now I feel properly displaced.

Rattled in a way that makes me understand how Mom might have felt twenty years ago when she threw a suitcase in a car and left home for good. Like she'd swallowed a snake that slithered and stretched until its fangs sank deep in her heart and its rattling tail banged inside her brain. You want to put it behind you, but you can't because it's inside you.

What I thought I knew of Mom's childhood was already limited. In the previous narrative, her parents died before I arrived on the scene. She'd grown up across the Ohio River in Tell City, Indiana, her dad a cop, her mom a phone operator at a trucking company. During late elementary school, they moved over to Kentucky and eventually to Lone Valley. In Mom's stories, college was the beginning of her life. I'd asked about kid things, of course— Did she like Happy Meals when she was my age? Did she sled when it snowed? Is granny bread called granny bread for a reason?—and she'd given roundabout answers that painted a thin, watery picture that might have belonged to anyone. By the time I was thirteen, nothing came of my probing except a heavily poured glass of wine, a long shower, and the Indigo Girls blaring beneath her bedroom door.

That was the most she talked about her parents.

Whose story was that? Some college roommate's?

She occasionally referenced Nockabout. More as Frankie's hometown than her own. Lying in the park, after we'd been evicted and before we moved in with Richard, I asked, "Mom, what about Nockabout? Couldn't we go there?" (I hadn't asked about my father's town because she'd told me from an early age, in no uncertain terms, that he was not and would not ever be part of our lives.)

"Oh gosh. Nockabout's beautiful, Ny. Simple. But beautiful. There are places in the state park that'll take your breath away, and I swear I've had to honk the horn to force the deer off the road. I'll bet I skipped a thousand rocks on the lake."

She'd sounded wistful.

"Let's go," I'd said, wondering where we might land for the night.

She had sighed and said, "I can't go back there."

There was no further explanation. She'd kindly asked me not to push—and while that had seemed deeply unfair, given the circumstances of us needing a place to sleep, I gave her space. Now I wish I hadn't.

CHAPTER 5

Richard rings as I'm passing a Walmart Supercenter in Columbia. His raised voice rockets through the receiver. "Where are you, Lion?" The next words are spoken through gritted teeth. "She's a blubbering mess."

"Good for her," I say.

"You've got a right to be furious, but I need ya."

"Thanks for the permission," I snap and then apologize. "Look, I'm almost to Nockabout. I'll be back tonight, but I need to get my head around this."

"Bad idea, Lion."

"Want to tell me why?"

"Nope."

Even from seventy miles away, I can see the canary's feathers poking out his mouth.

"Richard, don't take this the wrong way, but I don't care whether it's good or bad; it's the only idea I can stomach right now. Just handle her until I get back. Please."

"See you tonight." He's asking and also telling.

His fatherly tone makes me ache with thankfulness. Humans are supposed to be born to two people who love them, and instead we are born and love is a roll of the dice. At least I've rolled sixes in Richard.

CHAPTER 6

When I pictured the Nockabout Island Ferry, I imagined something far grander than its reality: a road ending in a graded ramp and a parking lot filled with broken concrete, weeds, and your basic small-town outdoor shopping strip. At the water's edge sits a floating shack with an aging sign about ferry services. Two round-trip routes during weekdays, three on Saturday, none for Sunday. Each trip is a dollar without a car and five dollars with. The little barge rocks in the water, its security chain clanking against the bow. I park, slide out of the sticky leather of the Honda, and stretch in the noonday heat.

Six fishing boats putter between our shore, the opposite shore, and what I can only assume is Nockabout. The island is smaller and closer than I expected. This town doesn't need a ferry; they need swimsuits. Or maybe a ramp and the *General Lee*.

The sun is high and orange, the sky swirling cotton-candy clouds across a bright blue horizon. Green River Lake is slicker than oil and prismed with a thousand diamond sparks. My mother didn't oversell the view; this sight is the epitome of craggy beauty that every Kentucky waterway seems to possess.

Unfortunately, the ferry is closed for another three hours. Someone has nailed a newly hand-painted, misspelled wooden sign to one of the dock posts: *Murder doesn't need your spectatership*. Evidently the press around the ADPA has brought renewed interest in the island's murderous history.

Up the hill, the three businesses in the shopping strip—Ned's Fine Jewelry and Pawn, Cecilee's Scissors: Dog Groomer Extraordinare, and Mary's Bait and Tackle—are hopping. While I'm debating who to speak with first, a young driver abandons her Chevy Equinox, engine running, and heads into Cecilee's with a dog under her arm. The simplicity makes me smile and, in a way, communicates more about Lone Valley than anything on Google ever could.

Three more cars glide down the hill and into spots near the ferry. Trying to avoid the appearance of a "spectater," I wing a flat stone across the surface and then another and another. Nearby, horns beep and a speedboat driver cheers at my next rock's ten skips.

"Hey," someone yells from the parking lot. "Hey, you." I turn around and a woman waves me to her car. She looks normal enough. When I'm closer, she lowers her voice and asks, "Is this where the tour starts?"

"Tour?"

"The murder tour," she mouths. She looks through me, searching for something unseen. "The guy said to meet at the dock near the spectator sign. That's it, misspelled and all. But he said it was a group. I don't want to take my girls on a murder tour alone with a strange man." The older of her two girls bends low enough in the passenger seat to gaze up at me and wave. One of her long braids falls into a cup of water in the center console. She notices and sucks the liquid out of her hair.

"Right, the murder tour," I say, even though she clearly wants to keep it on the DL.

I'm overheard. A guy with a man bun waves at us. "I'm here for that too. I only have a check. You think he'll take that?"

The woman looks doubtful and holds up three fifty-dollar bills. "We're not taking any chances, are we, girls?"

I'm not sure what sort of schmuck runs a murder tour in a place like this, but I'm hedging my bets that he'll tell me about Granny King. I play along, hoping I don't need fifty dollars, because the only things in the Honda are a couple of plastic gas station mugs and Burt's Bees lip balm.

In the time it takes me to skip a second rock ten times, a small passenger boat docks and one more car arrives. No one exits their air-conditioned heavens until the guy in the boat, who is carrying a honey-colored puppy under one arm and a yellow plastic sack in the other, leans against the "spectater" sign. The dog squirms and the guy kisses the wrinkle on her Lab-mix forehead before releasing her to run. She comes to me, sniffing, and I hear the guy calling roll. "Linda? Emily? Parson?"

The two girls with Linda make a total of five tourists. The guy looks over toward me and gives me a bro nod I take to mean that I'm welcome to join if I'm interested and have fifty dollars.

He says to the group, "I need to run my pup, Lucy, up to the hill to Ned and then you'll have my full attention." He sees the dog at my feet, strides over, leans into my ear, and says, "Act like my assistant and you can tag along for free."

I've never been hit on in a way I could confidently think, *I'm being hit on*, until now. Given the emotions of the day, I'm too whiplashed to enjoy it, even on a small level. And I feel shallow that I'm willing to use his attraction to get my answers, but then again, he's charging fifty bucks a pop for a murder tour.

When he returns, he huddles the group on the shore. "Don't be shy. You're in the right place. My name's Sam," he says. "Looks like everyone brought a life jacket." They're all wearing theirs and carrying cameras and iPhones in waterproof sleeves. Sam lifts an orange life preserver out of the boat and tosses it at me. "Got yours right here."

"Thanks," I say.

I need a ride to the island. I need information. And boom, up turns this strong-jawed, sun-kissed, dog-loving type. Who am I to look a gift horse in the mouth?

I note my co-tourists as we share first names with each other.

A middle-aged woman with bottle-colored red hair and wellies to match. Emily.

Then Man Bun. Parson. Twenty-five or so, wearing a vintage AC/DC T-shirt, khaki shorts, flip-flops, and a shark tooth necklace (which I really hope is sentimental rather than a fashion statement).

The remaining three: the mother, Linda, and her two daughters, one sixteenish, Ruth, and one eleven or twelve, Naomi. The threesome are painfully alike. Each has two brown braids that hang below their butts, straight black skirts that hit mid-calf, and Vans sneakers. All three have their iPhones out. Teen Braids faces Sam, likely recording him; Tween Braids takes a selfie with the group behind them. I feel the potential hashtags in her body language. #nockaboutisland #murdertour #thisiswhereithappened. The mom takes a picture of the "spectater" sign and smiles like a kid drinking sugar by the gallon.

Sam stands directly in front of his boat and addresses the crowd in a more formal voice. "As promised in the tour description, over the next two hours you will see firsthand the cabin where Cora and Francis hung out, along with Cora's sister, Elizabeth." It might be my imagination, but Sam pauses and looks at me—even though there is no way he knows who I am—before he continues. "From there, you'll be able to see the exterior of the King houses and property—"

I raise my hand and take a risk. "Will the grandmother be around today?"

"Yeah, we might catch a glimpse of Cassandra on her deck. Then we'll head down to the beach to examine where the body of Cora King was discovered, and finally, up the hill to Frankie's Camaro, which contains Cora's blood, the one piece of real evidence used against Francis Quick in the trial. Now, are you ready to get the real story?"

I touch the tiny scab on my middle finger where Granny Cassandra's ring lived and then I settle myself in Sam's boat.

CHAPTER 7

The aluminum-bottomed boat protests our weight and scrapes against the rocks and mud of the lake bed as Sam drags the tour lakeward. The muscles in his arms and stomach are taut—not in a way that suggests he works out, but in a way that says he works hard. Using perfect balance, he climbs aboard, shoves the paddle into the mud, and pushes off into deeper waters. He sits next to me at the stern, near enough to drop and crank the outboard motor and send us skimming toward Nockabout Island. Our thighs touch and I realize it has been a long time since someone my age has made contact with my skin.

"Do I know you?" he asks.

"I don't think so."

He's snapping his fingers, like he might call my name.

"I promise. This is my first visit to Nockabout."

"Okay," he says, disappointed.

Dragonflies skim and dive-bomb while a horde of gnats makes micro ripples. I am riding through a collage of nature: aquamarine water, Carolina Blue sky, gray clouds that look like dirty pillow stuffing. The greens—juniper, fern, chartreuse—steal empty pieces of the horizon. These trees, some full, some dead, create a kaleidoscope on the water. Everywhere I've previously laid eyes feels like a kindergarten sketch next to a Picasso. Mist kicks up from the boat's movement, and I smell the life that lives beneath the surface too.

Totally surreal.

This was my mother's home.

The rattle in my head returns; the fangs sink deeper and deeper as we near Nockabout's shore. Sam guns the motor across the last of the open waterway and then coasts into an island dock with fifteen slips. "Welcome to Nockabout Island. Home of miners, addicts, and murderers."

Maybe he and the radio DJ attended the same "Capitalizing on Local Tragedies" webinar. Or maybe this is what happens naturally when your tiny town is in the news.

When our tour reaches the place where the lake footpath meets the road coming up from the dock, Sam says, "This is Circle Drive. An unfitting title since it doesn't make a whole circle anymore. A rockslide took out a section near the mine years ago. Basically, if you're standing here at the docks, houses are all to the left and the Center's property is to the right." He points toward a large gated entryway and billboard that reads, *Island Behavioral Health Crisis Center: The privacy and professionals your family needs to heal.*

The font and branding are modern and properly medical. Beneath is a brass and bronze historical marker identifying the previous site and grounds of Wassily Sanitorium, a hospital dedicated to healing the white plague, tuberculosis.

"The building's awesome," Sam says.

Man Bun says, "Can we take a picture of the sanitorium before we start?"

The group agrees to the photo op. Sam leads us through the gate and far enough up the private drive to catch a view of the hulking half-hexagon hospital. Four stories high with a bell tower rising from the middle. The architecture is from the 1800s, right down to the gargoyles perched along the battlements and roof gutters. Building-wide solarium porches with large silver-tinted windows cover the front-facing walls. The mix of old and new makes the hospital appear almost hotel-like. Nurses cluster on the flat roof, their cigarettes sending out tiny puffs of gray.

Mom Braids says, "Girls, remember what I said about tuberculosis hospitals? They often functioned like small towns: no one in or out."

"That's about right," Sam says. "There's a complex behind the main building that butts up to the hillside of the mining property. And right over there"—he indicates somewhere out of view near the lakeshore—"is where the body tunnel comes out."

"The body tunnel? Right! I read about that." Man Bun

slicks flyaway hairs under his ponytail holder. He habitually tinkers with his earlobe. "So cool."

The woman with red wellies either already knows the Center is historic or prefers that Sam get on with the tour.

Sam says, "The guy that built the hospital also had the foresight to build the body tunnel. It's about a half mile long and runs between the hospital and the railroad so all the sick people wouldn't notice the coffins rolling out of here. The hospital cut a deal with the King family mining company to transport the bodies off the island. That's really what got Creed Senior interested in medicine."

"A lot of people died here," Tween Braids says. She sounds oddly excited by the idea.

"At least twelve thousand, according to the records Dr. Creed King Senior found when he bought the place."

"Twelve thousand and one," Teen Braids whispers to her sister. "His granddaughter. *Dun dun dunn.*"

My aunt is the *dun dun dunn* of a murder joke.

We return to Circle Drive and set off in the opposite direction. Near the dock, six or seven ranch houses have been built in a cul-de-sac cluster. They all appear occupied. Garden flags and flowers. Fresh mint and cilantro plants. I wonder if they are the homes of doctors or nurses. What else would make someone build a house this isolated?

Sam chatters away in his tour voice as we walk. "Now, during the time of the crime, the Center was in transition. Creed King Junior was officially taking over from Creed King Senior."

34

"Right, we read this on the internet," Tween Braids says, annoyed. "Where did Frankie and Cora meet? How did they all become friends? How badly did Frankie beat that Martin Jarvis dude? Mom said you knew things no one else does."

The mother face-palms at her youngest's impatience and shrugs at the group as if to say, *Who can control them once they learn to talk?* But, like her daughter, she leans into the conversation a little harder when Sam says, "I do know things."

Everyone walks a little slower as Sam talks.

"Frankie and Cora met in the nursery class of Wheelcreek Baptist, a speck of a church not far out of Lone Valley. My dad, Benjamin Stack, is the same Ben Stack who was dating Cora King prior to her disappearance." A satisfied sigh circles the five paying tour members, and Teen Braids jabs Tween with frustration for not understanding how important Sam is, even though she clearly didn't know either.

"Right," Sam continues. "My dad grew up in Sunday school with the Kings. I've included directions to the church in your packet, if you'd like to venture that way after the tour. We'll get to those other questions in time. But now I'll show you the cabin where they stayed that fateful summer."

"When do we get to see where she died?" Tween Braids asks, sounding annoyed by the copious backstory. Her mother and sister shush her with elbows to her ribs.

"After the cabin," Sam says.

Although his tone is polite, he doesn't totally manage to remove his annoyance. Fifty bucks an hour to deal with Tween Braids is barely breaking even.

"Is it a long walk?" asks Emily. She's plum-shaped and sweating profusely. Her wellies squeak with every wobble she takes.

"No."

Man Bun pipes up next. "And we'll be able to, like, take all the photos we want?"

Sam answers their logistical questions and directs us toward a lane that wraps around behind the Center.

Red Wellies asks, "No part of the mine works, correct? I read about diamonds. Do you know about those?"

"Diamonds . . . hmm." Sam has an extraordinarily kind face. You can tell he's spent a disproportionate amount of life smiling, and that smile buys him precious time to think of an answer. "The mine was an aggregate operation until 1959. That's mostly concrete and building supplies, not diamonds. Now, you could be talking about how Dr. Creed King Senior funded an exploratory medical lab here that used diamonds in some type of MRI technology. I think it was cutting-edge at the time."

"We don't care about diamonds. Show us the good stuff," Tween Braids says. "We want to see blood."

Everyone's eyes widen at the girl's morbid curiosity. Red Wellies curls her arms tighter around her chest. That's when I realize she's wearing a homemade T-shirt that reads *ADPA*. I start to ask her why she's here and Sam, who has

36

been following my pointer finger's involuntary move toward her chest, whispers, "Careful. This gets political and they won't shut up."

I jam my hand in my pocket and say, "Do all of these people want Frankie dead?"

"No," he says.

I think of the framed pictures of Frankie spread across Mom's bedroom floor. Spilled from the crate of memories. She's a smiling girl. Sometimes silly. Earphones pressed into her flared nostrils. A peace sign as she jumps from a rock into the lake. Up close and blurry four-by-sixes of her eyes crossed and her smile crooked. Everything about her is naïve and unsuspecting. I imagine if I asked that girl from twenty years ago how she feels about the hatred being flung at her now, she'd be in a state of disbelief.

Mom Braids bends down to tie the laces of one of her Vans. Sam ushers me ahead several steps as the rest of the group stops to wait for her, giving us the chance for a private word. "There's one of these ADPA crazies on every tour. I get the feeling it might be a conscience check. Like it's one thing to support the ADPA, but only if you're confident you're right. 'Cause if not, you're murdering people too. So Ms. Emily thinks, *Hey, I'll spend fifty bucks and confirm my position.* Question is: Will she go home tonight bundled up nice and cozy in her self-righteousness, or will doubt and guilt start to nibble at her morals?"

He brings his laser focus to me. "What's your opinion on Francis? Innocent? Guilty?"

I assume innocent, because my mother will die on that hill, but I've never really thought about it as a question I needed to answer for myself. When I don't answer, he says, "Hopefully this tour will help you decide."

CHAPTER 8

I 'd like Frankie better if she were innocent.

I think I'd like my mother better too.

Although Frankie's innocence wouldn't lessen Mom's lie. Or at least I can't imagine how it would. Maybe it's callous to admit, but Frankie's guilt or innocence is irrelevant to me. I won't sleep better tonight if I solve that mystery; I'll sleep better if I understand why I am not worthy of Mom's trust. All she had to do was be vague until she could be truthful. It's not hard to conjure up a conversation that wouldn't involve lies:

Me: *"Mom, can we go see your mom?"*

Her: *"I don't really get along with my family."*

Me: *"Why don't you ever talk about your mom and dad?"*

Her: *"My sister died and that made us all too sad to talk."*

There's no rocket science involved. There's certainly no need to change your name and lie to everyone. Especially if you stay in the same state, happen to be the daughter of a senator, and are alive in the internet age. I could probably pay thirty bucks for an internet search and reach the same conclusion as those reporters. The more I think about Mom's course of action, the less sense it makes.

The walk to the old summer cabin takes longer than pleases Red Wellies. Tween Braids has taken to dramatic huffing and kicking pine cones toward her sister's ankles. Meanwhile, her sister has decided she will get more out of her mom's money than an informational tour. There's a lot of one-sided leaning and staring at Sam going on. I admire her confidence and determination even though Sam is oblivious and keeps coming to the back of the group to check on me.

"You're quiet," he says.

"I'm thinking," I say.

A grove of trees nearly hides a semicircle of old cabins. There are six, each with paths between them that must have been neat and tidy back in the day. "This is a good photo op," Sam announces. He points at the foremost cabin with the peeling metal roof and missing boards. "This is where Frankie and Cora and Elizabeth bunked in the summer of 2000."

"Cora's family has a massive mansion on the island. Why stay in this dump?" Man Bun asks, massaging his earlobe until it's red.

Sam directs us to turn around. "There," he says, and we follow his gaze up the hill. A dense forest of pines and kudzu climbs nearly to the top and then several bald cliffs create beautiful overhangs. Atop one bald sits a massive stone and lumber home that is as much a spectacle as the view it must provide. The front walls come to a striking triangular point and seven picture windows rise on both sides all the way from the lowest deck to the green metal roof. In fall, the house would disappear; in winter, it would brag. Golden light pours outward, even though the sun remains high.

"It's like a mountain cathedral," I say.

Sam nods in agreement. "My dad actually refers to this place as Cassandra's Church. Cassandra, as some of you know, is the matriarchal head of the King family. Wife of the late Creed King Senior. Mother of Creed King Junior. Grandmother to Cora and Elizabeth. If you look to the left of Cassandra's, you might be able to make out the chimney of Creed King Junior and the senator's house, where Cora and Elizabeth grew up."

Cassandra's Church. A befitting title.

This was my mother's family home. The property wears its age like bourbon or wine; every year a polish on the one that came before. The timbers a deeper shade, the stone walkways lined with mature flowers and groomed topiaries. Each of the covered decks sports modern cable railings and shiny Adirondack chairs. Screened-in porches are tucked throughout the various four levels and stone chimneys jut from every turn of the roof.

What was it like? Walking away from all this wealth and ending up with more than a handful of days when

41

you didn't know where you'd be sleeping that night? What makes a person capable of such a difficult and drastic choice? I don't know that I want to know.

Monstrous holes pulse in my stomach; a wave of nausea rips from the bottom of my ribs to the back of my throat to behind my eyes. I step to the side of the trail and throw up. Only one thing is clear: whatever happened between my mother and her family isn't something I'll get to the bottom of today or tomorrow. Maybe never. I suddenly feel not only angry with my mother but sorry for her.

Sam's there beside me offering water before I can mumble an apology to the group. "Sorry. Got too hot."

"All the walking," Red Wellies says to Sam.

Man Bun isn't deterred by my state. "Can we climb up there if we want?"

Sam backs away and diverts the group's attention to give me breathing space. "Not unless you want to be arrested. Private property."

I rise in time to see Mom Braids tuck her daughters under her arms and memorialize the house at the top of the hill. "Now remember, Cora King was a girl like you. You shouldn't only watch out for the dangerous men in the world; you have to watch out for dangerous women."

"Mom!" Teen Braids is offended by the learning moment.

Tween Braids says, "If I lived here, on top of the world, *I* wouldn't get myself killed."

Sam takes over before anyone else adds commentary. "Let's get back to that question you asked earlier. If you have all that, why live in this dumpy cabin? I'll let"—he grins at me and I give a nod that I'm better—"my friend tell you."

I venture a guess. "Because no one wants to live with their parents when they're eighteen?"

"Ding, ding, ding," Sam says with snaps of approval.

"Aren't you a teenager?" Man Bun asks.

To which Sam answers, "I'm a thousand years old."

Red Wellies huffs at Sam's invented maturity and takes her moment to shine. "My brother interned at the Center and he said Cora hated the cabins and only stayed because the senator made her."

"Emily, I believe you are spot on there." Sam twists the cabin's padlock and forces the swollen door open.

There isn't enough room to gather inside. Sam leaves us in the breeze as he explains that the Center currently uses these cabins as storage and they're chock-full of stuff that should have been thrown away years ago. "Now, who wants to go first?"

Man Bun steps forward like he has been called upon personally. "What am I looking for? There's a bunch of stuff in there." The light he shines inside catches on spiderwebs and he shimmies with anxiety.

Sam says, "I cleared a path to where their bunks were. You'll find the signatures about waist high."

Man Bun holds his phone in front him like a weapon and ventures forward. Tween Braids grows hyper and begs to go in next; the mother, meanwhile, has a serious side conversation with the other sister that does not have to do with the tour.

Sam tells the group, "Your packets have the handwriting comparisons from Cora's schoolwork and Frankie's signature at the trial."

"I'm impressed," I say to Sam and tap on the packet.

"And I'm impressed you're upright. You're still pretty and pale."

"Takes a lickin' and keeps on tickin'," I joke, as I realize he didn't say pretty pale but rather pretty and pale. I can't help grinning and have to work to hide it from him. There's an exchange between us that keeps happening. Not in words, although he's not hard to talk to. We keep checking in with each other—our eyes coming together over the heads of the others. What I feel is complicated. Admiration, definitely. Attraction, probably. But more than that, a profound curiosity about how we got here. He's the son of Ben Stack, the boyfriend. I'm the daughter of the sister.

"Samwise Tour Guide!" Man Bun singsongs from inside. "What's your take on whether there's evidence that might save Francis Quick?"

"If there wasn't evidence twenty years ago, fat chance finding it now," Red Wellies answers first. I'm not sure anyone else notices, but she tugs on her cardigan and unbuttons the middle where the ADPA is more visible.

Sam takes that opportunity to issue a warning. "Whatever evidence hunting you plan to try—don't conduct it on the Center's grounds. Or the Kings'. You have permission to see

44

these cabins because you're with me. You wander around here without me and you'll find yourself in Green County jail. The administration values privacy for their patients and definitely for the senator's family."

And Sam values the price of his tours.

The tour, minus Teen Braids, is taken aback by the cut-and-dried nature of Sam's trespassing warning. Teen Braids takes it as a personal challenge and straightens her shoulders, creating new lines in her spine and chest that make me admit I underestimated her. She says, "Would you be willing to do a private tour?"

Sam's cheeks redden and he amps up the charm. "Maybe—if the price is right." He checks with me again—a gentle apology that seems to say, *It's only business, I swear.* The fact that he feels he owes me an explanation is interesting. We've known each other less than an hour. And while the flirting is nice, there are hints of real connection.

Teen Braids marches to her mother for a semi-discreet begging session. Lucky for Sam, Mom Braids is engrossed in photographing the signatures and little else.

I tease Sam as if we are old friends. "Someone has an admirer."

He laughs into the collar of his shirt. "I see how you are, Nyla Wagner."

I'm blushing and I don't play it coy. Reciprocation is a confidence builder. And today a decent amnesiac.

Inside the cabin, Mom Braids checks the images on her camera, loses her footing, and bumps into her youngest, who bumps into an aisle of stacked boxes. Boxes tumble in a crashing avalanche. The final collapse sends a group of canisters rolling across the uneven floorboards.

Red Wellies overlooks the mess on the floor. Her eyes are on the now exposed wall. "Would you look at that! Worth the price of admission."

She has her flashlight beam frozen on an inscription, which Man Bun reads out loud: "'I hate my sister more than anyone in the world.'"

Cora's handwriting.

A phrase follows, obviously penned by someone else.

Your hate will get you killed one day. Maybe even by me. ☺

That smiley face could go one of two ways: *I'm totally joking* or *I'm a psychopath.*

"Frankie wrote that?" Red Wellies says.

Everyone snaps photos.

"Doesn't match her handwriting," Sam challenges, his eyes on me instead of the woman. He's right; the handwriting is my mother's.

It's then I realize Sam called me Nyla Wagner, and I never told him my last name.

CHAPTER 9

S am discourages all accusations the group is trying to Sherlock from the handwriting. He sets us off walking again and locks the cabin door behind us.

"Whatever happened to her sister?" Man Bun asks.

"Elizabeth?" Red Wellies states.

"Yeah, the only sister who's been mentioned. Is there another? Like a secret sister or something ominous like that?" Man Bun turns to Sam for a definitive answer.

"I'm sure there's a reason we don't know," Sam says.

Teen Braids says, "Not true. The news broke today. Elizabeth changed her name after Cora's death and has been shacked up with this old guy, Richard Thorn, near Louisville. She's got a daughter too. She's, like . . . twenty. Maybe old Beth left Nockabout because she was knocked up. Or maybe she killed her sister and jetted. Or maybe the senator hid her away. I'll bet the reason is juicy."

It takes all of my willpower not to correct her. I'm eighteen. There's no way Mom left Nockabout pregnant. There is no way she killed her sister. And we are not shacked up with Richard the way she thinks. I do not out myself. I turn to Sam for support. He says, "This tour deals in facts. Not speculations. Now, if you don't mind, the beach is that way."

Being chastised by the cute guy knocks Teen Braids down a notch. She returns to her mother's side and Tween returns to her natural state of whining. "How far is it? Do we have to walk everywhere? This tour should have golf carts."

"This island is like two seconds wide. You're just lazy," her sister tells her.

No one else talks.

The wellies squeak up and down Nockabout Island's hills until the path crosses Circle Drive and dips down to the beach. The lake view lifts everyone's spirits. The soft shale and pebble beach crunches as we pick our way around the land shelf jutting into the water. Thirty feet ahead the shelf diminishes to nothing, the rocks cutting away dramatically. Sam tells us we will have to get our feet wet to reach the bit of shoreline where the cave and beach are located. Red Wellies clicks her feet together like she's either Dorothy in *The Wizard of Oz* or waiting on us to notice how intelligent she is for wearing proper footwear. No one gives her the pleasure.

Feet wet, we are rewarded by a half-moon-shaped cover. This is the sort of place where promposals come to life and couples get engaged. Being hemmed in with jetties on either side, you're left with a sand shelf roughly the size of a volley-ball court, visible only by passing boats. At the edge of the farthest jetty, there's a cavity in the rock. Green River Lake slides inside and disappears. The opening is narrow, no more than three feet at its widest. There's perhaps another four feet from the surface of the water to the hood of the cave.

"This is where they found her," Sam says.

"In the cave?" Teen Braids asks.

"Near the mouth. Partially on the beach. There's a crime scene photo in the packet, but I'll warn you again, it's not PG."

Man Bun holds up the picture against the beach and checks the comparison. "Wow," he says.

The water was much higher when Cora was found.

Sam speaks to this. "Heavy flooding that year is what the authorities believe helped to first hide and then later disclose the body."

Red Wellies snaps a photo and goes on a short tangent about how this couldn't be the location of the murder and it's likely the disposal site. "This is why the DA said a female could have committed the crime. Moving a body over land, if you're small and not particularly muscular, is difficult. Over water you can float her straight into that cave. Why else would someone risk stuffing her body here where it's likely to float up and be discovered?"

I can't help it. I imagine the scene as she speaks. A woman tugging a paddleboard through the water at mid-night. Ripples billow outward and the water kicks up as the swimmer struggles with her exhaustion and the added weight of Cora King. The body decomposes as she floats past where I stand on the shore. When I open my eyes, Cora's there, as she is in the crime scene picture.

"When you're finished," Sam says reverently, "we'll meet right up there and walk to what authorities claimed was the smoking gun in *State v. Francis Quick.*"

It feels as though everyone has only now realized Cora King was a real person. Even Tween Braids, who unbelievably has tears in her eyes, hides her face in her mother's chest. I take out the photo Sam included, force my eyes on it, and feel the opposite. This "thing" on the beach cannot be a girl my age. The decomposition has rendered her to sludge, bones, and teeth. Utterly unrecognizable.

For the second time on this tour, there's vomit in my mouth. This time I swallow it down. But not before Sam notices my distress and walks over to suggest I take another drink of water. I whisper, "That was my aunt."

"I know."

We do not discuss how he knows or when he figured it out. He is, after all, leading a paid tour that surely required additional homework on the King family. Which includes me. Thankfully, he gives me a minute alone and then rallies the group toward the final location on the tour. I'm not sure I can take any more.

Luckily, the last trek is short. Unluckily, it's steep. Everyone except Sam and me ends up bent over their knees, hands on their sides, complaining about the grade.

You can feel them oscillating between *This better be worth it* and *I want my money back*. Tween Braids is about to dissolve into a full-fledged fit about bugs and heat and being tired when Sam points at a narrow dirt driveway carved between the pines and oaks. "And this is it. Almost there," he says.

We've been staring at our feet for most of the hike. Now we look around as we catch our breath and discover we are minions in this landscape—everything older than us, larger than us, grander than us. The nature on the island causes two responses: admiration of its expansive beauty and claustrophobia. There is no way to escape the second feeling as we walk the driveway and are treated to drooping limbs heavy with pine cones and spiderwebs clawing at our heads. Sam leads the caravan toward a crumbling A-frame cabin built into the hill. Everything that can sag, sags. The roof, the paint, the gutters. But the house isn't our destination. We take the split in the drive and follow the left fork toward a garage with even worse posture than the cabin.

"Is that safe?" Man Bun asks of the misshapen garage.

Sam assures us that it is and promises in just a minute we'll be face-to-face with Francis Quick's 1995 pin-striped Camaro.

Coolness wafts from the garage as Sam lifts the door.

The group gives an audible sigh at the sight of the car. The Camaro is in prime condition—yellow with matte black accents, beautiful, not a scratch on the paint. Sam begins, "A few of the islanders have two cars—one island side, one

51

mainland—and boat back and forth. As you've noticed the island is hilly"—the group grumbles in agreement—"and if you're picking up supplies, trust me, you don't want to schlep them from the boat to anywhere without a vehicle and you don't want to wait on the ferry."

"How many people live on Nockabout year-round?" Red Wellies interrupts. She's engrossed in her phone; her face sours as something fails to load. I check my own and discover there is no signal in the hills of Nockabout.

"Changes all the time," Sam answers. "Maybe twenty full-timers. But in the summer the number is closer to two hundred. That number doesn't include the Center's patients either. Most of the doctors and nurses don't live island-side, but they're here for three-day shifts."

Red Wellies keeps deleting photos to create more storage. As soon as she's done, she frames the car and the group like she's Steven Spielberg.

"Anyway," Sam says. "Ramp Two, Weymeyer, was closer to Francis's house than the main ramp and dock. She didn't have two cars—just this baby." He taps the hood. "She left her, Dora Jean Wilcox, yes, that's actually what she called the car, parked at Weymeyer most of the time. She'd boat or swim over to the island for her volunteer job and bike. Nearly all the interns and volunteers had bikes. And most of them didn't make enough to regularly ferry their cars over and back."

"How'd a delinquent like her get a job at an establishment like the Center?"

"Ironically, it was the senator's idea," Sam answers.

"Why's all this business about the car important?" Teen Braids asks.

"Because the car spent most of the summer unattended," Tween says. "Like, duh."

Man Bun, who has stationed himself closest to the car, says, "I read the police didn't initially search Lone Valley. They searched Nockabout and the lake, called friends and family, but not until the second night she didn't come back to the cabin. By then, they figured she'd had an accident or left on purpose."

Sam says, "No one suspected murder initially."

"Weren't there rumors she ran away?" Man Bun asks.

"Yep," Sam says.

"What was her bestie supposedly doing? Other than ditching the body in the lake?" Tween Braids asks.

"You're gross," her sister says.

"No, you're gross." She makes kissy faces at her sister and Sam.

Sam cracks his knuckles. "According to witness statements, Frankie was as distraught as anyone that her friend was missing and joined the search immediately. Senator King called in a team to dredge portions of the lake. Divers and dogs spent days trying to locate her. Two weeks in, the assumption was that Cora had drowned and the body might never be recovered. They hosted a memorial and issued a death certificate."

"Did they check the cave?" I ask.

"Oh, there were loads of early theories about the caves, weren't there?" Mom Braids says.

"People around here love a good cave story," Sam says. "But like the lake, the entire mine was thoroughly searched. Cassandra King provided every resource to find her granddaughter. Owning the mining operation all those years meant the Kings made and curated the most accurate maps of the island. As you probably know, it took seven months and heavy rain for the body to surface on the beach—and Cassandra never gave up hope that Cora would be found."

I don't know what Cassandra looks like now or then, but her pain is almost an ethereal mist wafting above the Camaro.

Man Bun searches through his packet of papers. "And when did they find the Jarvis guy hanging from the rail bridge?"

"On the very day Cora disappeared."

"If the dude was dead, why was he a suspect?" Man Bun asks.

"Murder-suicide," Red Wellies says. "They weren't sure when he died in relationship to Cora King and therefore they couldn't rule out that he didn't kill her, stuff the body in the cave, and then kill himself over what he'd done."

Sam bobs his head with Red Wellies's conclusion. "Exactly."

Man Bun flips forward and back, the papers growing disorganized as he goes. "Going back to the car. To me it sounds like the Camaro was in the Valley and didn't make it over to the island all that much. How exactly did it get tied to the death?"

This is clearly Tween Braids's time to shine. She lifts her know-it-all chin and says, "Cora's blood was found in the trunk. Boom."

Sam gives her a tempered smile. "The Camaro was tied in when Cora's death was ruled a homicide by the medical examiner. He said a bone in her neck was broken premortem and wasn't part of the lake damage and decomposition. Now we have a dead senator's daughter, and we need someone to blame. The police turn their attention to the boyfriend, my dad; the best friend, Frankie; and Martin Jarvis, with whom Cora had previous romantic tension. The fact that Jarvis was already dead didn't help my dad or Frankie."

"Like, how did your dad get off the hook?" Tween Braids almost sounds as though she's found her conscience.

Sam sinks his hands in his pockets. "Oh, they hauled him in too. He took and passed a polygraph, same as Frankie."

"Frankie took a polygraph? That wasn't part of the trial."

"Excluded. They're inadmissible in most courts. Dad says it felt like the police drew straws on who to go after and ultimately they settled on Frankie because of her history of violence."

Mom has never mentioned the polygraph. I wonder if she knows.

To hear these strangers talk history, my history, like it is their own treasured family tale is disarming. They've debated death over dinner tables, discussed decomposition on long car rides. This is easy for them. Far off. The way Frankie was once far off to me, though now she feels glued to my face. But I know, when the tour is over, they'll go back to their blogs and theories and hashtags; I'll go home to Elizabeth King.

They keep arguing and I can't bring myself to follow the conversation. Tears have started to stream. I wander away from the group and clutch a tree to stay upright.

Man Bun says, "Like, why didn't they investigate the family or other friends? I mean, you all read what I did in that cabin. Cora had other enemies. Maybe even her sister. I can't imagine the senator was all too happy to have her precious reputation at risk if her daughter was maybe wilder than she wished."

Red Wellies puts her head back and laughs. "You must be kidding. You're blaming the senator?"

Man Bun is done with all the patronizing. He turns, hands on his hips. "Francis Quick scored a 31 on the ACT her eighth-grade year. She's intelligent. And intelligent women don't put the body of their best friend in the trunk of their own car. And if they do, they bleach everything." He gestures in the general direction of the lake. "Plus, this is not the only lake in Kentucky. If you're going to dump the body of your best friend, why dump it close to home?"

Red Wellies tucks her iPhone into her back pocket

and steps closer to Man Bun, whom she now seems to be evaluating and rejecting with a single lip curl. "You said intelligent *woman*. This was a teenager." She bobs from Sam to me to Teen Braids, our ages only now occurring to her, and says, "No offense." When she notices my tears, she softens. "It is very sad."

Too late for that, lady.

Tween Braids is the only one not staring at me. She takes up the banner where Red Wellies left off. "Maybe Frankie killed Cora on the island, ferried the car over, and then tried to buy time to get rid of the body when no one was watching. Shoot, maybe she had help. If I had three suspects, I'd definitely focus on the one with the record first."

The theory is astute. And that's almost nice since Red Wellies has insulted everyone under the age of twenty.

Red Wellies likes what she hears and adds, "Agree. I'd say Frankie's lucky they didn't charge her with Martin Jarvis's death too. Since that's who she attacked in the first place. Got lucky they ruled his death a suicide. The way I heard it from a girl at the marina, Jarvis and Cora had a thing, and Frankie was so jealous she beat up Jarvis one night."

Man Bun folds a little and turns to Sam. "Did Frankie plead guilty to that offense?"

"Yep. That offense was never in question. But Frankie never confessed to why she attacked Martin Jarvis. You'll see it there in the packet." Sam steps into the most central space of the group. "Remember, folks, this tour is about facts. You're here to see facts. No one thought the car was where the murder occurred. The speculation was it was used for transport. I think we should wrap this up."

He has said this for me.

His statement doesn't stop the argument. Red Wellies says she's been studying the case longer than Sam has been alive and that she grew up nearby and gave Francis Quick a campus tour of Lindsey Wilson College the same year as the murder. The group, even Sam, seems interested in this. I crouch on the edge of a fat pine stump and pick a clump of sap. I can hear them talking about her. They give me the same sensation as a candle flame. I like to hover my finger over a lit wick and feel the warmth give way to an almost burn, just to know the edge of pain.

"What *did* she seem like?" Mom Braids asks.

"Like a kid who wanted to get out of her hometown and my alma mater wasn't good enough. I doubt she would have been admitted anyway. Lindsey Wilson is a Christian school and she had a record. Of course, I didn't know *that* the day she came to tour campus. I found out watching the trial." She sighs. "You never really know a person, I guess."

The woman's self-importance is laughable. Saying she knew Frankie because she'd been her tour guide is like saying I know Sam after today.

Sam ends the conversation by raising the Camaro's trunk. He glances up the hill at me and says, "Nyla, I think you should risk rejoining us." To the group he says, "Remember. No pictures."

There is a delayed response to peer in the trunk. One by one, they walk forward, peer inside, and back away. A variety of expressions on their faces, from confusion to disgust. I have no idea what to expect when it's my turn.

I walk forward and shine my phone light into the trunk, bracing myself for the horrific.

There is a single circle of rust-colored blood, no larger than an M&M.

CHAPTER 10

I'm not sure if the rest of the group is meditating on the spectacular lack of evidence as Sam motors the tour across the lake, but it's all I think about. Twenty years of your life disappear over a nick from a fishhook or a deep paper cut.

One drop of blood. That's what she'll be executed for.

Back at their cars, the five paying visitors thank Sam for the tour. There seems to be a consensus he delivered more than they paid for and they will be sending others in his direction as a thank-you. Tween Braids gives him a salute and says, "I'd say you're three stars, but I'll give you four because my sister says you're hot."

Teen Braids shrinks into the front seat as Sam gives Tween a return salute. The lower lot empties except for Richard's Pilot. Sam and I perch on the hood, the quiet between us comfortable and solid. The June sun is lower now with miles of daylight left to shine. I should drive back and check on Mom, but I'm too stunned to leave.

"When did you figure out who I was?" I ask.

Sam picks at the skin around his thumbnail. "I wasn't a hundred percent sure until I said Wagner and you didn't argue. I knew Beth had a daughter named Nyla—"

"Even before the news broke," I say in mock horror.

"Even before," he says. He taps his temple. "Not just a hat rack, my dear. It wasn't even all that hard to figure out. Dad said your mom broke with the Kings because of Frankie, so I had a buddy of mine on the police force check the visitation log at Floyd. I was thinking if you leave all that wealth for your friend, she must be in your life. And there happens to be a great record of who is in Frankie's life. I was frustrated at first when my buddy told me there was no Elizabeth King, but then he said, 'There's an Elizabeth Wagner.' From there it was White Pages, Facebook, and photos from my dad to confirm her identity."

"You really are a thousand years old."

"Well, if you want to charge fifty bucks a tour, you gotta know the background."

"Is that what I owe you?"

"On the house. I coaxed you into it because you were downright beautiful and then I got lucky that you're a freaking undercover King."

His compliment causes me to stare at our shoes. Mine wear the sludge of the tour. His have lake mud caked around the flip-flops' soles and a piece of duct tape that aids one of the straps. There's motor oil encased in his nail beds and little crusts of sleep in the corners of his eyes. I wonder how long it has been since he's slept. Or if he sleeps at all. An alarm trills from the waistline of his shorts. He lifts a phone, checks the screen, and says, "Not me," as he tucks the phone back into a holster. "I'm on an emergency services team for the lake, but that wasn't us. Sorry. We were talking about something far more important."

I'm not surprised he's on an emergency services team for the lake. It doesn't take much to imagine him in navy pants and Boy Scout button-ups with patches on his sleeves. "I didn't know until today," I say.

"What? That you're stupid attractive?"

I swat his knee. "No, that I'm a . . . well, a King."

"No freaking way," he says without a single trace of the tour guide in his voice.

I tell him about my morning of reporters and Mom in her bed. How she's been there for three days since we found out about Frankie. "Please don't say any of this on your tour," I plead.

He's slightly annoyed and offended that I've said this—a sharp expression appears in his eyes that I haven't seen since he was dealing with Tween Braids. "I didn't tell them who you were, did I? But honestly, Nyla, I'd buckle up if I were you. Emily will likely figure it out by the end of today based on her amazing twenty-year study of the case." He uses air quotes around *amazing*. "She'll have your picture up on her website by tonight. If you have comment sections on any of your socials, I'd pause the accounts."

He's right. People are going to find out who I am. The past is the past, even when you're ignorant to its truths.

"What do I do?" I ask, when I really mean, *How should I feel?*

"If you're like me, you'll figure out how to capitalize"— he rubs his fingers together in a cash gesture—"so you can get out of the Valley. But since you're not me, I don't know. I guess it depends on if you like your mom. Do you like your mom?"

"What kind of question is that?"

"I mean, do you have her back even when she craps on you like she has? Or are you through?" He dusts his hands. "'Cause those are the stakes."

I look across the lake to Nockabout. From here, Cassandra's Church hangs over the hill like a tiny model house on display. He sees me staring.

"Oh, so you might try to meet the family?" He guesses thoughts I didn't even realize I was thinking. "Well, I've got good news or bad news. You won't have to try too hard. She's right there." He waves politely to a woman being wheeled toward the dock from the shops above. "Hello, Mrs. King!"

CHAPTER 11

Maybe everyone has had the experience of getting what they wanted before they actually wanted it, but I haven't. The things I've wanted have always moved at a glacial pace. Not today. Complex emotions lay like filo pastry layers right at the surface. I came to Nockabout to meet Cassandra King, whose name meant nothing, whose house I hadn't seen, who held no interest to me until those reporters erupted my world with a question about Elizabeth King. Now I've had a tour, a crime scene dump, a semi-significant crush, and the urge to get in the Pilot and drive away.

I take in every detail as she is being rolled toward Sam and me.

My great-grandmother is pushed by a pretty woman in her thirties who wears one of those scrolly *Blessed* shirts they sell at Hobby Lobby with bright white skinny jeans and Skechers. She's petite with frosted brown and blonde hair that has been chopped into a style rather than cut, and when she moves, her necklace catches the light and shoots prisms between us on the car's hood.

By comparison, and despite having a handicap that has challenged her mobility, Cassandra King seems larger and firmer than her caregiver. She's of a generation that only wears jeans in the garden and puts on her face every time she leaves the house. Today she's dressed in black slacks, low wedge sandals, and a bohemian silk shirt. Her hair is wrapped in the same yellow fabric as her shirt. Strings of pearls encircle her neck and wrists. The bracelets clink against her chair when she moves.

The caregiver leans into the ear of Cassandra. "That's Sam," she says loud enough for us to hear.

Cassandra raises her overlarge sunglasses, revealing cloudy pale blue eyes. "Sam, I sent your father home with two filets and if he doesn't share them with you, he's in big trouble." She wags her finger for emphasis.

Sam lets me in on his connection. "My dad's her grounds-keeper." *Of course he is. Because this planet is dime sized.* His response to Cassandra says he knows how to play the game. "I'll make sure he shares, Ms. King. Thank you for thinking of me."

She beams at his gratitude. Her comfort in doling out rewards suggests she exercises her generosity frequently.

I wonder how it feels to work for the Kings and how it would go over if Cassandra knew her groundskeeper's son was selling tours to her family's worst moment. I can't imagine it would go over well even though sending steak home with Sam's dad is a signal she treats her people with kindness.

"Hey, Anna," Sam says warmly.

"Samuel!" she responds formally and then cracks a smile.

Their relationship mimics aunt to nephew but is probably more hired worker to hired worker. These are the servants in a modern-day *Downton Abbey* and they probably have a language of hidden laughter and fist bumps, little off-color jokes told at their employers' expense. I'd bet anything Anna knows about Sam's tours and she'd die before she'd tell Cassandra.

Cassandra flourishes her hand in my direction. "And you are?" She raises the eyebrows that someone, likely Anna, has meticulously drawn on.

"Sam's friend, Mrs. King," I say.

"Ah. And does Sam's friend have a name?"

I don't know what to say. Does Cassandra know her great-granddaughter's name is Nyla? Does she even know she has a great-granddaughter? She might. Sam does. And she seems in full possession of her faculties.

"My friends call me Lion," I say.

Cassandra glances at Anna, as though she can't understand the younger generation at all, before responding, "Like the animal?"

"Yes, ma'am."

"Hmm. I rather like that. Sounds strong. Well, Lion, I do hope you and Sam don't get yourselves into too much trouble." At this she winks at Sam, her blue eyes sparkling, lowers her sunglasses, and taps on the handrest of her wheelchair. The clinking pearls are Anna's cue to push.

At the misspelled "spectater" sign, Cassandra raises her arm to stop. "Can you pry that off, dear?" she asks.

Anna manhandles the sign, twisting the weathered wood until it snaps off the post.

"Thank you," Cassandra says, and the two disappear around the other side of the ferry shack. The "spectater" sign sticks out of a nearby garbage bin.

"Give it a minute and you'll see her boat," Sam says.

Not much time passes before a sleek white fiberglass speedboat slips quietly across the water toward Nockabout, Cassandra seated in a special chair lift, Anna at the wheel.

"Wow. She looks good," I say.

"Yeah. That's a brand-new Boston Whaler with teak interior. Thing's like half a mil, maybe."

I shove at Sam's shoulder. "Not the boat."

He grins at the mistake and says, "Oh, right. Cassandra. She's about eighty, I think."

"She nice?" I ask.

"Uh, I'd go with tough before nice, but she's good to my dad. Anna too. Everyone who works for her gets a thousand-dollar gift certificate to Sam's Club for Christmas. I mean, what other caregivers wear diamonds with their T-shirts? I reckon Anna's trapped here until Mrs. King dies, but then she'll be set."

"I wish I knew her," I say as the boat slides into a slip on the other side of the lake.

Sam turns sideways on the hood and sits cross-legged. He's leaning shoulders over knees, directly toward me, in a way that's intimidating and intimate and uncomfortable. I can't meet his eyes, but I feel them digging into my face like two tiny shovels. "That's up to you, *Lion*."

"I thought it was. I came here thinking I was right and Mom's wrong, and then the tour and all these strangers and Cora and you and her . . ." I point toward the boat on the other side of the lake. "I don't know why I thought this would be simple."

"Do you know why your mom lied to you?"

"No."

He scooches closer to me and rests his hand on my knee as if we are old friends. I don't believe in reincarnation, but Sam and I on this hood feels ancient and repetitive, like we've been here before and we'll be here again. "I'm sorry."

"I'm angry and I can't tell if I should be."

Sam lowers his head until his face breaks my field of vision. "Your mom made a decision to lie to you, and sure, maybe it was even for a good reason, like she has too much trauma and stuff to come back, but that doesn't mean you can't have negative emotions toward her. Think of all the ones she has for her family. Empathy and anger might be unlikely friends, but they occasionally hang out and go for drinks, you know?"

There's wisdom in his words.

It's easier to make room for both emotions than settle on one. That idea gives me a little courage and I unclench my fist.

"There you go," he says and lies back on the hood like his work is done. "If it were me, I'd think about that boat. The house on the hill. The ice on Anna's neck. Play your cards right, Lion, and you're the heir."

My phone rings. It's Richard.

"You need to take that?" Sam asks as I deny Richard's call.

I sigh and slide off the hood. "I need to get on the road. I left Richard in charge of Mom and she's a handful. But would it be okay if I came back?" I feel shy and vulnerable asking.

Sam smiles, takes my phone from my hand, and types his info into my contacts. "You don't need my permission. For you, my dear, I'll even consider giving a private tour of Nockabout." He hops off the Pilot and says, "Now I gotta go get my puppy from Ned."

"You left your dog with Ned the jeweler instead of Cecilee the groomer?" I say as I send a text to his number that reads,

Hi. This is Lion.

And then I give him a sheepish smile.

He smiles too, reading my text, and sends back,

Hi. This is your tour guide to life.

A second text follows immediately.

And death.

"Indeed," I say aloud, thankful there's room for macabre humor.

CHAPTER 12

There's a fight ahead of me.

One I've been avoiding all day.

And while I feel rotten for ditching Richard, my instinct to leave paid off. I am more prepared to hear whatever Mom has to say about why she has spent the last eighteen years lying to me. And that preparation is the only armor I have.

I first spend the drive categorizing my emotions.

Am I upset she changed her name? No. That was her decision.

Am I upset she left her family? No. Not at this point in time.

Am I upset she has trauma about her sister's death that makes a Nockabout reunion difficult? No, that makes sense.

I'm upset she didn't tell me or warn me that someone might knock on our door and make me feel two inches tall about my own history. Especially since she's like a Vanderbilt of Kentucky.

I text Richard that I'll be home by dinner and he sends me an exclamation mark, which he cancels and replaces with a thumbs-down. Then I get another text that reads,

Dang fat thins.

A second later the phone rings, I answer, and he says, "Dang fat thumbs. I was typing 'fat thumbs' and the phone did that thing and made it 'thins.'" He huffs. "Be careful."

"How is she?" I ask.

"Packing."

Wow. He's practically growling. "Packing?" I ask.

"Yeah, I guess her MO always involves running away."

I white-knuckle the wheel. "Then she's going to hate what I have to say."

"Probably, Lion. Probably."

I practice my questions. I imagine her answers. I plan how I will counter, depending on which direction she goes.

I cannot go in soft.

I cannot have this conversation at all if I focus on the fact that she's fragile and has emotions that have basically strapped her to the bed these last three days.

Ignore her and be you, I tell myself.

When I walk in the house, Mom is standing at the closet below the stairs, pulling everything that is ours into the hallway. More twelve-by-twelve squares and old laundry bags. My arrival doesn't stop the braless zombie. Her shirt is stretched at the biceps and loose everywhere else. Her hair hasn't been washed and is up in a high ponytail with oily streaks. If Cassandra saw her like this, she'd probably have a heart attack.

I lean against the front door, fortifying myself. Richard, who is trying to change the volume on the television, freezes. A Netflix trailer for a Hitchcock film blares. I say, "I need to hear your side of the story. Don't tap out and go to bed. Don't pack a bag and run away. Stand there and tell me the truth."

Mom slides along the hallway door and collapses onto the threadbare carpet runner. She scratches the hardened skin on her heels. "It's not what you think."

"Okay," I say, hoping I sound calm. "What do you think that I think?" I cross the room and help Richard lower the volume of the television. He settles himself deeper into the corner of the couch like he might disappear. I rest my weight on the armrest of the adjacent loveseat.

Mom picks up a stuffed animal from one of the boxes and strokes its fur. "You think I don't trust you, that I'm embarrassed by you, maybe even ashamed of you. That I let you grow up poor instead of rich and probably somewhere in there you wonder if I ran away for a bigger reason than my mother is the senator who is frying my best friend like bacon in twenty-seven days."

I am disarmed by her answer, but I can't let up. "Let's not forget that you've been lying to me my whole life."

"Baby—"

"Let me run you through my day. No, let's go with the week. You find out Frankie is going to be"—I echo her word choice—"bacon . . . and you stop being a human being and turn into a sobbing lump that Richard and I feed and escort to the bathroom. After that, you sleep. There's no, 'Nyla, how are you?' or 'Nyla, I know this is hard on you too.' Instead, you leave me to open the door this morning to two reporters who tell me that you're not Beth Wagner; you're Beth King—"

"Baby—"

"—and your mom is a senator. Your dad runs a four-story rehabilitation facility. Your grandmother is a wealthy mining magnate. And you, you are the sister of Cora King. And your best friend, the one set to be—" The word *bacon* is on my lips again.

"Ny, stop."

I let it fall out again. "Bacon for killing her. Did I leave anything out? Because unless you've had a very serious case of amnesia for eighteen years, we have a problem."

"Are you finished?" She is anxious rather than angry, picking deeper into the skin of her heel. It'll bleed before long.

I am out of energy and out of the words I practiced in the car. I rush my questions, hoping to put everything in her court so I don't have to say anything else. "Did you think this through? Your lies? Leaving me out of your lies? Because it feels like a real mother wouldn't do that. When I asked about my father, you said, 'He's not an option for us.' That was an answer. Not the answer I wanted, but a legitimate answer. Wagner is a lie. My name is a lie. I've slept under a tree in the park with you and never once distrusted you. And to find out now that we're not in this together is incredibly painful."

"I've thought about everything," she says softly, and I can't help but hear how profoundly sad she is. How boxed in she has felt by her past. "Baby, I've wanted to tell you, to share that part of my life, share you, but I couldn't. Not until—"

"Not until what? Frankie died? You had nowhere else to go? Someone else called you on my existence?"

"Nyla, I left home at eighteen. My sister was dead. My best friend was headed to prison because of my parents' accusations. You can get mad at me all you want, bless. God knows I've been mad at me, too, but I didn't know what to do. Every day I stayed there my anger grew. I almost couldn't find myself anymore. That's scary. Scarier than losing my family even. Yes, I got dramatic and changed my name because I foolishly thought someone might come after me." She laughs.

"I kept it that way, I guess because it felt like loyalty to Frankie. Loyalty to you. And us. That we would be something different from where I came from. Those lies were a protection, and I'm not sorry. And maybe that means I didn't trust you, or maybe it means I didn't put the burden of my secrets or my choices or my mistakes on you. You're old enough to get your head around the fact that I'm a human *and* a parent, who is doing the best I can for the people I love." She pitches the stuffed animal that's been resting in her lap into its box. "Now, bless, I'm going to give

75

you your pity party because it's earned and we all need that sometimes, but then I'm asking you to put it away and help me get us out of the press. We do not want my family here."

"Mom, I not leaving Richard's for some jack-in-the-box town in Indiana or Ohio or Tennessee where we know no one and you don't have a job. That's not the answer. I think you should pack a bag rather than a closet and buckle up for the ride. Nockabout's coming to you regardless."

"We're never going to Nockabout."

"Too late. I've already been. Cassandra says hi."

She stands, eyes wide with horror. "You wouldn't . . ."

"Wouldn't what?"

"Betray me."

"Betray *you*?" That's painfully laughable. "You love Frankie more than you have ever loved me. How is that supposed to make me feel?" I hadn't meant to yell, and I hadn't even known my jealousy until it rocketed from my mouth.

"Oh, Nyla, you've got this all wrong. All wrong. Where are you going?"

I'm on my way toward the steps and out of our ridiculous, convoluted conversation. "I'm taking my pity party upstairs to be alone. Maybe I'll get in bed and stay for a week. A chip off the old *Wagner* block." I pound my way up the steps and into my room.

CHAPTER 13

I don't know why, but I text Sam a comment like we're right in the middle of a conversation. Talking to him—venting—seems better than anything else I can think of to do.

That went well.

Sam texts back.

Bad news, Lion.

And then Emily's website. She's written an article on today's tour and this woman is like the Rita Skeeter of Kentucky journalism. Four paragraphs are dedicated to my presence and how I, like my mother, never identified myself as the daughter of Beth King and instead claimed to be Nyla Wagner. Which never happened. I never claimed to be anyone.

Sam: You planning to come back to the Valley?

Nyla: Yes.

Sam: ☺ Think of what we can charge if you come on all the tours.

Sam: That was a joke.

Sam: I'm not that shallow.

Nyla: I know. I wish I knew what I was walking into.

Sam: Talk to Frankie. She can help.

Nyla: Night, Sam.

Sam: Night.

CHAPTER 14

I meet Richard at the toaster the next morning. He's popping his frozen waffles in for a second go-round. "Will you take me to Floyd? Or at least get me a phone call with Frankie?" He glances at the ceiling, to where somewhere above us my mother is pacing in her bedroom. I hand him the maple syrup and butter dish and pour myself a cup of coffee. "Please."

He's in his robe. The local paper is spread out on the table and he looks longingly toward the front page. "Let me eat and get dressed. We'll give it a whirl," he says. "Even though I don't think you should have yelled at your mom that much. Some? Sure. But you got all roar-y, Lion. First time I've seen you with all that rage. I didn't like it all that much."

He's said his piece, and for my part, I kiss his temple and say, "It needed to be said."

He bops the cooked waffle on the tip of my nose. "She's right about being human, though. Good parents do the best they can. Sometimes it's enough. Other times it's not."

Richard doesn't have any children of his own, but he's a retired social worker, and he says that's like having a million children all at once.

Five minutes later, he's behind the wheel of the Pilot and we're on our way to Floyd Penitentiary. He doesn't ask me about Nockabout or why I want to talk to Frankie or even if I've thought about what I will say if I'm able to see her. Instead, we talk about how he hopes Betty White will live forever and why Americans are obsessed with British royalty. We're at Floyd's gatehouse an hour later.

The penitentiary looks like it has been built on a Minecraft server, square upon grayish-white square. Standard razor wire fencing stakes the complex's edge and grassy surrounding fields. Two fire tower structures rise above opposite corner perimeters. Their guards are mere shadows from this distance, the long shape of their rifles poised against the railing making them seem like toy army men rather than a real threat.

Richard forks over IDs to a guard at the gatehouse. The guard, Chip Rodriguez, offers a cheery "Hello" that doesn't match his uniform or the sidearm holstered to his belt.

"We're here to visit Francis Quick. I understand that the ADPA allows extra visiting hours to those who lose their appeals."

"She know you're coming?" Chip asks.

"No."

Chip taps the roof of the Pilot, thinking. "Let me phone and get permission before we do your walk-around.

Back up and park in that spot and I'll let you know when I get word."

Three other cars enter and exit the prison before Chip returns to where we are sweating through our clothes in the Pilot. "She's agreed to see you." He conducts a brief search and then hands two visitor's badges through Richard's window. "You're good to go, Mr. Thorn, Ms. Wagner."

The visitors' lot is barren. When we reach the entrance hallway, a guard who might have been manning his desk for more than a hundred years tells us, "Hold up there; we need a little looky-loo at all your belongings." When he asks me how a woman "as purdy as you" doesn't have a wedding ring, I answer, "My mom would shoot me if I got married this young."

"Well then, maybe if she's as purdy as you are, I'll look for her in here."

Really! This is federal security at its best. With a firm jerk, Richard tugs my shirt toward my knees. A warning. He must see the lion in me again.

Thankfully, the guard hands us off to one of his buddies.

Excitement and fear grab my stomach with an iron fist.

I am meeting a murderer or a victim. I think again about that one drop of blood in the Camaro's trunk and the photo of my dead aunt's slime on the beach. I don't know that I'll know if Frankie's guilty or not, or if I'll have a sense of her after one meeting. No matter what happens in the next thirty minutes, for the first time I'll lay eyes on the woman around whom my mom has structured our entire existence.

81

CHAPTER 15

The pale green tile of Floyd Penitentiary squeaks underfoot. Although freshly mopped, according to a dingy A-frame sign, the hallway is basically a kid in charge of his own shower for the first time: wet, not clean. Whatever expectations I had going in, Floyd falls well below. I am not creeped out or feeling agoraphobic. The cement walls are bland except for the occasional educational or legal advice poster. The first prisoners we pass hug the opposite wall and carry Bibles. One hums the chorus of "How Great Thou Art" to herself.

After many turns I lose track of our position. Each section of Floyd has its own guards and we are a short parade. People come out to see us, and everyone, from guards to inmates, is interested in who is visiting who. We pass an empty visitation area that's straight out of every middle school cafeteria I've ever seen.

"We've got you set up outside. Safer," our guard explains. For Frankie or us? He goes on. "Haven't had many visitors except press and investigative journalists." He laughs. "I thought the woman who usually comes to see Quick would be here, but I haven't seen her since the ADPA news. Hope she's not sick or anything. She's real nice to us."

Of course she is.

Meeting outside throws me. Will Frankie be chained to a table the way inmates are on television? When we reach the exterior door, Richard says, "Would you like to do this part alone?" He seems to be second-guessing himself.

"I want you there," I say.

He nods.

Outside, the sun flings gridded shadows of the surrounding fences on the concrete walkway. The larger yard around us has a track, basketball court, and softball field. They're empty. I wonder if Floyd made sure we'd be without an audience or if the privacy is happenstance. Our guard leads us along to an eight-by-eight gated enclosure. The wind has picked up, and the two red aluminum chairs inside the pen rock on their own.

"We'll bring her," he says.

After we are locked inside, I take a deep breath. Richard paces our cage and seems to sink deeper into his trucker hat.

I hear the threesome. Dragging chains. Gates opening. Closing. Slide and *click*. The nausea rises in my stomach and begins to bounce like a ball. Two guards escort

Frankie—one short, stocky female with rounded shoulders who reminds me of a *Despicable Me* Minion and a dude so skinny a whisper might blow him over.

Francis wears her Crayola yellow hair in two messy braids. A puzzle book is rolled in her hand, a golf pencil tucked behind her ear; a half-cocked smile spreads on her lips. She is five nine or ten with a tight, muscular frame. She moves with an athletic grace that my mom will never possess, no matter how much muscle she packs on. In another life, I'd peg Francis as a retired soccer star who still picks up a few games a week. Her eyes are wide and alert, happy even. She's almost identical to the photo Mom has of her from twenty years ago.

The female guard shoves Frankie between her shoulder blades. "Walk faster, Quick." She almost comes to a complete stop to lock eyes with me.

I have an out-of-body moment during our miniature stare session. I swear I feel another, wiser version of myself whispering into my ear, "This is bigger than you think it is." Like I need to hold this moment tightly because I'm going to remember it for the rest of my life. By the time Francis joins Richard and me in the enclosure, her smile is enormous.

"You're here," she says. "Wow."

This is not at all the reception I expected.

The male guard unlocks the shackles on her ankles and wrists and she rubs the raw, irritated skin and stretches toward the sun. The gate slides into place, leaving the three of us inside, and Richard pushes a hundred-dollar bill through the chain fence toward the female guard. "Can we have an hour?"

"Thirty minutes," the guard says and snatches the cash. She and her partner disappear around a nearby corner building.

Richard and Francis evaluate each other, and I can't tell if it's curiosity or distrust. Frankie finally caves. "You look good, Richard. Thanks for the JPay."

I don't know what that means, but Richard seems to. "Everybody needs Cheetos."

"Cheetos before dying," she says and lifts a fist in triumph.

"I know, kid," Richard says and grips her forearm with support.

He calls her "kid" the same way he calls me "lion." I always assumed Richard waited in the parking lot when he brought Mom to Floyd. He must have come in more often than he stayed in the car. Frankie turns to me—our eyes lock again in a trance-like state.

She pushes through my outstretched hand into my personal space. She is close, so close, and taller than me by four or five inches, which puts me eye level with her shoulders. I am a lone antelope in tiger territory. I smell soap and sweat and meet her blue eyes with steel of my own. To which her lip curls into a tentative smile. She raises her hands until they are directly between our faces, her palms facing upward. "I've never hurt anyone in my life." Her voice is southern, low, gravelly.

"Okay," I say, unsure why she needs me to believe her. I am no one.

She exhales. "Good. Whew, glad I got to say that."

I guess if you've spent twenty years incarcerated for a crime you claim you didn't commit, everyone you meet has the potential to join your side. I can't blame her for gathering troops, no matter how few they may be.

Frankie quickly becomes wide lips, bright teeth, and breathing room. "I *am* very glad to meet you," she says and glances over her shoulder at Richard before taking my hand, a gesture I had extended during her approach and left frozen in the air. Now her fingers tighten, appraising mine, squeezing until we are both uncomfortable. "You're strong too."

"I run," I say and then wince. How ridiculous does that sound?

"Keep up the good work."

Five words of praise set my cheeks on fire. And then I blush extra because I am blushing and I have a hint of why my mom has circled Frankie earth-to-sun for all these years. When Frankie draws you in, it's fast and hard. I can hear her gravity bending me in her direction.

"Do you know why I'm here?" I ask Francis.

Frankie drops into one of the aluminum chairs, unrolls the celebrity edition of a word search, and begins doodling in the corner. "Not yet, but I'd love to know. We have thirty minutes and that means twenty-five, so unfortunately we should go about this fast."

It all spills out. "Tell me about my mom. And Nockabout. Cora. Who killed her?" This history is the centerpiece of the table Mom has set.

Francis's eyes are a never-ending story. I wonder if Richard sees them as I do: the innocence and the flames. In them, two Francis Quicks coexist: the prisoner who works word searches and accepts last-minute interviews with her best friend's daughter and the terrified woman who will be executed in twenty-six days. Frankie says, "I don't know who killed Cora."

"Did Mom and Cora get along?"

"Bethie and Cora, they were." Frankie blows out a huge breath that vibrates her lips. "They were antonyms and synonyms. Depended on the day."

Frankie's use of the name Bethie reverses Mom's age, and I have a rare window into who my mother was twenty years ago. Bethie, not Elizabeth King. Certainly not Elizabeth Wagner. As for Frankie, she's remembering. "Cora was a momma's girl and Bethie never really fit the King mold. Cora was bombastic; Bethie was measured. Not hesitant, but thoughtful. Studious. Always had a plan and moved like she lived in a minefield. Cora started dating when she was like five; Bethie's never had a date in her life."

"Except with my dad," I say.

Frankie nods. "Yes, except your dad." She continues, "Cora was hard and smart and stubborn and we loved her for it. She could convince you to do anything for her, and I mean anything. Bethie was strong in a different way.

87

Strong enough to go her own way even when no one else would."

There is no doubt Frankie loves both sisters.

"But they got along?" I ask.

"They had each other's backs. You had to with their family," Frankie answers.

"What does that mean?"

Frankie leans forward in her seat and chooses her words carefully. "Let's say she could have listed 'Being a King' on any résumé."

That's loaded. "And you were Cora's best friend first?"

"We were the same age. Bethie's a year younger. Cora and I were paired in school, and during summer we'd all do a triangle thing, but Bethie and I didn't get close until I went to juvie. And then obviously closer after Cora died."

"Did Cora have enemies?"

"Well." The weight of Frankie's sigh is painful. "More like loyal opposition."

"What do you mean?"

"She could do us all wrong and we'd forgive her. We knew she did it and she'd do it again, but we didn't care because she was her. Sounds dumb now, but none of us would have hurt her over it."

"Who's us?"

"Ben. Me. Your mom."

"Martin Jarvis?" I throw his name on the pile like he was one of them.

Frankie tenses. "Twenty years ago, I would have bet

a million dollars he killed her. Even though they said his time of death was before her . . . I don't know. He's a central part of this, but that specific part"—she growls with frustration—"I'm not sure."

"Okay, if not him, who? A stranger? Martin's partner?"

Frankie lifts her hands in a *Who knows?* movement.

I ask the question that brought me to Floyd. "Would you say it's safe for Mom to go home—to Nockabout, I mean? For me to meet the Kings? My family?" That's incredibly strange to say aloud.

Frankie looks quizzically at Richard. "You're not letting her go there, are you?"

"This one's already been." He wings a thumb in my direction.

Frankie's gaze snaps to me. "You went?"

"Yeah, right after the reporters told me my last name isn't Wagner."

Frankie drops her face into her hands. "Oh, Nyla. Oh, sweetie. I'm sorry. That's not the way she wanted you to find out."

My jaw flares with anger. "No. Definitely not. She never would have told me if she had her way."

"That's not true. She planned to tell you. If you want to blame someone for making your life complicated, blame me, not her. She's protecting me, and soon she won't have to anymore." Frankie stares at the guard tower. "Nyla, you're going to do what you want to do, but think about this: Have you ever known your mom to hurt you on purpose?"

89

"No." The answer is swift and true. Prior to this, Mom has done everything to protect me.

"Then," Frankie says, "maybe even the lie was protection. And maybe that says a lot about how strongly she doesn't want to go back to Nockabout. That place killed her soul. Killed more than that."

I stand, my back to Frankie, my cheek pressing into the wire enclosure, my fingers curled around the rusted metal. "She loves you more than anyone else," I say. "Why wouldn't she at least go back to fight for you? If you're innocent, and she's your greatest defender, she could have faced the past and figured it out."

"Or she could die." A pause. "Or you could die," she adds.

That's not at all what I thought Frankie would say, and it knocks me backward. Mom said she left for emotional reasons. "I'm sorry this is happening to you. I really am. But I want my mom to be my mom. That's it."

"Me too, kiddo. Me too."

When I turn, Richard's fingers are curled over Frankie's. I hear him say, "Leave it all on the field, Frankie."

I have no idea what that means, but Frankie's response is a piercing, tear-filled look at me. "You're mad at her right now, but do something for me? A favor for a dying woman?"

I nod.

"Give her a hug for me." Frankie extends her arms. "And then try to forgive her."

I step into Frankie's embrace, and she is ribs and love

and muscle and sadness. And then she is ripped away and my arms are empty.

I hear, "Quick, get off that kid," from far closer than I imagine possible. The guards are in the enclosure. The skinny guard raises his baton to strike her and catches me in the forehead on his backswing.

I fall into the fence and Frankie screams and lunges toward me. This time, when the guard brings his baton down, he brings all his force. Once. Twice. A bone breaks the second time and she screams in pain. From the ground, I can't tell whether he broke her nose or cheekbone, but there is no mistaking the crack. Her hands cover her face; the blood drips between her fingers like a horror film. Richard holds me as the Minion woman drags Frankie away.

There's a tremor in Richard's voice when he tilts my forehead for a better view. "Lion, you're gonna need a stitch."

Some blood on the concrete is mine. I press my hand to my forehead and feel the stream dripping into my ear and down my cheek.

At the entrance to Floyd, the guards and Francis appear to halt; each guard strains to shove her through the doorway. As they wrestle, I read the crude prison tattoo above Francis's elbow bone. *Jane.*

"Don't go to Nockabout," Frankie screams. "Let me die and it be over."

Blood leaves a trail between us like breadcrumbs.

I am standing in a puddle.

The baton rises again. And before the strike . . . "Tell her I love you," she yells.

Frankie collapses, unconscious, and they drag her indoors.

CHAPTER 16

My back muscles are already smarting from where I fell into the fencing, the swelling under way. In the silence, my head feels like it's experiencing a tornado. The migraine will be full-blown by the time we're back at the car. I hope I can see to get there. Richard has torn off a portion of his sleeve and has it pressed to the gash on my forehead.

"You're okay," he says.

"I'll live." I immediately regret my choice of words.

Our escort guard returns and Richard, who has always been calm and cool, tells him in no uncertain terms that Floyd'll hear from his lawyer. This guard is about ten years old, turtles inside his uniform, and says, "I can get you a Band-Aid or a cotton ball."

"No thanks."

We reverse the long hallways and locked corridors. My back, numb. My brain, electric. The cut bleeds through the fabric of the shirt. By the time we return to the desk for our checked belongings, word has reached the front. The ancient guard strongly discourages us from bringing a financial suit against Floyd over the mishandled "incident" and hands me a towel.

That bone-cracking baton strike reverberates in my ears, making me nauseous all over again. And then her voice. *"Let me die and it be over."*

What is *it*? And then I hear her yelling those final words to my mom: *"Tell her I love you."*

There are very few certain things in this world. Very few.

But after the last hour, I'd stake my life on Frankie's innocence. There's no way that woman killed anyone. Much less her best friend.

CHAPTER 17

When we arrive at the Honda, we lock ourselves inside. "They broke her nose, maybe her jaw," I say, and Richard says, "Yeah, and they knocked you pretty good too. Let me get a look at that cut."

I remove the torn piece of his shirt and check my forehead in the mirror before turning for his evaluation. I am a mess. The corner of the cut is deep; the rest, a scratch. The blood's clotting. Richard's glove box overflows with paper napkins from Wendy's. I clean up the various paths and smudges of dried blood on my face. The corner continues to bleed.

"Keep the pressure on that side," Richard says. "We'd better get you to a clinic."

"Don't pay for that," I argue, and make sure I can't see the bone or anything. "I'll steri-strip it at home."

He shakes his head. I can't tell if he's impressed or disapproves. "You know, you don't always have to be such a lion."

"Right," I say, because if the last few days have taught me anything, it's that there's no time to be a mouse. "Richard, she didn't do it."

"No," he says. "She did not."

The confidence in his voice is deep. Like he isn't relying on my opinion but his own. That feels nice. To have him in this with me. Strange to believe my mother has been right about Frankie all these years.

Richard moves his hands around the wheel, flexes his fingers, and says, "I'm from there." Another pause. "Grew up in Lone Valley, like your mom and Frankie. I left a year after the murder. Took a job in Lexington, then Boone County, then wound up in Radcliff. Got married. Got divorced. Your mom came to me needing help—and I helped. You grow up in a place like ours and one of your own asks for help and . . . well, I guess she was the dose of home I needed without paying for the gas."

I am speechless.

His confession contains a few side glances in my direction. No eye contact.

"Okay," I say.

He laughs with disbelief. "You're angry with her and fine with me? Maybe we should go to the clinic and get an X-ray."

"Richard. You're not my mom. You haven't been lying

to me my whole life about who you are or who I am. Plus, I don't have time to be angry with you too. I need you to help me make her go back."

"Why? After everything Frankie said."

"Because of everything Frankie said," I argue.

"Bethie won't do it." He's immovable on this conclusion.

"Then I'll do it for her. Alone if necessary. I'm eighteen." Richard struggles with what to say next and I continue, "Here's what I know. You don't believe Frankie killed Cora and Mom doesn't believe Frankie killed Cora and now *I* don't believe Frankie killed Cora. Who she is plus how little evidence there is equals not guilty. I'm not saying I'm a detective or smarter than all the other people who tried to figure this out, but I'm at the center of something I didn't ask for. And if I don't try to save Frankie, there is something seriously wrong with my head. And Frankie's right, if Mom lied to me, there's a reason. She might be scared to go back, so I'll go back for her."

Whatever happened all those years ago to Frankie resulted in more than Cora's death; layers and layers remain. Allegiance cost Mom her family. Even if Frankie dies, I want to understand this piece of the past.

I text Sam.

Nyla: Met with Frankie.

Nyla: She's innocent.

Nyla: Want to help me prove it?

Nyla: (It might increase your tour attendance. $)

Sam: In the middle of huge stuff. Stay tuned.

Richard drives and I recline the passenger seat until the back meets two cases of Cokes I forgot to bring into the house earlier in the week. Cold sweat slinks along my spine. Muscles across the top of my back throb in time with my head. The daylight dances on the other side of my eyelids, and I attempt to block light and memories and thoughts with my forearm. Only after taking long, measured breaths do I feel any amount of calm.

Richard pauses at the guard shack to reclaim our IDs. The same guy from earlier leans nearly through the windshield to see me. "Heard things got a little dicey."

Richard pats my knee. "We'll send you the bill."

"Good luck with that," the guard says.

I don't open my eyes. The migraine is in full assault mode. No matter how tightly I close my eyes, nothing keeps the documentary from playing: The baton strikes Frankie. She is that limp doll being dragged over the threshold while I watch helplessly from my own cage.

We're nearly back to our exit, having forgone the stitches, when I lift the seat to the upright position and say, "Hey, Richard."

"Hey, Lion."

"Did you see Frankie's tattoo? The Jane tattoo?"

"Uh-huh," he says quietly. A quick glance in my direction and then, "I believe that was Cora's middle name."

That's my middle name too.

And I find it's nice to have something of hers.

CHAPTER 18

At home, the garage door is at half-mast and Rod Stewart blares rock at the neighborhood. There's no further word from Sam, but I get an internet notification of a diving accident on Green River Lake that would definitely count as huge to him. I shouldn't be, but I'm disappointed. I thought huge had to do with Frankie's case rather than a lake emergency.

Mom's working out, which is preferable to her pity coma. I understand her a little better than I did when I left. These weights, this workout: it's control, not strength. She probably can't even see how strong she is.

"You should get in the shower and let me break the news to her about . . ." He taps the skin of his forehead.

I agree that she'll flip out if she sees the blood and head inside as he walks slowly and deliberately toward the garage. I'm relieved he's telling her about the encounter.

He'll likely recount the entire experience and they might even strategize together on how to dissuade me from Nockabout. From what he said in the car about his departure from his hometown, he seems to have his own reasons to stay far away.

I'm making my way up the steps when Sam calls.

"Hey," I say, surprised. I took him for a texter, not a caller. "You okay?"

"Too much to type so I called. Hope you don't mind." He's breathing crazy hard. Either winded or excited. "I just did a rescue dive."

"That's great."

"No. Not great. I pulled a girl out of the Cora cave. Same age as your aunt was. Same look too. They could be sisters. That's unbelievable, right? Two girls. One alive. One dead. Same age. Same place. Twenty years apart, but this one's right before Frankie's execution. What the heck is going on?"

I don't say anything. Anything I said would be conjecture. *Green River Lake is popular. Frankie's case is in the news. Tourist probably went exploring and got in trouble.*

"You there?" he asks.

"Yeah. Thinking."

"Think about this, Lion, because I haven't gotten to the interesting part yet. This girl had a diamond tester in her pocket. Because she needs to know whether a stone is a diamond or not in an aggregate mine? And it's the only thing on her. No ID. No camera. No phone. No swimsuit. No

100

flashlight. Nothing that says 'I was swimming and got into trouble' or 'I was exploring and got lost.' Not only that, she's skin and bones. No way she was healthy enough to dive that cave in the first place. What's a girl in those circumstances doing with a diamond tester?"

He's got a point. "Who is she?"

"Nobody on the rescue team recognizes her. Ned said she might be a college student and that makes sense, but . . . a diamond tester. Totally weird coincidence. Remember Emily the blogger, 'the expert' asking about diamonds? And now this girl turns up in the same location? Come on. No such thing as a coincidence."

"Maybe," I agree, not wanting to tell him that Emily probably isn't the only one with a diamond theory.

"If you saw her, you'd agree." In the background noise, there's a commotion. "Wait. What?" he says to someone on his side.

I picture him there on the beach. Wearing his swimsuit and diving gear, dripping wet; his phone to his ear, goggles pushed into his hair. He's tall and lean. A young Adam Driver without a crooked nose. A pleasant picture. Far better than the one in front of me. I'm standing in front of the shower door, head throbbing, partially naked, not willing to turn on the water while I'm on the phone.

"Lion, Anna's here. She claims the girl is a patient from the Center. That she snuck out last night."

"See?" I appreciate Anna's reach. She is the Mary Poppins of Nockabout.

Sam lowers his voice and the background noises dull. I picture him stepping farther away from the crowd gathered on the beach. "Lion, I'm telling you, I've got a weird feeling that she's connected to Cora."

"Okay," I say.

"You asked if I wanted to help you. This is me helping." He's disappointed by my response and I rally to explain.

"Ignore me. I got smashed in the head by a guard at Floyd who was trying to beat Frankie for hugging me. I'm not at my best and I'm actually bleeding. Give me time to shower and sleep and we'll meet up tomorrow and figure out a plan of action."

"Do I need to beat someone up?" he asks.

His protective streak delights me. "Sure. Except no. Because then you'd be in prison, too, and I'd have no one to help me." I give a weak laugh.

"Promise you're okay?"

"I'm better than your cave girl, but clearly not up to full mental acuity. Get back with the dive team, talk with Anna, find out all you can, and I'll meet you tomorrow at the Lone Valley dock at 10:00 a.m."

CHAPTER 19

Rain pounds the windshield on the drive to Nockabout. I didn't tell Mom and Richard anything; I took the keys and left, coffee in one hand, purse in the other. The migraine I've had since yesterday nags instead of screams. Nothing ibuprofen and sunglasses won't fix. With a bandage the size of New Hampshire on my forehand, I leave my hair down for a little coverage. The red waves hang below my chest and feel like a million pounds of hair. Not my favorite look, but today was never going to be my favorite. Not in this rain and humidity. Not with that bandage. The minute I step into the rain, I'll be sporting my favorite poodle updo.

I follow the signs to the ferry, feeling more comfortable navigating this time. A scattering of cars populates the lower lot, and except for a navy sedan, the upper lot is filled with minivans, golden retrievers, and dads running their weekly honey-do errands. I park near the water and Sam hops in the passenger seat without me even seeing him walk up from behind.

He's wet but not soaked and has to dance around the stuff I've left on the seat and floorboard. "Pull back up to Ned's, will you? He's got a little table inside." While I drive, Sam parts my hair near the cut on my forehead as if it's the most natural action in the world. He's looking at the bandage, and I can smell chai or something spicy on his breath. "You need a Captain America or Wonder Woman Band-Aid, if you ask me." He's serious then. "How's your noggin feeling?"

"Fine. How are you?"

"Glad you're here. Disappointed I had to pull a cave rescue for you to come back and visit me."

"You don't know. I might have shown up for the two o'clock tour."

He clicks the side of his mouth. "That one's rained out today, but I'll let you pay me fifty bucks to make up for yesterday's."

"No chance."

"Yeah, I didn't think so."

I like that he teases me, that he wants me here. I find myself smiling and he catches me. "What?"

"Nothing." It's against my better judgment to let on how much I enjoy him.

"You were thinking about us. Go on and admit it." He's cheeky and enjoying himself as he says, "You were like—here we are in a murder movie and you're the gorgeous girl and I'm the handsome guy and we're going to get together by the time we solve this. Am I right or am I right?"

"Are you always this confident?"

For a split second the bravado thins as he questions if I like his confidence or find it annoying, and then it's back, full strength. "Fake it till you make it."

It's probably safe to say he has made it.

At Ned's, we duck inside and manage to stay mostly dry. A bell over the door rings our arrival, but no one is in view. A grinding noise is coming from the back of the shop. Tucked into the front corner of the shop is a bistro table and chairs with a gorgeous view of the lake. Sam plunks down and I do the same, even though I wouldn't mind taking a stroll to see what Ned's Fine Jewelry and Pawn has to offer.

Sam yells, "Ned. It's me."

The noise stops. *"Hola. ¿Qué tal,* Samuel?" a voice calls from behind the shower curtain acting as a door.

Sam's eyes are laughing when he tells me, "Ned has been learning Spanish." A dramatic pause. "For about twenty years. He and Dad were in school together."

"I heard that, and we weren't. Your father was a lowly freshman when I was a senior." There's humor in his tone. The man peeks from behind the curtain and searches the floor. "And where's my Lucy?" he asks.

"She ate a shoe," Sam says and raises his mismatched tennis shoes for us to see.

"I thought maybe Mr. Famous TV Man needed to be free for interviews. Do you have one here?" he asks, gesturing to me with approval. "Ned." He greets me with a wave. "Pardon my mess. Day in the life of jewelry."

"Nyla," I say.

I don't typically like men who wear yellow gold necklaces and diamonds in their rings; Ned has both and they fit him perfectly. He's balding and has the distinct starch of wealth and the unique bent of someone used to serving others. The hair on his arms is the same rust color of what is left on his head. He uses his paunch as an armrest and looks back and forth between Sam and me. "It's very nice to meet you, Nyla. What do you think of our local hero?"

"He's decent," I say.

"Oh, I like this one," Ned says to Sam. He holds up a finger like he has just the thing and then ducks behind a counter and returns with two Cokes. "I'll leave you to your corner booth then."

We thank him and he heads toward the back. The bell tinkles again before he can get through the shower curtain.

Anna, the caregiver from the other day, ducks inside. Drenched and dripping, she extends a black velvet drawstring purse toward Ned. She notices us in the corner, smiles, and says to Ned, "Cassandra's, of course."

"A cleaning?" he asks formally.

"A stone needs resetting."

Ned peers into the bag. "And how's the patient today?"

Sam and I lean toward their conversation, unsure of

whether he means Cassandra or the girl Sam rescued on the beach. Either is likely fodder for town gossip.

"Cassandra had me at the Center this morning before six." Anna's aware we're listening. She looks in our direction with a silly screwed-up face that indicates she is a fan of sleeping much later. "Sam, you'll be pleased to know she's stable."

"They took her to the Center instead of the hospital?" I ask.

Ned beams with what can only be called hometown pride. "The Center has a small, state-of-the-art treatment room and the very best doctors and nurses. The transition to inpatient care will be safer and easier for the girl from there."

Anna walks behind Sam and squeezes his shoulders. "Boy howdy. You should have seen your dad this morning. Ben was whistling. Like legitimately happy. Talking about how no one could have made that rescue dive but you."

"He did not," Sam says dismissively. To me he says, "Dad is more of a grunt of approval guy."

"Okay," she agrees. "He didn't use those words, but I knew. And he was whistling. That part's not an exaggeration."

Sam's cheeks redden and he tucks his chin toward the table; I suppose he's unsure of what to say in light of Anna's and his father's praise.

Anna asks, "The girl didn't say anything to you that I could pass along to the doctors, did she? Anything about how long she was in the mine or cave system? How she got there?"

107

"Nothing," Sam says.

Did Anna see the diamond tester? She seems to know about everything else.

The caregiver leans against the windowsill and toys with one of the wilder chunks of her hair. Water drips from the strands and onto the carpet. "Dr. Creed thinks a visitor smuggled in drugs and she jumped from the second-story porch and ran. No telling how she ended up on the beach. He's got half the nurses up there calling her Houdini."

Ned says, "Cassandra probably wants Creed's head on a platter."

"Oh yeah," Anna says. "'The press will eat us alive for this.'" She imitates the elderly woman's voice and nails the power and fragility. "'Anna, get up there and make sure no one sues. Anna!' At three this morning, mind you. 'There's already news speculating what Rebecca will have to say about her husband's clinic losing a patient. And then there's the situation with Elizabeth.'" I flinch, but Anna is wrapped in her tale and doesn't notice. "Like I can control the spin of anything. Houdini isn't coming out of sedation anytime soon. They've got her under. Probably the best thing for her. Definitely the best thing for Cassandra's health." There's obvious love for her employer in the teasing and something else too. Frustration maybe? Weariness? "Anyway, if you could put a rush on that resetting, I'm sure it would calm her down."

Ned lifts the velvet bag. "Diamonds are a girl's best friends."

I tense under the table and Sam presses his tennis shoes against mine. We're both thinking the same thing—Emily's diamonds and the diamond tester. Anna curses the rain, bids us goodbye, and hurries out of the shop.

Ned says, "Well, I've got polishing to do."

Sam hops up with a request of his own. "Before you start, can I show Nyla your workroom?"

Ned scratches at grinding dirt that's caked on his cheek and grins. "I guess Cassandra's cardiac care can wait a few minutes."

The workroom is wonderful. Messy and a brand of chaos that only an artist can love. I see immediately why Sam wanted to share Ned's natural habitat. Wall-sized tools and ovens and a very expensive computer setup with design software. A diamond ring design spins in circles on the home screen. Soldering irons hang over worktables. Scattered plastic bags and coiled metals and loose stones and adorable bins with hundreds of tiny drawers and a million other things I can't identify but are very cool. Not at all what I expected from the bowels of Ned's Fine Jewelry and Pawn Shop.

"This is where the magic happens," Sam says. "Ned's one of the best jewelers in the world."

"Could you say that to my dad?" Ned jokes and then adds for my benefit, "He's still disappointed I'm not a dentist."

"Leaving the practice to pursue a passion isn't a crime," Sam says.

"You're only on my side because I'm teaching you to cut stones."

"Maybe," Sam says. "All right, we'll leave you for our Cokes and corner table. *Adios, amigo.*"

"*Adios.*" Ned lifts a dismissive hand without turning around. He's seated now and anxious to get working from the way his posture curves and his eyes linger on Cassandra's cinched velvet bag.

On the way to the front, I ask, "How'd he go from dentistry to diamonds?"

Sam's sigh is deep. "All has to do with his mom. Been in the Center for twenty years. Early onset Alzheimer's. Super tragic. Now, I'm piecing this together from a bunch of conversations, but basically, Ned and Dr. Damron disagreed on her treatment. Enough that Ned left the family practice and they stopped speaking. He needed to fund a life that kept him close to his mom, so he turned a hobby into a world-class business."

I'm impressed with Ned's ability to land on his feet. "That's sad about his dad though," I say.

"Yeah. He'll tell you he doesn't care, but he makes comments like he made earlier. And he let it slip one day that his dad has an undergraduate degree in Spanish."

I say, "So you think he's learning another language to—"

"—impress the dad he swears he hates. Yep, I do."

"Man. Parents," I say, thinking about the differences

in how one child reacts versus another. Ned, the son who won't leave. Beth, the daughter who jetted away in a crisis.

"I've been thinking about what you should do about all this," Sam says.

"Yeah?"

"What if you blow it up?"

"Blow it up?"

"Yeah, put it on your socials. Call those reporters back. You heard Anna. Press will get this family's attention. You want to investigate anyway, and sooner or later Emily's website will get back to Cassandra. Beat her to the punch. There's no way your mom can avoid coming home then."

"You are seriously underestimating her ability to run," I say. "Besides, what if they hate her? What if they actually asked her to leave way back when and she's too embarrassed to tell me?"

"Trust me. They didn't. According to my dad, she broke their hearts."

"You're sure?" Heartbroken wasn't the impression I got from what little she said about her folks.

"I'm sure it'll be tense. But think about it, Lion. Beth comes back here to face the music and that gives you and me plenty of time to figure out who is the Houdini diamond tester and who in the world killed Cora."

"Mom won't."

"Do it without her. You're the granddaughter of a senator. You'd get an interview in a second."

I don't want to call the reporters. That's a loss of control in my book. Who knows how they might cover the story? Mom could even end up being a suspect for conspiracy theorists like Emily. Especially if yesterday's tour gets ahold of her handwriting sample. She flat out mentions killing her sister. If I take Sam's advice, the attention can't be on Mom.

But if it's not on her, who then?

And then I realize what we can do.

CHAPTER 20

H ow's the camera on your phone?"

"Sucky," Sam says.

"We'll use mine. It's one notch up from sucky."

"And what exactly are we doing?"

"You'll see."

Forty minutes later, the rain clears and I have nearly memorized my script. I don't need the video to be great. I don't even need it to be public; I need Mom to believe it is.

We frame up the shot. Nockabout behind us, boats crossing in and out of view. Sam holds my phone and says, "Tell me when."

I flip my hair up and down, coaxing body into the limp strands. The pad of pavement beneath us holds the day's heat like a sauna. Steam burns off the puddles.

"When."

He shoots a finger at me and I begin, trying my best to summon the tour voice he used the previous day.

"Behind me is Green River Lake in Lone Valley, Kentucky. The island you see is named Nockabout. Twenty years ago, a body surfaced on a private beach, right over there." I point in the general western direction. "The girl, the *victim*, was my age. You know her as Cora King, the daughter of Senator Rebecca King. And you likely know by now her best friend, Francis Quick, was convicted of her murder. In twenty-five days, the ADPA will take the life of Francis Quick. Did she commit the crime?" I glance over my shoulder at the beach. "Well, according to the justice system, yes. But if you look at the miniscule evidence used to convict her? There's another conclusion."

I address the camera directly and with conviction. "Hi. You're watching *Death Daze* with Nyla Wagner"—I breathe—"and over the next twenty-five days I'm going to take you on an unflinchingly honest investigation of Cora King's death. Starting with one fact you likely don't know. I am the daughter of Elizabeth King, and Cora was my aunt. Do I want justice for her? Absolutely. And I'd love for my mother, Beth King, to feel safe returning to her hometown and for the real murderer to be caught. But . . ."

I bait the word with silence and let the boats motor past in the background. "But if new evidence isn't found, well, you and I both know what will happen. Francis Quick will be executed by the state of Kentucky under the ADPA." I jump straight into a tiny bit of commentary that will hopefully ease Mom's mind. "Now, I am more than aware that the public's opinion on the ADPA depends on political affiliation. I am aware that neither side"—I make air quotes around *side*—"finds the practice foolproof. Not even my estranged grandmother, Senator Rebecca King. She has long stated that she's not pro-ADPA for personal gain or revenge, but because she, along with the majority who backed the ADPA, proclaim the procedure is a necessary evil to overcome the financial crisis in the United States. This is not a political video meant for one side or the other." I give a smile that should please my mother and say, "It's more than that. This is a quest for justice and truth. This is my challenge to every Sherlock like me. Help me solve the murder of my aunt, Cora King."

Another deep breath and then the close. "Tune in next time to *Death Daze* and we'll take a tour of Francis Quick's Camaro."

I smile and Sam makes a cutting motion.

"That was great. You could actually do this."

"No way," I say. "Now we send this YouTube link to Mom." I send the private link and then a text.

We have to go back now. Cassandra has seen this.

My heart pounds as I hit Send. She's going to kill me. Frankie might too, given how adamant she was that I not come back to Nockabout.

"You ready to have a good time?" Sam asks.

"No murder, right?"

"Nope."

"No tours?"

"Uh," he stammers. "No tours with blood. I was thinking we'd go for a boat ride."

"Only if you feed me," I say.

Sam and I grab sandwiches and boat the less popular sections of Green River Lake. Despite his agreeing to no tours, I convince him to walk me step by step through the rescue of Houdini. After that, we talk about everything except the murder. He's easy to be with, and even if we didn't have the last two days in common, we'd be friends.

By the time I climb in the Honda that afternoon, I have thought about kissing him more than once. The prospect of spending more time in Nockabout entails perks beyond getting to know my family. There's an incoming text from him when I pull into the drive at home.

Sam: Trouble. Big Trouble.

I don't know what that means. He's texting again. The three dots are there, but my mom is already charging across the yard toward my window. Here's the rage I expected. I need to play it as cool as I can or she'll see through me.

"I cannot believe you," she says. Richard has come to stand on the porch. He gives me nothing about how I should handle her.

"I know you're mad," I say, hoping that if I empathize long enough she'll let me talk.

"Mad? I don't even know what I am right now." She's freaking out—the vein in her temple is hitting its pulses double time. "Granny has seen this video?"

I say the first thing that seems plausible. "Her care-giver, Anna, showed it to her."

Mom throws her hands up in the air. "I can't believe you did this."

"Oh, I think you're pointing at the wrong person."

"You're playing a dangerous game, Ny."

"You're blowing this out of proportion," I say.

"Have you seen the views?"

I'm about to get busted. I was not counting on her under-standing privacy settings on YouTube—on her knowing or caring about numbers. Game's up.

I lift my phone, prepared to show her the lack of YouTube stats, and read Sam's message on my notification screen.

Sam: We were live. Video's been public this whole time.

This is the BBC's coverage.

A link follows.

I click and hear an English voice say, "Meanwhile in America, the most picked-up livestream of the day is from Nyla King, the granddaughter of Kentucky senator Rebecca King. Now, Senator King happens to be one of the most ardent supporters of the controversial Advanced Death Penalty Act passed less than three months ago. Those following the story have watched hundreds of incarcerated men and women on death row face their final appeal, and likely their final meals. Eighteen-year-old Nyla King has something to say about that. And her family."

Oh my gosh.

"The BBC?" she says, her anger deflated, her tone dubious.

I go with it. "Mom, this is good. No! Great. People are talking about Frankie on a global scale. You want to save Frankie. You don't do it through Jimmy the Lawyer; you do it by going home." With the pressure of a viral video, the idea suddenly seems less appealing, but there's no room to backtrack now.

"I can't," she says, but I can tell she's considering.

"You have to. For Frankie. Mom, the world's arguing about the ADPA. Hollywood. Wall Street. DC. Facebook's on fire. Twitter. Twitch. Everywhere and everyone who has an opinion has or is going to watch. This is our chance to find justice for Cora and Frankie."

I watch her face move through emotions like hands on a clock, until finally she arrives at acceptance. "We'll go to Nockabout."

As I hug her, I watch Richard. He gives a head shake that feels almost audible. *Guess you're getting what you want*, it says.

He looks scared for me. For all of us.

PART II

CHAPTER 21

N ever assume adults can move quickly. At basically anything. Especially not travel. They need to plan and buy batteries and bottled water and reroute mail and think through what might happen in the event of an earthquake, even if you're nowhere near a fault line.

Nockabout is less than two hours away. I've gone twice now with hardly more than a coffee cup. Mom and Richard find my approach wanting. Never mind Frankie's on a tight schedule; they cannot be rushed.

Richard won't go without a gun, which he doesn't own. Mom "needs" her weight bench, and the Pilot isn't large enough to transport it and us. So after booking a two-bedroom Airbnb in Lone Valley under Richard's name, the two of them spend most of that night in the garage transforming an old trailer into a roadworthy pull-behind and then making a trip to a pawn shop and Walmart.

Taking her weights to our Airbnb isn't all that surprising. In times of stress, Mom either works or works out, and we're all anticipating the stress ahead. Coverage hasn't slowed down; the snowballs have built into a country-wide division. There are marches planned at county and city courthouses from Seattle to Miami. My video struck a nerve that pierced the body of America. One reporter went so far as to call me the "Voodooist for the American conscience."

All I can reckon is the world was poised to have this fight and they needed a rallying point, which I accidentally provided. I've gotten voice mails from every Tom, Dick, and Harry news affiliate. They want a cover photo and a time-line. When will I release the next video?

I shouldn't, but I spend the evening watching social media expand and contract around all news related to Frankie Quick. People come out of the woodwork to share their interactions with Cora and Beth King and Frankie Quick. They're entertaining. Some aren't so favorable. Most are from run-of-the-mill attention-seekers. And if you ever want to know what people think about you, all you have to do is go viral.

A girl on my track team writes:
Beth Wagner is an avid steroid user who got her own daughter hooked in order to win. That's how she beat me in the 400 at Regionals.
A girl in my political science class:
There's no way Nyla Wagner is a senator's

granddaughter. She was the worst group project partner evah. We got a C-. What an embarrassment to the great Rebecca King.

A guy I went to the movies with on a group date writes: Family seemed normal to me.

And then there are other "character" witnesses.

Carl, Mom's grant cowriter for the school system: Beth Wagner is a saint. Doesn't matter what her last name is. She's done more for the county than most people will do in a lifetime.

Leslie Willick, a former landlord: I never had trouble out of the Wagners. Never saw any meth or weapons or weird kinky sex stuff. They had bedbugs once and even hauled the mattress to the dump. Now, you know a woman who hauls a mattress to the dump ain't involved in nothing criminal. She coulda put that on the street for the garbage man.

Estelle489 responds to Leslie's post: Maybe there was blood on the mattress she didn't want the garbage man to see.

Sam sends me a few of his favorites. They include random photos of me that were probably taken by the school yearbook crew. One is from freshman year—I had braces and decided to grow out my bangs. Whew. Not attractive.

Nyla: Glad you saw that one.

Sam: Me too. If I ever need blackmail, I'm ready.

Nyla: Whatever. Everyone's already seen it.

Sam: Good point. Not to worry, there are far worse ones of me.

Nyla: Doubt that.

There's a pause and Sam sends a photo that I have to agree might be worse.

Nyla: OMGosh. How old were you?

Sam: Twelve and obsessed with Dad's Bon Jovi collection.

Sam: Want to shoot the Camaro video tomorrow?

Nyla: Yes.

Sam: What time will you be here?

Nyla: Question of the year.

My brain processes *pop, crack, pop, crack* out of sequence. But I know immediately that it's gunfire. Richard must be testing his new pistol in the backyard.

Pop. Pop. Louder now. Closer. Uncomfortably close.

Pop. Pop. Pop. The lights go out.

A window in my bedroom shatters. Shards drop to the carpet. I tumble off the opposite side of the bed and cover my head. I send Sam a text.

Someone's shooting at the house. 412 Maple St. Call 911.

Pop. Pop. Pop. Pop.

"Mom! Richard!"

I don't know if they're in the garage or if they finished and came in. I was consumed with Sam and scrolling on my phone.

Staying in a crouch, I creep downstairs. I am between the front door and the kitchen hallway when the large bay window in the living room explodes inward. Four feet away, a brick lies on the coffee table. And then a canister hits and rolls.

Another *Pop. Pop.*

And then the smell of gas.

CHAPTER 22

I lay splayed across a musty blue-and-gold rug that runs the length of the hallway. Mom's arms, elbows, and head form a cage around my skull. Her body atop mine, shielding me from whatever might come next. She pulled me down and under before I realized she was in the room. We must look like a scene in a military movie. "Crawl toward the kitchen, Ny."

Richard yells, "Beth!"

"Coming," she says, and we army crawl in the direction of his voice.

Behind us, gray smoke rises from beneath our now-concave coffee table. A second cloud originates from closer to the television. The two fogs meet and mix and seep in all directions.

"The brick was wrapped in paper," I mutter.

She swats my backside, sending me in the direction of the kitchen. "Go, go, go. There's no time."

But I've already reversed toward what my brain has identified as a probable note. The gas spreads fast, overtaking the air with a peppery heat. My nose drips from the acidic attack. My fingers close around the brick, the rubber band, the plastic bag. And then Mom is tugging me backward. She coughs and grips my hand tighter. We reunite with Richard in the kitchen, Marnie the cat, who never appears for anyone except Richard, in his arms.

The back door opens onto a large porch with floor-to-ceiling windows. Nothing on this side of the property seems askew and yet the idea of crossing into the open, after the gunfire, doesn't appeal. Mom pauses at the glass doors, gathering her wits. I am longing for clean air and cough hard enough bile slides up my throat. "Do you see anyone?" I ask, looking across the shadowed yard.

In the distance, sirens wail.

"Can you run, babe?" Mom's voice is husky, a whisper. Tears streak her cheeks and neck. I nod and Richard does as well. He removes the wooden dowel blocking the track and slides the door in two shoves. Marnie claws her way loose and darts up a tree.

"Garage," Mom says, and then, "Film this, Ny. Go live right now." Her face is nearly grayed out; the dark straps of her tank top show dark against her skin.

There's no time to evaluate if this is sound logic. "Where are you going?" she says as I move toward the living room one final time. I hit Record and my scratchy voice matches the foggy feeling of the room. "This is *Death Daze* with Nyla

Wagner. Two minutes ago someone shot at our house and threw a gas canister through the front window." I do a quick pan of the clouds behind me. I'm not sure what to say next and end up saying, "This is heating up, people. Why attack my home unless I'm right about Frankie's innocence? Bye for now."

"Good job," Mom says. "Now . . . garage. Richard and I are right behind you."

The siren is near.

I've done a lot of running in my life. Nearly every morning since I turned eleven. Three to five miles on school days, eight to ten on weekends and summers. Pushing my body isn't foreign; I've asked it to sprint when it wanted to walk plenty—but never like this. I bust through the yard, hoping no one is waiting outside to pick us off. The brick feels like a counterweight, making my right side out of sync with my left.

In the three seconds it takes to leave the illusion of protection provided by the porch for the illusion of protection in the garage, my head screams a yin and yang chorus: *You're all going to die; you're not going to die. You're all going to die; you're not going to die.*

The garage is ten steps away.

Five.

I skid across the loose gravel and slam into the garage. I hold in a cough, unwilling to draw more attention while exposed, and wrench open the door. I don't stop until I hit the workbench on the rear wall. I cough until I choke. My heart pounds against my knees as I tighten into a ball, waiting for Richard and Mom. They are there and huddle around me. Tears and snot drip over my lip and into my mouth. I listen for more gunshots but hear only sirens and Richard wheezing for air.

Mom's arms remain cocooned around me in the tightest hug my lungs allow. "We're okay. Someone wanted to scare us. They're gone. They're gone." These are her mantras.

She's correct. By the time officers announce their arrival in the garage, I'm pretty sure whoever did this is long gone.

"Is anyone injured?" the officer says, hurrying inside.

Mom uncoils and makes a rapid assessment. "Check Richard's lungs."

I agree. That much smoke plus exertion can't be good for a man his age. Their attention to Richard gives me a moment of privacy with the brick; time to see if the thrower sent a literal message. They did.

Rubber-banded to the brick is a Ziploc bag. Inside is a flash drive and note. *Play this on* Death Daze, *you freak.* I slip the Ziploc into the pocket with my phone and turn my full attention to the officers and rescue workers who are crowding into the garage. "Site's clear," one woman says.

I step forward and hand off the brick. "Someone threw this through the bay window in the living room," I say.

The officer is surprised by this. "You brought it with you?"

"I was standing in there when it hit."

He takes the brick gingerly and calls for an evidence bag.

My legs wobble as I walk toward Mom and someone offers me a bottle of water, which I down. A female EMT touches a stethoscope to my chest and fingers to my pulse. "You feeling okay?"

"Other than adrenaline, yeah." My voice cracks at my attempt to whisper and I take another long drink.

"And this injury?" She indicates the bandage on my forehead.

"Not from tonight."

Another EMT does his best to address Mom's and Richard's care. A police officer says, "The 911 operator said shots were fired. Are you aware of any injuries other than the gas inhalation?"

"Minor cuts to my feet," Mom answers, and he removes a lawn chair from where it hangs on the wall and helps her sit. He lifts her bare feet toward the light and I see the blood.

"I'll get those fixed up for you right here, ma'am."

A radio chirps and the ambulance eases closer to the garage.

"Any idea who would do this to your house?" an officer asks.

"I've got a theory," I say and take out my phone. "I'm guessing one of these idiots." It takes me several minutes of searching below the video I posted inside the house. Already there are hundreds of comments, maybe thousands, given the number of posts I pass before the page reloads. When I find what I'm looking for, I enlarge a section of comments for the officer.

Beth Wagner should be killed with Frankie Quick.

Strap Beth to the chair for what she did to her sister.

The Wagners are liberal scum who should be eliminated.

Take the fight to them. Justice forever. Defend the ADPA.

The ADPA is the constitution. Let all opposed burn.

On and on they go.

People hate or love Mom. Love or hate Francis Quick. Love or hate Senator Rebecca King. I count four death threats on one screen alone. They are venomous in a way that makes no sense. How can strangers be so hateful with strangers? It's almost like someone has removed all the gray area from the earth and we're left with only black and white opinions.

Hate isn't the only response. Curiosity is a close second. Around the world, armchair investigators are caught up in a twenty-year-old case. They want to know:

Has Nyla seen this or that trial document?

They add screenshots of trial paperwork and hand-writing samples.

Is Nyla aware of Francis's juvie record?

More screenshots and JPEGs.

Loads of similar questions and documents populate a new FreeFrancisQuick.com site.

Mom's coughing turns to amazement at what I'm showing them.

A wheeze comes from Richard and then, "She told you this is dangerous."

"Who, sir?" the officer asks. "Who told you this is dangerous?"

"Frankie."

That's not the answer he expected. He hitches up his belt and focuses in on Mom. "Okay, walk me through the night one more time."

We give our accounts and are interrupted by the arrival of a young officer. He carries two large evidence bags. Each holds a security light and its mount. They're shattered, bullet holes at their centers. "Confirmed, boss," he said. "Bullet holes. Twelve-gauge shotgun from the looks of the damage."

Our officer agrees with the analysis. To us, he says, "We'll track the IP addresses of those who've commented on your channel and see if there's evidence the person who did this is among those yahoos." He sends the agent on his way with the directive, "Call IT Carl in the morning and see what he can unearth. In the meantime, I'll get these three settled in a hotel."

"Beth, do you still want to go back to Nockabout? After this?" Richard asks.

Mom flexes. Not like a bodybuilder. Like she's steeling herself. The attack has woken her up. "We have to. Whatever I face going home can't be worse than what Frankie's faced every day the last twenty years. I shouldn't have let it come to this."

"You know she'll find out," he says.

132

"Yes." A bittersweet expression crosses her face. "And I'll deal with it."

"Mom, Frankie'll understand," I say.

Richard and Mom look off in the distance. "It's complicated," they say together.

CHAPTER 23

The police send us to a hotel for the night. The first available moment I slip away to the ice machine room, call Sam, and tell him everything. He's as amped as I feel, maybe more. "What does the jump drive have on it?"

"I don't know yet. No way to check."

"Girl, go to the lobby," he says. "Use whatever crusty room that motel calls a business center."

He has a point. I hold the phone against my leg and pop my head in the hotel room. Mom is fully dressed and sitting cross-legged on the center of the bed. Richard is back in his bathrobe, checking the hotel amenities for a hot tub. "Says right here they've got one."

"Only you could remember to bring a swimsuit at a time like this," Mom says.

"I'm going in search of a donut. Anyone need anything?" I ask, hoping to avoid one of them offering to come along.

"Not unless they have a bourbon donut," Richard says.

Mom shoots him a distasteful glance and says, "I need protein, but I doubt they have that."

"Oh, come on, I'm sure they have a chia seed and kale dispenser down there." She throws a pillow at my head and I toss it back. "I'll be right back," I say, grateful we've found a way to laugh.

When I have the phone back at my ear, Sam says, "You two have a good relationship."

"Mostly." I direct the conversation back to him. "What about you and your dad?"

"He's all right."

"And your mom?"

In a no-nonsense way he says, "Rehab."

"The Center?"

He scoffs. "Can't afford that. Hers is more court ordered. Adderall. Not meth. She was housekeeping and stole it. Got caught. Been in and out of rehab and jail since I was twelve."

"That sucks."

"That's addiction." He makes a noise that I chalk up to acceptance and frustration and then says, "Tell me you found the business center."

I have. The Wingate Inn has a room off the lobby shrouded in mini blinds. Inside are three middle-aged computers and a fax, printer, copier combo machine. I choose the farthest unit, even though no one is rustling in the lobby, not even the night manager.

The USB contains two files. An MOV and a JPEG. We decide to start with the MOV.

"It's loading," I tell Sam and then switch to video so he can watch.

When the dials stop spinning, we're treated to a grainy zoomed-in scene. Three-quarters of the screen is high-polished wood flooring and one-quarter is two pairs of legs. Girls, according to their choice of sandals. The volume increases as the videographer inches the camera forward. The picture remains limited to legs, but two voices can be heard. They're raised and agitated. I don't recognize either, and we pick them up midconversation.

Girl one: "What're you gonna do?"

Girl two: "I don't know. Use makeup until it goes away." *(Pause)*

Girl two: "You can't tell anyone. I'm serious. Someone will get hurt."

Girl one: *(Huff)* "You mean your mom's precious career. Because I really think she'd rather you not get beaten—"

Girl two: "You don't understand. Let this go. Please. If anyone asks, we were playing tennis."

Girl one: "I'm not worried about your mom's career right now."

Girl two: "Well, you better. That's who's paying for our tuition."

Girl one: "Man, Cor . . ." *(Deep exhale)* "You never should have cheated on Ben to begin with."

Girl two: "Don't bring that up. And he cheated on me first."

Girl one: "I'm not sure I'd call what he and Bethie did cheating, given the circumstances."

Girl two: "Are you seriously on her side? Because you don't know the whole story."

Girl one: "Yeah? Tell me."

Girl two: "It's weird family stuff that wouldn't make any sense."

Girl one: "Because I'm poor?"

Girl two: "Because you don't have to deal with being a King." *(Huff)* "Come on, Frank. You know what the press would say about the program. 'Senator Rebecca King's pet project fails youth of Green County, Kentucky.' That's the spin they'd put on it. It would never be about Martin. And then the program would die, and it shouldn't. Not because of him."

Girl one: "I don't care. That jack-off does this again and you should kill him. Shoot, if you don't, I will."

Girl two: "Yeah, that'll play well in the press."

Girl one: *(Evil laugh)* "Maybe I knock you out and hide you from him."

Girl two: "I wouldn't put that past you and Bethie."

Off camera, a voice calls, "Tatti, where are you?" and the video shuts off.

"Oh my gosh," Sam says.

"I know."

"What's the JPEG?"

A screenshot from an iPhone appears. It's the Notes app. The cursor sits at the end of the sentence.

Stop Death Daze *or this gets released.*

CHAPTER 24

S am and I don't say anything immediately. I flip the screen around, recline the desk chair, and readjust my baggy sweatshirt. I look a mess and do my best to raise the camera angle and sharpen the planes of my face. Not that Sam cares. He's outside and he's wearing a long day too. Nearby Lucy whines.

He ignores her yips. "Okay, that's Cora and Frankie talking."

"Yes," I say.

Sam bites his lip. It's hard to process all the pieces of the conversation. We watch the segment again. And by the third time, I have the story.

Cora indicated that Martin hit her and that he participated in the senator's summer youth program.

Cora wanted Frankie to lie about the origin of the bruises.

She believed the altercation would reflect poorly on her mom's career, and that career was the family's golden ticket.

Beth wasn't being told because of some tiff the sisters were having over Ben that involved cheating.

Frankie suggested that Cora fight back against her aggressor (Martin?), and then—big kicker—she said she could protect Cora herself by removing her from the equation, in a way very similar to how Cora actually died.

"This video's bad for everyone. It pits Mom and Cora against each other over your dad, which gives them all motives. Plus, it has Frankie endorsing violence and then ties it all up with her verbally threatening Cora."

Sam stares up at the sky and he is all jawbone and eyelashes in the moonlight. "Yeah. And honestly, I'd say it's a current threat for the senator. She's known all over the country for her Leap program. Other states model Leap because it reduces drug abuse and the incarceration of minors. There are even rumors of her getting a VP bid."

"Those are high stakes for her."

"For the kids around here too." Sam pulls Lucy into his lap and buries his mouth near her collar. "I took Leap," he admits. "That's how I learned to dive, and I'd hate to see it go away."

His opinion helps frame Cora's state of mind and her willingness to take a bruise for the greater good. "Okay. Who is Tatti?"

"Dad might know. I can ask." Sam nods. "If they're

talking about Martin Jarvis, and I'm assuming they are, no wonder Frankie pled guilty to the juvie crime. Someone had her on tape threatening him." Frankie's voice is in my head. *"I've never hurt anyone in my life."* I'd been focused on the murder charges and didn't catch the contradiction to her juvie record at the time. "You think whoever shot this video blackmailed her back then?"

"Maybe. They're blackmailing you. And they shot at your house tonight."

"But why? Sam, the timing doesn't make sense. This video has been around for twenty years. It could have been released a long time ago. Or used at the trial. I think whoever rubber-banded the jump drive onto that brick doesn't really want the video seen. But they want us to believe they want it seen so we'll back off *Death Daze*."

Lucy stops the conversation by licking Sam's neck and ears. He has to hold her away from his body to get her to stop and nearly drops the phone in the process. "Sorry," he says, even though I'm not. Lucy is the only levity tonight. Sam continues, "You think we need to stay focused on the fact that whoever attacked your house tonight wants you to stop investigating Cora's murder rather than get caught up in the details of the video."

He's nailed it. "Yeah," I say. "We need to figure out who stands to gain if the *Death Daze* craze goes away."

"You're going to ignore the threat?"

"I don't have a choice. We lose traction and Frankie dies for sure."

"Ny, Frankie's basically strapped to that chair with needles in her veins already. You're not going to save her. If you do this, you do it for your mom or yourself or to make a case against the ADPA. But don't set yourself up for an improbable outcome."

He's right and I don't want to hear it.

"What about you?" I ask. "Why would you do this with me?"

He chuckles and says, "Publicity." In a serious voice, he adds, "Think about it, Lion. I'd rather not pull your body out of a cave."

That's a sobering thought.

"I'll see you tomorrow, Sam."

"Buenos noches, amiga."

CHAPTER 25

There's a knock at the hotel door.

I uncurl from Mom's body and tug the covers to my chin, uncertain if the knock is in my dreams or real.

In the night, I snuggled against Mom's back and she turned instinctively in her sleep and held me. A whispered "I love you," and then a snore. I'm sure she doesn't remember. It took a long time to fall asleep after that. I lay awake thinking about what Sam said—how he doesn't want to pull my body out of a cave—and wondering what I should do with the channel.

Going live gives the anti-ADPA-ers a boost and keeps Frankie and others like her in mainstream media, but puts us at greater risk. My family is sleeping in a hotel room because someone shot up Richard's house to threaten *Death Daze*. That's a clear, harsh message. And I can't ignore

Cora's murder. If Frankie didn't kill her, whoever did could be in the area.

I have a million questions about Martin Jarvis. And Frankie's time in juvie. And I'd love to get Mom talking about Cora—about what she was like before she died. I'd like to gauge if cheating with Sam's dad was a onetime thing or was it not really cheating at all? Will Sam's dad know who Tatti is? Will the police turn up any leads from last night through IT work?

The knock comes again, firmer.

I rub my eyes. This time I wake up enough to check my phone: 6:50.

From the other bed, Richard turns on the bedside light. "We don't want any towels," he says grumpily.

The knock sounds again.

Mom doesn't stir; her breathing is smooth and deep. There's no telling when she fell asleep.

"Seriously," Richard says, scratching his chin and sitting up in bed. "Who knocks this early?"

"Maybe the police," I say. Richard's only wearing boxers and it'll take him longer to get moving than me. "Coming," I yell loudly enough that whoever is in the hallway stops knocking. I open the door the width of the security bolt and peer into the hall.

Anna's there in her raincoat with bag-like bruises under her eyes, despite her best attempt to hide them with makeup. She extends a pristine card with *Elizabeth King* written in perfect calligraphy script. Her expression is apologetic as she says, "Cassandra asked me to deliver this first thing this morning."

"Well done on the first thing," I say, and then realize she has driven two hours in the rain to arrive before seven. "Gosh, what time did you leave Nockabout?"

"Early," she says, and I can tell she wants to roll her eyes but stops herself. "I'll wait in the lobby for your answer." There's practiced patience on her face. She's well versed in delivering things for Cassandra. Well versed in waiting until Cassandra gets whatever Cassandra wants.

I let the door close.

Richard is out of bed. "Who was that?"

"Cassandra's caregiver slash personal assistant."

That rouses Mom. "Granny's here?" Mom props herself against all the pillows on the bed. Richard has opened the drapes three inches wide, and the gray, rainy day sends an easy light into the room.

"Nope. Her card." I fling the envelope across the comforter into Mom's lap.

Mom's right hand covers her mouth as her left tucks the letter against her heart. "This is the handwriting of my childhood."

The envelope is the kind that should be sliced by an ornate golden knife adorned with a carved eagle. I imagine Cassandra in her pearls at midnight, seated in front of a huge oak desk, dabbing a pen into a vat of ink as she considers what to write to her only living granddaughter.

The brick through the window felt lighter than this.

Mom scans the note. "It's an invitation. To come home. She says she is not well and would like to meet her great-granddaughter, the film producer. And since she's Granny"—Mom almost manages to laugh—"there's a cash reward for my cooperation and a formal RSVP for Anna to return."

"What's her price?" Richard asks.

This time Mom does laugh, full and hard, with an air of incredulity. "Typical Granny. Five thousand dollars if I agree not to fight with my mother. Twenty-five hundred now." She lifts a folded check in the air. "Twenty-five whenever I choose to depart."

Richard says, "Guess I'll cancel the Airbnb."

"'PS,'" Mom reads, "'I have secured you a boat and escort for your time in the Valley. My lawncare man's son, Sam.'" Mom raises her eyebrows.

"I didn't tell Sam to offer that." Although I'm pleased he has.

"Your Sam works faster than you do."

Your Sam. Now there's a turn of phrase. She has no idea. "Heads up," I say. "Ben Stack's her lawncare man."

Mom disappears beneath the covers. "I hate going home."

CHAPTER 26

I expect Sam to be there when Richard parks the Pilot and trailer in the Nockabout Island Ferry lot. He's not. Neither is the ferry. The baby barge chugs across the water, two cars aboard like turtles on a log. I glance up the hill to Ned's shop, wondering if Sam might be up there at the corner table watching. Anna answers the question I don't ask. "He's waiting at Cassandra's for you. I'm supposed to make sure you tour the Center and then deposit you on her doorstep for lunch."

Anna's wide mouth stretches into a yawn. "I hope you get to sleep after that," I say.

"I doubt my nap is on Cassandra's agenda. She's like having a newborn with colic. They tell you to sleep when the baby sleeps, but what if the baby never sleeps? You'd never know she was eighty-seven." Anna laughs good-heartedly.

Mom catches Anna's wrist in kindness. But at the

initial grab and squeeze Anna appears caught off guard. She steps back and clasps her necklace with her free hand. It's not until Mom says, "Thank you for everything you do for them, for us," that Anna relaxes.

I get the feeling today is going to manufacture many awkward moments.

"Sorry," Anna says, having been caught flinching. "I can't believe you're back."

"Me either," Mom says.

"Now, come on. We'll take the boat and I'll come back later for your car and belongings."

"Only if that will give you a break from Granny," Mom says.

Anna folds her rain jacket over her forearm. "Deal."

She leads us to a vessel smaller than the Boston Whaler. Also luxury. Also teak. She's comfortable behind the wheel. I'm guessing she could manage anything. On the ride over, the waves kick up and the running motor provides enough sound coverage that I can ask more about Anna.

Mom says, "We didn't cross paths much. But she's Granny's type for sure. All bootstraps and elbow grease. You'll see."

"How did Granny meet her?"

Mom slides her hands along the boat's silver railing. "Cassandra King knows everyone in the Valley. But Anna was one of Mom's Leap kids."

"Sam told me about Leap."

"Oh, I'm sure he did. Rebecca's *famous* Leap program."

It's interesting that she refers to her own mother as Rebecca. When you run away and change your name, some manner of distance is normal, but this naming feels like it predates her escape from Nockabout. I wonder if she called her father Creed, or if he, like Granny, has garnered more affection than the senator.

"Did you and Cora do Leap?" I ask.

"Mandatory. We took piano and skeet and programming and cooking and whatever else made Rebecca look good." She shows me the back of her hand and indicates a thin line I'd mistaken for a wrinkle. "I got that for not correctly memorizing 'Für Elise.'" She shows me another. "And this for 'Prelude in C.'" And another. "And this one was from Cora when I beat her in the Annual Clay Pigeon Competition."

"Your mother meant well," Richard says.

Unless I'm imagining his defensiveness, Richard has a soft spot for Rebecca, brigadier general of piano and all things Leap. Mom cuts her eyes in his direction, signaling she doesn't appreciate his betrayal. "Anyway," Mom says to me, "the lake hasn't changed much. I'm sorry you had to see it by yourself the first time."

"I was with Sam," I admit. *And five other people.*

"Ah, yes. Sam."

At the Nockabout dock, Anna loads us onto a golf cart that rivals the fancy boat and drives to the portico of the Center. Her tour conveys the same historical and modern hospital information as Sam's. The bulk of content is directed at Mom. Everything is "Creed's achievement this" and "Creed's achievement that." Anna offers an apologetic smile. "You already know this stuff. I'm just—"

"—following directions," Mom finishes. "Let me guess. 'Anna, make sure you remind Bethie what it means to be a King.'" Her imitation is identical to Anna's from earlier.

"Something like that." Anna checks her watch and continues a recitation of King's medical achievements.

The tour makes me think about Houdini—the girl with the diamond tester. How would she have escaped without notice? The Center is not exactly bustling. There's little to no traffic in the hallways. All patient doors are closed. The felt message boards containing patient last names feel more like the home section of Target than a hospital. There's a central nurses' hub that makes escape improbable, and Anna has already told us they lock the elevators at dusk every evening. Only staff have keys to the stairwells.

When a nurse exits a patient's room, I peek inside. The room could be the home page image for a high-end hotel. Anna's current spiel includes an overview of the meth crisis in Kentucky and how "no one has done more work than your family to bring healing and restoration. There's even talk of the prestigious Lasker Award."

"Are all the rooms that nice?" I interrupt, having never heard of the Lasker Award.

"Yes," Anna says, and then a conspiratorial elbow in my direction. "Nicer than my digs, for sure."

The elevator reaches the fourth floor—the tour is almost finished—and when the doors open, a man in a medical jacket stands waiting with his arms crossed, his clipboard tucked to his chest. He's Richard's age and made of thin muscles, sharp lines, and tailored clothes. I recognize him from framed photos in the lobby. Creed King Junior. My grandfather.

Mom goes rigid. Richard is trapped behind her. The elevator dings and the door begins to close. Creed reaches out to stop it and says, "Bethie." His voice is reverent and warm—an invitation to hug him that matches his outstretched arms.

"Daddy."

I nudge her forward into the room and he takes the movement as permission to embrace her. They're human puzzle pieces that should fit, but her muscular arms hang limp; she casts a sideways glance and mouths, "Help me."

Richard taps Creed on the shoulder and says, "You've done an amazing job with the hospital, Creed. We've been enjoying our tour."

"Dick." Creed greets Richard and releases Mom.

"Creed."

They say more saying each other's names than most people do in autobiographies. I really hope our time here doesn't involve the two of them in the same room very often.

"I'm Nyla," I say.

"Ah, yes, our very own Spike Lee. The girl with more power than all of us combined."

I take action first and thrust out my hand. We shake and I keep it real. "Dr. King, we were shot at last night."

Richard swears under his breath at my gumption.

Dr. King retreats backward and pins his clipboard to his chest again. "Call me Junior. Someone says Dr. King and I look for a real hero instead of myself." That quip is supposed to be charming, but it comes off practiced and forced. He moves on. "I heard. In fact, I might have been the one to suggest to Mother that she—"

"—invite us to stay," Mom finishes. "Bless that. And what did *the senator* think of your invitation? Am I walking into a lion's den?"

"Sugar bug, between my wife and my mother, I'm never out of claws' reach." He chuckles. "You'll have one of your talks. It'll be fine. A reunion long overdue."

It's Mom's turn to nod.

Creed beams at me. "I'd say the senator is most interested in *you*. She's not happy having our story in the spotlight, but she's very impressed with your coverage and scope."

"And should I expect one of her talks?" I ask.

He turns on his heels to face Mom. "You've done a good job with this one. You too, Dick," he says, the laughter now somewhat fake.

Richard doesn't give him the satisfaction of responding.

Thankfully, an overhead speaker pages Dr. King to the third floor. I've never seen a man look more relieved. He asks, "Bethie, can we expect you all for dinner? Mother will want it."

"We'll see."

"I hope so." He quick-walks toward the exit stairs and

152

stops abruptly, as though he just remembered his manners. "Anna," he says.

"Dr. King," she says.

Their exchange of names is odd and formal, reading more like a rivalry in which Anna has the upper hand. And yet we stand in Creed's hospital and Anna's role here is tour guide and message girl. His hostility, or perhaps the fragility that seems to cloak him, feels unearned.

Anna, having done her duty in staging this casual reunion, tells us we are relieved of touring the final floor. She presses the down arrow to call the elevator.

When the door slides open, Ned is standing there holding a bouquet of daisies stuffed in a Mason jar.

He recognizes me and then his gaze shifts to Mom. From the exchange between them, she is up to her neck in history. "Ned Damron!"

Bright red splotches streak his cheeks and stretch below his collar. "I heard you were coming." He stares at the flowers in his hands and then back to me. "Nice to see you too, Nyla."

"*Buenos tardes,*" I say.

Ned is pleased by my greeting. "*Buenas tardes, ¿como estas?*"

"*Bien.* And that's my entire Spanish dictionary," I warn.

He smooths the polo shirt where it stretches over his belly and grins.

Mom gestures to the flowers and raises her arm in a question.

"For Mom," he says. "She's still chugging along."

Mom looks sympathetically toward the hallway. "I'll stop in and say hi."

"I wouldn't bother." Ned shifts heel to toe and works the flower stems until one snaps. "Mom only recognizes me intermittently and she has a restless roommate. If you get Ms. Rey singing, there's no stopping her." Ned shakes his head, like he has endured more hours of Ms. Rey's music than anyone should.

Mom touches his arm. "I'm sorry."

"Me too, Bethie. I heard about the attack on your house. Scary." He shrugs out of her touch and shuffles away, leaving me wondering if he's glad she's back. From the expression on her face, she's asking the same question.

Away from the hospital and back in the golf cart, Richard whispers in my ear, "You ready to figure out which one of these monsters killed Cora?"

"Depends on how many more tours I have to take."

"You got a doozy coming up," he says as Anna turns off Circle Drive, gears down the golf cart, and we start the long ascent toward Cassandra's Church.

CHAPTER 27

Anna parks the golf cart in front of Cassandra's house. The view is pure wow. The patio stone alone is more expensive than Richard's house. Everything is manicured. I wonder if even the spiders ask Cassandra's permission to spin webs.

There's a cutting garden in a raised bed bursting with buttercups, blue flax, iris, English wallflowers, and crown vetch. It takes little to no imagination to picture Anna standing at the kitchen sink washing and arranging the buds in Cassandra's favorite vases. Kentucky wildflowers are no doubt spread in vases throughout the house.

Sam is shirtless and helping a man twice his age unload sod from a flatbed truck. He flicks sweat from his forehead. "Cassandra's napping so I told Dad I'd give him a hand."

Ben Stack raises his chin and offers a curt wave, and then he's back to the sod with renewed vigor. If he cares

Bethie has come home, he's not showing it. Ben is handsome and toned; his skin has been leathered by summers, and it likely stays its rusty color all year. He's an older version of Sam with deep-set eyes and narrow lips. Even though he's wearing baggy denim work clothes, there's no doubt this work won't let him gain an ounce. He has none of Sam's gumption, and I can tell by the simple way he works the dirt that if he weren't working for Cassandra, he'd be breaking his back for someone else.

Sam jogs over to the truck, wipes down his stomach with a towel, and grabs the T-shirt he's left thrown over a tree branch. "Hey, Lion." Richard chuckles softly at his use of my nickname. Sam hasn't noticed. He's busy telling Anna she can hand us off if she wants. "You're bound to be exhausted if you left as early as Cassandra says. Go on. Get out of here. I'll take care of them."

"You're sure?" Even though Sam is nodding, Anna checks with Ben, who drops his chin to okay Sam subbing in, and says, "She's planning dinner at five."

Mom asks, "Does five still mean four forty-five?"

Anna clears her throat and laughs through a yawn as she climbs in the golf cart. "You'd be better to arrive at four thirty."

With the logistics settled, Sam surges right past subtle introductions and hugs me. "You smell like dirt," I say and squeeze him back. "Mom, Richard, this is Sam. Sam, this is my mom and my, like, granddad."

"I'm the one with the shotgun," Richard says.

"Noted," Sam says. "Come on. I know they've dragged you this way and that. And I doubt you slept all that well at the hotel. Let's get you to the pool house and I'll get back with your stuff as fast as the ferry will allow. But don't go thinking I drowned if I don't show up by dinner." He realizes the faux pas and turns bright red. He trips over himself as he apologizes. "Sorry, ma'am. That was waaaay insensitive. I meant the ferry's not fast or regular. Sorry again."

"It's okay, Sam," Mom says. He's right about her being tired. I hear it in her voice when she adds, "And thank you for taking care of us. I can get us to the pool house."

As Sam runs down the drive at a sprint, pausing briefly to make a melting gesture at me, I wave off his worry. Hustling to get the car makes a deeper impression on Mom than his verbal misstep, but I'm glad he cares what she thinks of him. Even in the middle of the mess we're in, that bit of normalcy acts as an anchor. Especially given how many notifications have pinged my phone. The video from last night has more than a half million views. That's . . . that's a lot.

Internet famous isn't something to trifle with. From the conversation on the way to Nockabout, neither Mom nor Richard has extrapolated what *Death Daze* means for me. They're thinking of Frankie. They're hoping for traction. They've forgotten my very vanilla online history. I've never even posted photos of my dinner or selfies of me wearing new earrings. I watch zoo livestreams and the Dodo.

Not to mention that the internet is forever. Any job, school, group I want to join or attend: a simple search of my name and my opinions on the ADPA will be there. I don't even know what I think of the death penalty. That's not a great place to be.

But I'm here.

And we're at the pool house.

One of our apartment complexes had a pool house that consisted of a concrete floor, a urinal and toilet in the corner, and three shop vacs in various stages of decay. This is a miniature of Cassandra's Church, adjacent to a sparkling inground pool, complete with waterfall. One toe in the water tells me it's heated. "You grew up here?" I say with amazement.

"I know," she says, almost in disbelief.

I try to imagine her and Cora.

Two girls my age laying out, splashing each other, inviting boyfriends over, drinking diet soda, and eating whatever Anna's predecessor brought out on a silver tray.

CHAPTER 28

Richard's car is delivered in time for us to dress for dinner. Sam wishes me luck, and I promise to text him proof of life when the ordeal is over. I'm hoping to ask if his dad knows who Tatti is when there's no one around.

Mom and I are sharing the bedroom, and there are two queen beds with luscious duvets and silk sheets. Richard claims the living room couch, and although I feel bad that he doesn't have a bed, it's a seven-piece sectional. We dress in silence, except for Richard announcing the A-list Twitter accounts that have retweeted the original *Death Daze* video.

Mom applies a thick eyeliner and says, "Granny is probably fit to be tied. If I weren't nervous myself, I'd suggest you stay here." Those nerves give her an unintentional cat eye, which she asks me to fix.

I tilt her face to the light. "Her note said she's not well."

"That probably means she's running half marathons

159

instead of fulls." Mom laughs, and I am forced to hold her still while I finish drawing the line. During the final examination of my work, she says, "But really, she's not the one to worry about. Granny's harmless. Rebecca's the peach. Speaking of, you should wear my ring. She'll notice and love that." She flicks her earlobe to show off her own diamond studs.

"Right," I say. I need to get the pieces to Ned and see if he'll fix it for me before I have to tell her I broke it punching the steering wheel. I change the subject. "If you don't like your mom, why bother trying to impress her?"

"It's what daughters do," she says.

I check my own reflection in the mirror. I've chosen a baggy summer sweater that falls off one shoulder, a pair of white shorts, and platform sandals. An intentional mimicking of Anna's style. I have a feeling that Anna knows to play to the crowd and following her example might get me places.

In the mirror, I watch Mom sprawl across the bed and thread her fingers through her hair. She's messing up the pins she spent fifteen minutes placing. I cross the room and take her hand. "You can do this," I say. I'm not an expert on terrifying emotional experiences, but I feel confident applying the label to dinner with the Kings.

Mom turns sideways on the bed and looks at me. "Do you like me?"

"What? Yes." I do. I always have. She's strange, but an acceptable strange.

"I thought so, but I'm processing why I don't like my

mom, and I got all insecure for a minute. Like, is the part of me that can't stand her immature or stalled and has that ruined my own attempts at motherhood? Or what if I'm perpetually stuck at eighteen when it comes to my parents? No one tells you how to feel about your mother when you're an adult. You get to hate your parents as part of becoming independent when you're a kid, but now . . ."

"Sounds like a question for a therapist." I have a feeling she will find out at four forty-five if her feelings are relevant. We all will. "What was it like back then? What started the hate?"

She has a fast answer.

So fast, it must have been processed with more than one therapist.

"I never felt loved. But I had to listen to her talk about love. Love and service. Love and service. Love and service. That was her commercial. I posed for Christmas cards that read 'From Our Loving Family to Yours.' And I remember thinking, *Seriously?*" She sighs at the irony, and I do my best to keep a neutral face.

"What I mean is . . . when she's one person out there and the world loves her, it's confusing. Because you're a kid who knows your mom used her signature stamp on your birthday card, but they don't have any idea she couldn't pick up a blessed pen. They think she's wonderful." She weaves her fingers back through her hair and dislodges a pin. "But maybe there's not much difference in a mom who does that and a mom who lies about her childhood."

"None at all," I tease and quickly say, "Mom, it's all the difference in the world. I mean, you came back here for me." There's a tinge of falsehood as soon as I've spoken, because I honestly believe she came back here for Frankie.

"Ladies, it's four twenty-six," Richard calls from the living room.

The three of us walk the stone path in silence. The air smells of sod and Richard's cologne. We are saved from ringing the doorbell by Anna, who throws open the front door. "Come on in. Everyone's in the dining room."

Wow. They weren't joking about getting places early.

Everyone is three people. Creed has swapped his work clothes for khakis and a golf polo and waves from the table. The senator, who is much older than her profile pictures, doesn't look like the politicians on television. She isn't donning a power suit with her hair blown out and her nails manicured to a lovely shade of navy. This powerhouse bites her nails to the beds and is wearing only a hint of eye makeup. She paces the rug in front of the window, cell phone against her ear. She lifts a finger that I take to mean she'll be right with us.

And then there's Cassandra. The queen of the afternoon sits in her wheelchair, hands folded in her lap and a diamond-studded tiara in her willowy gray hair. "Welcome," she says with the grandeur of someone who has broken a bottle of champagne on the hull of a ship.

The awkwardness commences. Rebecca strides forward, phone tucked into a purse. Hands go out. Toes are physically stepped on. There's a moment I am so self-conscious I breathe into my hand and check my breath and try desperately to remember if I put on deodorant.

The senator has either decided to pretend or ignore what this meeting truly is. "There's my girl," she says, "and Richard." It is Richard who catches her off guard, Richard who forces her to take a sharply inhaled breath that she can't hide.

"Becky," he says.

Rebecca blushes, but then she turns to me. "Hi, Nyla. My assistant says I should hire you for the marketing team. We see you're quite adept at spin."

I'm unsure of my response when Creed throws out a life preserver. "Let's not work the campaign tonight, dear. Our beautiful, prodigal daughter and granddaughter have returned home and Mother has killed the fatted calf, literally. I hope you like veal, Nyla." The absence of Richard's name isn't a slip.

"I do," I say, even though I've never eaten veal and am not what I would consider an adventurous eater.

Cassandra clicks her pearls against the armrests of her chair and everyone stops talking. She flicks her index finger in a downward motion and without discussion everyone takes a seat at the table. "I hired waitstaff so none of us will miss a moment of delight." Her sarcasm is wicked and perfect. When Granny stares off out the window, I give Mom a "Wow" under my breath. Granny is a force. Mom understands the kudos I'm feeling for the older woman, but she's not the only one. Creed, who sits across from me, leans over his place setting and says for my benefit, "That one's a wizard. Been that way all my life."

"Creed, don't suck up to me while I'm formally meeting my only great-granddaughter. Nyla, or shall I call you Lion?" She turns the full power of her baby blues on me. "Tell me exactly what you plan to do with *your little show.*"

Should I explain that I never intended for *Death Daze* to be a show? How would she take the discovery that my fame is accidental? I imagine confessing that Sam and I got the settings wrong on the video. Cassandra King would hate that, I think.

I'd do better to click my own cheap bracelets against the table and announce I plan to run for president. I plaster on the most confident smile in my arsenal and say, "I plan to overturn the ADPA. Hopefully before Frankie is executed. I'd love to interview you"—I glance around the room and meet each individual's eyes—"all of you. Senator, if you don't have time to film something formal, maybe we could do yours on Zoom or Facebook Live."

The invitation renders the senator speechless.

Creed holds his lips closed with his index finger.

Mom squeezes my thigh until I flinch. Richard is sucking his lower lip so hard it'll be fat all night. The room waits for Cassandra's response.

I had a drama teacher tell me not to be scared of silence. According to her, silence is a weapon. "Use it like a knight with pawns on his shoulders," she said. I don't play chess, and I have no idea if that makes sense in the game, but I've never forgotten the concept. Saying more makes you look weak, and you never want to do that after you throw down the gauntlet.

Cassandra toys with us by resting her forehead against her gold charger and caging her slender arms around her head. It takes three very long seconds to realize she is laughing hysterically.

"Oh, Nyla." She lifts up from the table barrel-laughing. "I haven't loved anyone so much since . . . well, ever. You may have been called a Wagner, but, girl, you've been raised a King." As a faith statement to my mother, Granny adds, "A true King, I mean. None of that mumbo PC jumbo Rebecca favors."

Creed says nothing to defend his wife, but unfortunately, Richard takes the opportunity. "Cassandra," he snaps. "Why can't you step over people instead of on them?"

The senator sends daggers at Richard and excuses herself from the table. Not before saying, "Nyla, I'd be honored to be on your show. And it truly is wonderful to meet you tonight."

That is not the response I anticipated.

I call after her, "Thank you, Senator."

Cassandra's cackling, enjoying that she has run her daughter-in-law into the other room. "Oh, I love getting the gang back together. Feels good. Doesn't it, Junior? To know there might be an heir worth leaving everything to? Because at this rate, it's Ben, Anna, and Ned all the way."

"Mother." Creed's voice is sharp, but he says nothing else.

Wow. Guess that explains the tension between Creed and Anna. This is not a family where you play hardball once. This is a family where you get up every day and sink your teeth into someone and pay your dentist to swap the X-rays. No wonder Mom left when she did. I can't imagine how they might handle the direct aftermath of a trauma.

Creed says to me, "I wasn't kidding about what I said at the Center. Rebecca admires *Death Daze*, in her own way. And despite what your mother has told you, we've only ever wanted justice for our . . ." He's not able to speak his daughter's name.

Knowing I won't keep the upper hand, I take one more risk. This time with a far more humble voice. "Honestly, as long as none of you killed Cora, you've got nothing to worry about with my little show."

Everyone stares and then chuckles, not like I'm funny, but like they need to fill the space with noise. But while they're laughing, Cassandra says under her breath, "The person you should ask left the room." And then she winks. Or at least I think she does. With a woman like her, it's hard to tell.

CHAPTER 29

That night I dip my feet in the pool, lean back against the warm concrete, and video call Sam. I explain the strangeness that was dinner. Which did not contain veal because Granny fell asleep on her charger and Creed had to call Anna for her medicine. The three of us excused ourselves to the pool house, where Richard showered off his cologne and Mom and I took off our bras and makeup in favor of pj's.

"You're kidding. No food?"

"Someone who works for Cassandra showed up with doggie bags twenty minutes after we left."

"I ate on the tractor," he says, and the camera view wobbles as he hops backward to sit on the roof of Lucy's doghouse. He's already taken out his contacts and is wearing rimless glasses that mostly disappear into his face. He smacks a bug off his skin. "And now the mosquitoes are munching on me."

"I think maybe Cassandra is sick for real. Like that part of her invitation might have been accurate. Mom says no, but tonight was bonkers."

"The person to ask is Anna," Sam says.

I explain my Creed versus Anna theory. "What does your dad say about the Kings?"

"Nothing."

"Like nothing at all or nothing noteworthy?"

"Like, the man is practically mute. Tomorrow, after we film the Camaro video, I'll show you the real Ben Stack. One glimpse of his man cave and you'll understand."

"What about Ned?" I ask. "He seems to know the family pretty well."

"I hadn't thought about that, to be honest. Ned's Ned. He plays with rocks and visits his mom. He's grateful to Creed for the Center, but I've never gotten the feeling that Creed likes him all that much."

"Hmm." I can see that. Creed is a personality, and from what I can tell Ned is a worker bee and not the type of man Creed would hold in high regard.

Sam lifts Lucy to the phone's camera and animates a low, silly voice. "What's the plan for *Death Daze* tomorrow?"

"Well, Lucy, I've got an angle to run by you."

"That's good. But I like treats better than angles."

Sam lowers Lucy out of view and laughs at his puppy. "What's the angle?"

The idea came to me at Cassandra's. "We need to blame someone else. Even if we're wrong."

Cassandra blamed the senator at dinner. Sam and I need to do the same. The idea worked my brain over hard. I've been able to think of little else, but it has to be done carefully. Frankie has lost more than one appeal. Her critics frequently recount that in the comments section of *Death Daze*, which tells me the only retrial we'll get is in the press. The goal has to be to keep people talking and hope they apply enough pressure that the governor stays the execution.

"Everyone with a social or a stream needs to feel entitled to a seat on a new jury. To do that, reasonable doubt won't be enough; we have to hand them a new killer."

He's quiet. "We're ignoring the jump drive threat completely and plunging forward."

"Yes. Unless you want to stop."

"No."

"Did your dad know who Tatti is?"

"Tatti was Cassandra's corgi from way back when. Which doesn't tell us anything about who shot the video. He said everyone knew the dog because Cassandra carried her everywhere."

That leaves us to banter about the question of who to blame. The most logical approach suggests the other original suspects the police identified and eliminated: Ben Stack and Martin Jarvis. We'd never point at Sam's dad, so that leaves us Martin. Since he has been dead for twenty years, that's not going to be easy. Plus, his time of death is problematic.

The next morning I bring our questions to the *Death Daze* audience and I bring them hard and fast. When the interview begins, I'm seated in the Camaro's trunk to showcase the lack of blood. Then I sit in the driver's seat and swing Frankie's senior ID lanyard hanging from the rearview mirror. The pendulum arc of the lanyard mimics a clock and I stare the camera down and speak.

"Francis Quick has twenty-four days left. Twenty-four days because of one drop of blood. I don't know about you, but that got me in the gut. I feel duty bound to ask: Who else could have killed Cora King? If not for Frankie Quick, for my aunt. Maybe even for myself. I'd hate to lose my life because someone got a paper cut in the trunk of my car."

I let the weight of that statement land. In the silence, and as if I've cued her, Lucy howls. She's staring at wild turkeys, but the audience doesn't know that. The mournful bail accentuates the video perfectly. I take a breath and say, "Sad, isn't it? The police had another suspect. A local guy. Older than Cora. His name was Martin Jarvis. That's right; the same man Frankie Quick went to juvie for attacking. Now, we don't know what caused that event, but we can guess how Martin Jarvis might feel about Cora and her best friend, Frankie, following his stay in the hospital. Antagonistic. Antagonistic enough for revenge? That's the question.

"I'm not claiming to know, but I'm asking you, listeners, to bring me your evidence. The good. The bad. Tell me he couldn't have done it. Tell me this is a classic case of murder-suicide. Tell me everything I need to know about

Martin Jarvis, and hopefully the next time *Death Daze* returns, Senator King will be live with me."

When the phone is down and the camera is off and I stop shaking, I can't remember half of what I said. I practiced so many times before we went live that it's hard to know what I missed in the final product. I could watch it back, but seeing the channel gain and lose followers in real time might give me a panic attack.

Sam wipes my phone screen with the sleeve of his shirt and lays it in my palm. "You nailed that, Ny. Bringing them in, inviting them to be part of *Death Daze*, crazy smart." He dusts the top of Lucy's head. "You nailed it, too, little girl, didn't you?"

"She did. We should pay her royalties for that howl."

Sam grins. "You can make her check out to Samuel Stack. That's S-t-a—"

"We'll stop at the bank after you take me to that man cave of your dad's."

He drops into a ridiculous curtsy/bow that is adorably dorky and then leads me from the Camaro's garage to the shabby A-frame carved into the hill. "This was my grandpa's house," he says as we cross concrete blocks overgrown with moss and weeds to reach the porch. Sam scoots a moth off the facing and then uses his boot to pry open the bottom right of the door. The movement is practiced.

Inside, the house feels more like an abandoned outbuilding. A freestanding pellet stove. A blue couch without cushions. Cobwebs and dust and uneven floors. The groaning wood planks sing as we walk. Lucy settles herself by the front door and Sam tells her to stay. The house isn't large by any stretch of the imagination, but it's configured with small rooms and hallways designed to block the light. As if whoever lived here was allergic to the sun.

We move from entry room to hallway, hallway to kitchen, kitchen to a door off another hallway at the rear of the house. The dark is all-inclusive. No windows. I feel the earthen hill pressing at the ceiling; a damaged place in the corner drips water onto the old linoleum, and green vines spider away from cracked plaster in all directions.

Sam slides an empty bookcase to one side and reveals a punctured hole between the wall studs. Cool air prickles my skin. He steps through the opening. I poke my head inside and smell the dirt, the peat, before I lean around his body and get the view I expect. Darkness that stretches on and on. Sam lifts a lantern off the ground and checks the brightness of the bulb. That first lit glimpse shows off endless U-shaped supports and wooden trestles. The trestles closest to the house are buried, the earth having pressed its way forward over the years. Between the first two are wooden shelves with dozens and dozens of Mason jars and jugs.

"Cellar?" I ask.

"Man cave."

"Did you bank on me not taking you literally?"

He holds the light up near his face and grins. "Maybe." Then he shares the story. "My great-grandfather built this house into the hill, linked it indirectly to the mine for his,

172

uh, business." He continues, "White lightning. Moonshine. There's a room about thirty feet along the tunnel where he made spirits. He'd smuggle them to the miners and into their lunch boxes. That part of the mine collapsed years ago, but the still room's in good shape."

"Are all the Stacks entrepreneurs?" I'm only half joking.

Our laughter fills the corridor. Dust trickles from the ceiling through the light. I test the strength of the closest trestle. Sturdy and unmoving. The surrounding dirt feels like concrete. "You're sure this is safe?" I ask, not liking the idea of the collapse he mentioned.

"I'm back here pretty often," he admits. Which is not an answer to the question.

I wonder what's in his father's room that brings him here "pretty often."

Whether it is for his support or mine, he takes my hand. We must look like a classic book cover. A guy and a girl, standing a Christian distance apart, holding hands. The dark abyss looming in the background. *Nancy Drew and the Case of the Whiskey Mine.* Bourbon bottles and beer cans and the occasional tree root interrupt the path.

Thirty feet in we reach a narrow opening on the right side that you could easily miss. Sam hunches and ducks inside; I follow. I don't know what I expect to find. A generator that powers a mini-fridge and TV/DVD combo with a couch. Maybe a gun safe or a hobby table. When he raises the lantern, I let out all the air in my lungs at once.

"I know," Sam says in response.

The room, maybe two hundred square feet, contains shoeboxes. Floor to ceiling in neat rows, five to six boxes deep.

Each box has a label. Some, years: *1985. 1991a. 1991b.* Others are specific: *Olympic Torch Run 2002.* Others, far vaguer: *Traffic Miscellaneous. Whitby Abby Ghosts. Ledbetter Florist.* Sam walks to a specific section and removes rows until he locates two particular boxes. "We can't take these out of the cave." The practiced way he states this rule tells me he was told that long ago and probably many times over.

These boxes remind me of my mother's twelve-by-twelve crates.

"Dad saves things, files them. Old things, family things. His life, his father's, mine. There's a ticket in an Adidas box over there from the first movie he and Mom saw in the theater. There are scraps of fabric and toys and the fronts of T-shirts and packs of cigarettes and playing cards. There are love letters from middle school girlfriends and deeds to properties we don't own anymore. There's a whole box of plastic lizards that's labeled *Knight.*"

"He lets you look at them?"

"More like he doesn't stop me. This is the way his brain works. In these organized boxes. All these compartments. The good and the bad—"

"—and the ugly."

"I'll let you be the judge of that." Sam lifts the lids of the two boxes he's chosen and places their contents on the floor. In the first there are photographs.

He's collected hundreds of pictures from the summer of

1999. Nockabout is front and center: the mine, the Center, the ferries, all that gorgeous blue water, the senator's Leap program. These capture the strange exoticism of a rural life. Dirty roads and make-out lanes and field parties. Cora's there. Alive. Looking like a sorority girl in her red bikini and hip cocked to one side. She's got an overlarge pair of blue Ray-Bans. There are at least twenty different poses of her wearing them low on her nose and giving a sexy eye smile over the top of the lenses.

Mom's there too. She is very Bethie, very not Elizabeth Wagner. With her skinny arms and tomboy clothes. She wears one-piece swimsuits and athletic shorts and most of the time a Life is Good cap that's too big for her head. Instead of sunglasses, she wears almost permanent suction marks from goggles. Aside from predictable clothes, she's a chameleon. Confident and beaming in one image and then broody in the next. And I don't think she ever used sunscreen. Anytime she's wearing a tank top, skin's peeling off her shoulders.

There are King family photos at Granny's pool house. Multiple shots of Ben, Cora, and Mom. They toggle who puts their arms around who, and you can almost see the battle for this boy as you flip through. Ben is better looking than Sam, but not by much.

Frankie's there too. Between Rebecca and Creed. Sitting with Granny. In the group pyramid photos. Pretending to give Ned a knuckle sandwich. Jumping off a cliff doing a herkie. Her forehead resting against Ben's arms. She has a simple style: cutoff shorts that show the length of her legs; fitted T-shirts that almost always have sweat stains around the collar; ankle socks and black Adidas trainers; Nike cotton headbands in every color. Her hair is less blonde and more auburn, and she's got this wicked awesome dimple that makes me wonder how a jury convicted her of anything.

Ned makes a few appearances. He's much thinner and always has a cigarette above his ear, a Solo cup in his hand. Maybe he's high. Or tired. His eyes are always bloodshot. Anna's in several photos. In one, she's sporting pigtails and flashing a peace sign. In her little cotton shorts and dinosaur tie-dyed shirt, she's the very picture of a Target child model. Behind her, there's a guy doing pull-ups from the mouth of a cave. It could be Martin Jarvis, but the background is too fuzzy to confirm.

All these characters, pictured twenty years before I met them, ignorant of all that is to come. I wish I'd been there then, even though that's stupid because I came from them.

The second box has heaps of notes. Squares of tightly folded notebook paper. A collection rubber-banded together and others scattered and loose. We sit on our haunches with the letters and lantern between us. I feel like an ant in a shoe store stockroom.

Mom's handwriting is here. Messier than her writing is now, but clearly hers. She's written Frankie's name. The others are a bulky stack addressed to Bethie. I touch Sam's knee, more questions hanging in my mouth. I understand what they are—not long ago I'd had a Steve Madden box like one of these hidden in my closet below a bag of old clothes—however, I don't understand why Ben had them initially or why he kept them.

Sam lifts the Converse box and its label closer to the lantern. *Camaro 2000.*

"When did you find these?"

"Last night. I came up here looking for stuff we could film." He glances toward the corner of the room. "Dad doesn't always come home and I check here to make sure he's not trapped or drunk or whatever. Anyway, these were in the Camaro when the police released it from evidence."

"The police read these?"

Sam shrugs. "Probably. They kept the car for a while, I think. They're from when they were our age. Before Cora died. They're the letters they sent back and forth while Frankie was in juvie."

CHAPTER 30

First-person insight into my mom and Frankie's relationship directly before Cora's murder is huge. Sam fumbles through the notes, discards some, and lays others in an ordered stack. "No dates or anything, but I think I've got them in a good order," he says. "You want me to leave you here for a minute with them? I can check on Lucy."

His question reminds me that the price of admission is to leave these here.

"How worried should I be?"

"I didn't sleep much last night."

Those notes are a roller coaster I want to ride, even though I'm not sure I have the courage to stay in line and strap myself in.

"Stay," I say to Sam.

And he does.

Bethie,

Thank you for your letter and for what you said. You can't imagine what it means to me in here. This is the strangest time of my life. I keep going back through every pleading word and muddy detail and stupid decision that led me here. And I don't know, Bethie, I thought I was doing the right thing. Now I'm afraid I've screwed up my life forever. Thanks for sticking with me through the worst.

Frankie

Frankie,

Not hard to stick with you at all. I'd bet a hundred thousand dollars you didn't attack Martin. I saw you that night and your migraine was so bad you couldn't see straight. You told me you were headed home to sleep. And unless you are an incredible actor, I'm betting you were out of it all night.

So when you say "every pleading word and muddy detail and stupid decision that led me here," I'd love to know more.

You're safe with me.

Bethie

Bethie,

Martin got what he deserved, even if I'm not the one who dealt him justice. How is that for a subtle confession?

Frankie

Frankie,

If you didn't attack Martin, who did?

Ben? Ned? Daddy? Bless it all, just tell me.

And regardless of who, why in the world would you plead guilty? That's what I can't figure out.

Bethie

Bethie,

Best answer: I made the decision before I realized the consequences.

Does it help to know my dad liked the idea of me standing up to Martin? Don't get me wrong; he was upset, but when it came down to it, he got eye to eye with me and said he'd heard enough rumors about Martin to believe he deserved what happened to him. He was proud and I went with it.

Frankie

Frankie,

I've always liked your dad. Especially since my folks parent the tri-county youth more than they do us. Their parenting sounds more like . . . "You know the drill, girls. If a reporter calls the house, you answer, 'No comment.'" Mix that in with a "Pearls are timeless," and I can consider myself raised.

They haven't even noticed Cora and I are fighting. Dad woke me up at three this morning yelling at a guy in Toyoko on the phone about a new drug trial and Mom is in full-scale Leap program mode. Speaking of, I did hear her tell someone that you never completed the entire Leap program. I'd say she's more worried about program results being tarnished than if her daughter's best friend beat a dude senseless. She hasn't stopped to ask why or how you being in juvie might affect you or me and Cora.

I've tried to get Cora to explain what happened and she won't. I can't tell if she's still angry with me over Ben or she can't talk about anything to do with Martin or she hates me. Just tell me who so you don't have to do this alone.

Bethie

Bethie,

Think through the whole situation again and tell me your theory. That feels safer than me writing it down.

Also, I know this is a long shot, but would you ask your dad about giving me my old job back at the Center this summer? I'm going to need a respected reference to help me get into college now that I have a record to deal with. Ask if he'll let me work maintenance. Maybe that would fit in with your parents' whole rehabilitation theme and they can get positive press or something.

Frankie

Frankie,

I told Dad he was rehiring you this summer and he agreed. Cora says she's planning on going to Europe with Granny, but Granny hasn't mentioned that at all.

As for who really did it—I don't even have a guess that makes sense. Could we maybe talk about this over the phone? I'll pay for a phone card or whatever you need.

Bethie

Bethie,

I'm not sure if what I did will ever make sense.

It'll be easier for me if Cora is gone this summer. Tomorrow at 3:00. I'll try to call.

Frankie

Frankie,

I'm reeling from our conversation.

I hate this for you. Hate it for her, too, but what she asked you to do is wrong on top of wrong.

And then to basically abandon you during the trial and not talk or write you while you're away . . . after all you've done for her . . . is incomprehensible to me. She's supposed to be your best friend. She's acting insane. And maybe that's trauma, but still.

Why didn't either of you tell me about Martin? You could have. We could have figured this out together.

You don't deserve any of this, and regardless of

how much it might hurt my family, I think you should push Cora to tell the truth and maybe get this over-turned. People will understand her side. Maybe not everyone, but most people. I'll be there for both of you.

Bethie

Bethie,

I've put a lot of thought into this, and here's my decision for now: Cora's already been punished enough with what Martin did to her. No woman should expe-rience that. What I did kept her from telling the story before she was ready, and that feels right to me, regardless of the consequences.

And as far as not talking to me, I got a letter from her this morning. And get this, she said since Martin got out of the hospital he's been acting like he can't remember anything that happened. Not even before the attack. Evidently he and Ned were on the lake this week and he waved at her like he used to at the dock. Like there was zero memory of what happened between them. Wigged her out. She said it was like the twilight zone. You should check on her without telling her you know. Like a little sister would.

Frankie

Frankie,

You're going to hate me. I did less checking and more threatening. I gave Cora a week to set the record straight. I told her if she didn't, I would tell Granny. Take it straight to the top, right?

Cora didn't handle it well. Cried and begged—you know how she can be. She promised she would confess but couldn't yet. There was this whole pity party about how I didn't know the whole story and if I did I would keep my mouth shut. She claimed she was working on something big, but she wouldn't tell me what.

I don't believe her. I don't know how you can either. If you're banking on her bailing you out, don't. Set her straight, Frankie. Tell her how you feel and what she's done to you, and if she doesn't tell the truth then, I might kill her myself and recruit Ben to help. Lord knows he's got as many reasons to let her have it. Seriously, talk to her.

Bethie

There was more of their back-and-forth. More of Bethie trying to convince Frankie that Cora needed to be held accountable. More of Frankie trying to convince Bethie not to talk to Granny until Frankie was out of juvie. At times, the rage they generated was hard to read. In the end, Frankie came over to Bethie's side. They planned to confront Cora together.

CHAPTER 31

S am."

The mine absorbs his name.

The lantern dims, flickers, and dies. Sam turns on his iPhone flashlight.

"I know, Lion."

"These notes make it out like—"

"I know."

"Were they part of the trial?"

Sam looks from the notes to me. "How could they have been? If Frankie went to juvie for a crime Cora committed, wouldn't that have exonerated Frankie, or at least vouched for her character? They went for the death penalty because of her prior assault record on Martin Jarvis. And these show that record is false."

"That wouldn't necessarily exonerate her," I say, thinking through what the notes might have meant to the jury.

"Both sides would have wanted to suppress these. If you're the prosecutor, they give reasonable proof that Mom is guilty. If you're the defense, they illustrate Frankie had a motive."

"True."

"Where's your dad in all of this?"

"I don't know. Frankie gave him the Camaro when they sentenced her. He said she asked him to keep it running for her." He laughs, but not in a way that suggests he finds anything about the situation funny. "I need to show you something else too."

The cavern is pitch black. Sam knows exactly where he's going; he shines the light so I don't trip into the boxes and send them in every direction. He leads me to a set of oversized metal file lockers that are so piled with boxes they almost disappear. The metal protests and we both steady the shaking tower of shoeboxes. We move slowly, unwilling to risk a total collapse.

Once the locker is open, I'm looking at an old, dirty backpack with a monogram: *CJK*.

"Cora Jane King," I say.

My heart beats hard and fast; Lucy can probably hear it back in the house.

"The real kicker is what's inside." Sam unzips the bag to lift a steel hammer and a pick-like weapon from the pack. "This is a rockhounding kit. Take a look in there." He shines the light directly into the front pocket, illuminating a hand-held mechanical device. "And that is a diamond tester that is basically identical to the one the girl I pulled out of the cave had. Look, if we keep at this, Lion, we could—"

"—figure out our parents did this instead of Frankie," I finish. My whisper is heavier than the hill above us.

CHAPTER 32

"S am!"

Sam and I jump at the sound of his father's voice. I drop the diamond tester; Sam releases the backpack. The weight of the pack landing on the metal file causes the piece to tip forward, and as it does the boxes arranged on top teeter and fall. Sam stops the majority of the avalanche, but several are upturned in the narrow aisle, their contents spilling out. Lucy trots over to help as Sam says, "Dad, we were . . ." He can't make himself finish the sentence, and although I have no more than a glimpse of him from the phone light, I feel him shrinking with shame. In the end, he gives a shaky, "I'm sorry." All while Ben Stack stands wordlessly at the entrance to the room.

I react, laying my hand over Sam's. The top of his hand feels like ropes and decking splinters. And when I turn his hand over inside mine, his palms are even more callused and rough. For a moment our eyes meet and we're transported out of this situation and into another. A hand in yours can work magic—a magic that says no matter how bad things are, you aren't as alone as you feel. Lucy nuzzles under our hands until we're both in a position to pet her nose and head.

His father gives no indication of when or if he will speak. Sam gathers the fallen papers and coupons and knickknacks and crams them into the open box. They are a pair of long faces that mean nothing to me and much to them.

"Dad?" Sam finally asks.

Ben shoves his hands deep into the pockets of his jeans; his hips are so narrow the material sags lower on his waist. They're dirty at the knees, like he just got up from the sod.

"Dad?" Sam says again. This time with urgency. "Tell us what you know. Please."

"About?" This single word seems to cost Ben.

I imagine Ben at my age and figure into the equation that he was my mother's type, my aunt's type. He's also the type you'd give your Camaro to. Was he more back then or was he merely handsome and convenient? Could he have been a pawn between Mom and Cora—the guy whose jockeying affection allowed them to wound each other? Based on the brick thrower's video, that's a possibility.

"That summer Cora died," Sam coaxes. He drops to the earthen floor and wraps his arms around his knees. I do the same and we wait for Ben to join our tiny circle. He abandons us first—moving silently along the corridor. I can't tell if he went right or left. Lucy follows him as far as the entrance and then comes back to us. Sam shakes his head like he knew this would happen, but then Ben returns.

His father doesn't sit; he leans against the singular exposed trestle while tilting his ear toward the ceiling like he's waiting on the world to collapse.

"Sir, what if we ask you questions?" I say. The idea that this man will tell a story seems impossible.

Sam takes my cue. "You're with Cora. She cheats on you with Martin." Ben shrugs, like he can't and won't fathom the relationship between Martin and Cora. "Then what, Dad?"

"She came back to me, but Martin was still there."

Ben's hatred for Martin does not feel twenty years old; it's ripe.

"She kept you both until he got violent?" I ask.

A nod.

I keep going. "Then Martin got more violent and Cora fought back."

"But Frankie agreed to take the rap." Sam phrases this like truth rather than a question and earns another nod from his dad.

"She served six months for nothing." Ben's hands push deeper into his pockets, his fingers balling into fists that make the fabric bulge. Years later this choice of Frankie's infuriates him.

"What did Cora do during those six months?" I ask.

"Got distant from everyone and disappeared for long periods of time. I figured at first she went running back to Martin." Ben turns his finger in a circle to indicate a cycle of abuse. "I asked her about it and she said I had crap for brains. Told me she was scared of him remembering everything. Even claimed he broke into her bedroom."

"When?" I say as Sam asks, "Why would he do that?"

"She took something from him back before the attack, but his break-in would have been"—Ben stares up at the ceiling—"maybe a week before she disappeared. Around the same time Frankie got out of juvie. I think Cor messed up Martin pretty good with that bat of hers, and whatever argument they were in that night got fuzzy in his brain."

The picture of Cora's mental state leading up to her disappearance remains hazy, but she must have been freaking out if she thought Martin's memories were coming back. To think any day he'd realize she, not Frankie, attacked him. Or that any day he might remember whatever it was she stole from his cabin.

I keep at Ben while he's willing to talk. "Do you know where she went when she kept disappearing over those six months Frankie was in juvie?"

"She had the rockhounding equipment," Sam says, and then suggests to his dad, "And you maybe let her keep it here?"

"No. I found her backpack in the mines after she went missing."

It isn't hard to imagine Ben finding the pack and

tucking it away in his secret place. "And Martin Jarvis?" I ask.

"Found him swinging from the rail bridge."

My insides squirm. Ben found Martin. That should have set Cora's case on fire and left Ben holding the gasoline. I ask the next question. "Do you believe he killed her and then himself?"

"Couldn't have. I was with her right here"—Ben jabs at the packed dirt floor with his work boots—"before I found his body. He was definitely dead before she was. Sorry, I know you want that to be different. Saw you asking on your show."

I glance at Sam. He, too, seems surprised his dad is watching *Death Daze*. "Did Cora see Martin dead?"

Ben's eyes narrow and shift toward the boxes on the other side of the room. He doesn't answer. Maybe he doesn't know. Finally, he says, "Whatever existed between them was toxic. To both of them. All I know is she took off toward the mines and that was the last time I saw her."

I ask so Sam doesn't have to. "And you didn't go after her?"

"No, I did not."

"What did you do, Mr. Stack?"

"Left. Hiked down the hill and discovered Martin hanging from that old section of rail bridge that's up near the body tunnel entrance, called Ned and the police, and then spent the next few hours being questioned."

"That's it?"

"Basically."

"You're leaving out the polygraph you took. You're leaving out that you were a suspect," Sam says, holding Lucy tighter.

"Son, I suppose I'm leaving out a lot, but nothing that'll tell you who killed Cora. Only that Martin couldn't have. Cora died. Frankie went to jail. Bethie left. I stayed here."

He states the history factually, resolutely, without bitterness or challenge. There's no fat to the body of this man or the stories he tells. He's given us so much, but nothing satisfying. "You must have thoughts on what happened." I sound squeaky and desperate.

"I drank buckets trying to avoid thoughts of Cora and Beth King."

"Okay, Dad. One more question and then you get out of here and call your sponsor, okay?" Sam senses the dangerous vulnerability we've drawn out in Ben by resurrecting the past. "You saw Cora on the day she disappeared. Do you know where else she'd been?"

"She'd tried to confront Martin, but she wouldn't say about what. That happened at his house. Then she went to Frankie's, talked to her dad. Then here, I think. All fits the police timeline." He whistles and Lucy stirs and meanders his way. She pauses halfway between the men and turns to look at Sam.

"Go on," he says and the dog obeys.

I study Ben Stack, his stooped posture, his sadness. I hope that twenty years from now I'm not also wearing the fate of Cora King in every ounce of my being.

CHAPTER 33

The outside air is between boil and blister. Or maybe the cave was cool and we forgot how hot and sticky we were when we climbed the hill. Sam and I break a sweat on the way to the pool house. I want to talk about what happened and I also want to leave him alone. He's not inside himself the way his father lives—but there's no doubt he's processing. It's only after we reach the driveway that I realize we've been walking in step together, his arm around my shoulders, mine around his lower back. He's as comfortable to me as new socks and a pair of Vans, and they're about a ten on the comfort chart. Right up there with fingerless mittens and a Sherpa-lined blanket in winter.

Halfway up I risk asking his opinion on our next step. "Should we check the channel and see what has turned up on Martin Jarvis or let it go?" I'm fairly discouraged. Dead men can't kill anyone, and everything lessens the notion that Cora's murder was random. She was up to something and that something cost her life.

"Let's talk to Frankie's dad. See if he remembers anything about the day Cora disappeared. Dad's right. There are timelines of June 2 online, but I've never seen them place Cora at Frankie's dad's house on the day she disappeared. Ever. I'm pretty sure the last anyone saw her was a fisherman who had a time-stamped picture of her boat crossing toward Nockabout at eleven forty-five."

I take out my phone and pull up the documents Sam's referencing. He's right. They have four data points for Cora on June 2. She was up and gone from the King house by 6:30 a.m.—confirmed by the front-door security camera. She was spotted docking a boat at Weymeyer at 8:00 a.m. by a family out skiing, and then back again at 11:45 a.m. According to a later document from AT&T, authorities knew Cora's cell lost service at 3:07 p.m. No way to determine if that was her choice or someone else's, and several occurrences of that behavior happened in the months leading up to the disappearance. It was assumed at the time she turned her phone on and off to save the battery.

Like Sam, I don't remember anyone coming forward with information on Cora's whereabouts from 6:30 a.m. to 8:00 a.m. when she was island side or 8:00 a.m. to 11:45 a.m. when she was in Lone Valley, and nothing at all from 11:45 a.m. to 3:00 p.m. Seeing the timeline again—right in front of us—and putting it up against the new information from Ben lets us pencil in possibilities.

Sam says, "Check those FreeFrankie.com people. They had testimonies up about the timelines of other people too."

He's right.

They have Mom's police statement from June 3, in which she states she didn't see her sister the day of the disappearance. Beth was out of the house by 7:15 a.m. and at Green County High School by 8:00 a.m. to take the ACT. There's a registry that puts her there, which I suppose should give me comfort that even if the jump drive video leaks or the juvie letters are found, she has a rock-solid alibi for Cora's and Martin's deaths.

"What do you want to do?" I ask.

"Why don't you see if you can interview Mannie Quick, Frankie's dad? Get him to confirm what Dad said about Cora stopping there on the second. I'll call my buddy on the force and see if he has anything on Martin Jarvis's suicide."

"What if we talk to Ned?" I say. When it doesn't immediately click for Sam, I add, "About the diamond tester. Maybe they're used for something other than diamonds. And Frankie's letter to Mom puts Ned and Martin together on the lake. Plus, I'd like to ask him to fix a ring for me."

Sam swings around to face me and sighs. "You're losing your Band-Aid, Lion." He lays his hand on my forehead and gently tugs free the end of the bandage that hasn't sweated free. He leaves his hand on my face, up near my cheek. I tilt upward toward him, feeling the heartbeat of the kiss we both want to happen. He's bending closer to my lips when we hear a very faint *click, click* from the tree line.

"Hey!" he yells.

Two shadowy figures freeze. The taller of the two lowers his camera and runs into the woods, his buddy following along behind, holding on to the waistline of his jeans so they won't fall off.

"You know them?" I ask.

Sam shakes his head. "It would be better if I did."

Two random guys in the woods, waiting to take our picture, reminds us both we're being watched, and maybe not by curious bystanders.

Our brick thrower is out there, and he, or she, has had plenty of time to reload.

CHAPTER 34

I hadn't intended to tell Mom and Richard about the guys in the woods. They ask where I've been all morning, and I find it easier to express the fear in my stomach from the click of that lens than of the big hulking terror that's building. Why does truth have to live on such a narrow ledge?

Mom and Richard do what people who love you do. They tuck me between them on the sectional and ask if I'd like to watch *Pitch Perfect* for the hundredth time. This is our family movie. You wouldn't believe it, but in the right mood, I can get Richard to shove aside the coffee table and do the entire dance scene at the end. He's an awful dancer, and that makes it oh so wonderful.

"I can't today," I say. "I need something else."

"Name it." Richard pops off the couch like a young man and digs through sacks on the counter in our makeshift kitchen. He tosses me a bag of gummy bears and says, "And there's Yoo-hoo in the fridge."

I am grateful neither of them suggests we leave Nockabout. I'm scared, but I don't want to quit yet. "Will you take me to meet Frankie's father?" I ask. "I'd like to ask him about the day Cora disappeared."

Richard and Mom exchange looks, their faces teeming with questions. Richard raises an eyebrow that seems to mean, *Yes to meeting Mannie?* Mom's features are lost in silhouette when she walks closer to the window. From that position, she whispers, "Okay."

An hour later, Mom raps on the door of a run-down ranch on the Weymeyer side of Lone Valley. The man who answers bears no resemblance to Frankie. Mannie Quick is a large man with eyes the color of dawn light—a gray that leans toward blue. They bulge, not in an unattractive way, but in a way that makes him seem like he thought too hard once and now his eyes are stuck in a state of perpetual curiosity. It's hard to imagine him fitting into, much less driving, the Volkswagen Bug parked by the garage.

He greets Mom with affection and surprise. "Bethie." There's that name again. The name that sends everyone back in time twenty years.

"Mr. Quick," Mom returns and leans through the doorframe to kiss him on the cheek. It is the kiss that makes me realize she drove here without directions. Just like Nockabout, Mannie belongs to a vibrant and hidden past.

"This is Nyla," she says with a wave of her hand.

His jaw drops cartoonishly, an expression that reminds me of the quintessential television aunt who pinches your cheek and says she can't believe how big you've gotten. Mannie ignores my extended hand and wraps his arms over my shoulders. Unsure what to do, I hold on above his belt and lean my ear against the lower section of his ribs. He holds me like a tow rope in the river, like I am part of wherever he's heading next. "Thank you," he says, "for believing in my kiddo."

"You're very welcome. Mom taught me."

He lifts his hand in an apology. "Sorry, sorry," he says and dabs at his eyes with a handkerchief. There's an implied neatness in his clothes, in the square of folded white cotton in his hand, and in the living room behind him. A no-nonsense approach. That neatness makes me nervous to ask questions, especially the ones I've come to ask.

Mannie leads us through the living room and into his tiny eat-in kitchen. There is a water glass on the table and a hunting magazine on the placemat. He carries the glass to the sink and stacks the reading material under a small clock radio before pulling out chairs.

We're barely in our seats before Mom asks, "How are you since . . ."

She doesn't say the ADPA; she doesn't have to.

Mannie lifts his enormous shoulders. "How any father would be. How are you? Other than fit as a fiddle." When Mom also shrugs, he asks me, "And you? Our superstar." His eyes protrude toward me like they are on springs.

200

"I'm . . ." Well, what am I? "Hoping you might be able to help me help your daughter."

"Anything." He thumbs toward a computer setup across the room. "But I'd rather not film unless it's absolutely necessary."

"My next interview needs to be with the senator."

Mannie says, "I can't stand that woman." To Mom, he bows slightly. "Sorry. She's your mom, but . . ."

Mom reminds him of her allegiances. "You know I left. And you know Frankie and I . . ."

I pounce before the two of them have a nonverbal conversation I can't possibly interpret. "Sir, it would be helpful to know if Cora came here on June 2 looking for Frankie."

The question catches Mom off guard, but now that I've asked, she wants to know too. We're both leaning forward, thumbnails jabbed between our upper front teeth, waiting for his response.

Mannie stares out the window. "She did."

"And you never told?" I ask.

"Not even Frankie, I'm ashamed to admit. Not sure why I'm telling you now." Mannie stands and paces over to the sink. He swivels the empty glass in his hand and holds it under the faucet without turning on the water.

"You thought Frankie would think you hurt Cora?" I guess. "Because of how much you hated Cora for letting Frankie take the fall for the Martin Jarvis attack when you learned the truth?" I catch my mother's eye before I say the next things that may or may not surprise her. "Cora is the one who attacked Martin, and Frankie took the blame either to save Cora the embarrassment of the senator finding out or to save the integrity of the Leap program."

Mom inhales sharply. Mannie bends in half and puts his head on the stainless steel rim of the sink. "Frankie doesn't know I know about that. Did she tell you?"

"No," I say. "I read letters Mom and Frankie wrote to each other when Frankie was in juvie."

Mom's ankle taps the leg of the kitchen table. I put my hand on her thigh to steady her and then say to Mannie, "Tell me what happened when Cora came over on June 2. What time was it? Elevenish?" I guess, trying to fill the timeline.

He fills his glass, lifts it to his lips, sips, and says, "Before lunch. Maybe eleven, maybe a bit after. She knocked and I answered. She was wanting to talk to Frankie and I said, 'No. She's not home.' But she was sleeping in her room. She woke up with a migraine and I made her stay home from the ACT even though we'd paid eighty dollars for that stupid test." He sighs over the decision he has clearly berated himself over for the last twenty years. If she'd gone to that test, she'd have the same alibi as Mom. "She'd argued with me, 'Dad, you know I need to get a good score. Dad, I've gotta go up from a 31 and try to do something that'll make them forget my record.' I knew she was right, but she couldn't even walk in a straight line, much less take a test."

I understand. I get migraines like that, and even the idea of thinking hurts.

202

I need to keep him talking. "So Cora's at the door and you don't let her see Frankie. Did she say why she came over?"

"No."

"Did she have anything with her?"

Mannie thinks hard. "I don't think so."

"You don't know or you don't think so?"

He massages his forehead. "It was twenty years ago."

"And your daughter has twenty-three days to live. Please. I need you to think." This comes out harsher than I intended and I regret my tone.

"Come with me," he says. Without another word, Mannie leaves the kitchen for the narrow dark-paneled hallway. He opens a door with a Switchfoot poster. "This is her room."

He hasn't done much to change her space. The preservation of her teen style is museum quality right down to the half-naked cowboy poster on the wall, the large boom-box system on her dresser, and a row of shooting trophies that read *The Senator's Competition*. There are photos everywhere, taped to her panel walls and inside the rim of a large mirror above the bed's headboard.

Mannie's only addition to the room is a well-worn rolling chair, placed at the center of the once-white carpet. I understand immediately that this is where he comes to sit and spin and watch the memories of his daughter the way I might watch television.

"Look at this," he says of a framed collage. There's a large picture of Frankie wearing a hideous black V-neck drape and ugly pearls and then encircling that photo are eleven others from the Green County school system. Frankie was not always beautiful. I watch her grow from a girl with uneven bangs to a skinny, freckled preteen to a girl my age who would make anyone swoon. I glance at Mom, who smiles, and I say to Mannie, "Mom did one of these for me."

"Look again," he says.

"Mannie!" There's a warning in Mom's voice. A pleading.

Whatever Mannie might have said next, he stops, removes the frame from the wall, and holds it against his chest. "That's my girl and there's nothing I won't do for her. Or for you."

I'm out of my league. I don't know how to conduct an interview. I go with what I've seen on cop shows and hope that something comes out of my stumbling approach. "Okay. It's June 2, 2000. Cora shows up. You hate her for letting Frankie take the fall. She wants Frankie, and you lie so she'll leave. Is there anything that stands out?"

Mannie is practiced at falling into the rolling chair. He collapses; it slides and comes to a stop at the edge of a purple throw beside the bed. He has his eyes pinched, remembering. We watch him mentally retrace the steps of that day. "She had her purse with her. A black velvet one."

Mom scrunches her nose in confusion.

"What?" I ask.

"Cora didn't carry a purse. Ever. She had a backpack with her initials monogrammed."

Mannie is defensive. "You're saying I'm wrong?"

Mom backs down. "I'm saying that specific bag wasn't a purse."

"Anything else?" I ask.

"Yeah. She drove left out of the driveway and she normally would have gone right. Doubt it matters. It's documented that another family saw Cora at the Weymeyer dock a little bit later, but you said to mention anything that stands out."

"Thank you, Mr. Quick."

"Would you mind taking a walk with an old man? There's one more thing I could show you."

"Sure," Mom answers for us both.

"Just Nyla," he says.

I can hardly say no. On our way out the kitchen door, he tucks an empty gallon bucket over his arm and leads the way into the yard. He is sure-footed in his size-thirteen shoes, and I wonder how old he is. Young enough he doesn't sag; old enough he's cautious with his steps.

"You're retired?" I ask.

"Something like that."

"You were a teacher?"

"Administrator."

We exit through a wooden gate, cross a gap in the hedge-row brush, and walk into an open expanse. No more than five feet away, a brown rabbit freezes like a statue. We watch its eyes widen before it bolts under Mannie's fence. Hundred-year-old trees scatter left to right across the property. Water collects in the low spots. "That's a pecan orchard," Mannie says and keeps walking until that piece of land becomes another.

High on the next hill sits a ramshackle barn: the only man-made thing on the horizon. Everything is green, yellow, and brown. Color differentiations show the growing seasons and separate one field from another. Corn has been planted, plus beans—though I can only identify the corn and rely on Mannie to explain the rest. We cross a creek on a wooden plank, and on the other side are row upon row of green bushes, low to the ground. The corn smells fresh and earthy; whatever grows here exudes sweetness.

"It's early," Mannie says apologetically. "They're small, but good. Even better with a whack of sugar." He takes two sugar packets from his pocket and places the empty bucket on the ground between us. His knees sound like popcorn as he kneels, picks a small bloodred strawberry from the vine, and tosses it to me. "Try that."

The berry is perfect. "Are they yours?"

"They are. All of this is."

Mannie settles on the ground and tosses more fruit into the bucket. We pick berries for nearly an hour in silence. I do not understand why we are here, only that he's given me something and this is what he asks in return. Sweat pours off us in sheets and drips onto the vines like rain. Our fingers are stained pink from the juice.

"Tell me about her," I say when the bucket is too full to add another berry and the time has come for our whacks of sugar.

"Francis? Or Bethie?"

"Both."

His expression warms. For this conversation, he returns us to the pecan grove, eases our backs against two trees, and uses sanitizer from a hook dangling off the bark. "I come here a lot," he says, swinging the sanitizer. We eat handfuls of berries. They melt and crunch, their sweetness perfect. Their delicious smell almost drives away the alcoholic zing of the cheap handwash.

Mannie begins, "Frankie was a handful when she was little. Never stopped talking. I guess the first sleepover she had, Bethie and Cora spent the night in her little room and they all laid out on pallets. I remember coming by to check on them—one o'clock, two o'clock, two thirty in the morning—and Frankie was chattering away. At three, I went in to tell them they had to go to bed, only to find out that Cora and Beth had fallen asleep at midnight. Frankie claimed this was her only chance to tell them everything she wanted to without annoying them." He laughs at the memory. "She didn't stay that chatty. And we definitely found our attitude in middle school." This time he whistles long and hard, impressed by the very thing that used to drive him crazy. "Oh, she had a fast lip and a quick wit. Sounded like you on your videos," he says.

"They were always close? Her and Cora and Mom?"

"Met in preschool. They were thick as eyelashes on a drag queen from moment one. Nothing alike except for growing up in this place. Never mattered to any of 'em.

207

Now, the King girls struggled under the weight of their momma's reputation, but they were far more down-to-earth than they deserved to be. I think they'd have stayed that way if Cora had never taken up with Jarvis." Mannie stretches his long legs away from where he's been holding them against his chest. "Mr. Stud. All Hollywood out here and dirty jerk down here." He dances a hand over his pelvis, disgusted. "You know what I'm saying?"

I nod for him to skip those details.

"Cora had always been steady with Ben, but Martin got her all stirred up. I don't know if they dated or hooked or whatever they called it, but it didn't take him long to show himself. You know the next part. Cora flipped and beat him up and then what? You get the best-hearted criminal in the world, if you asked her dad." He flushes with love.

"Still?" I ask.

"Still," he says. "You'd love her."

"We met."

"So you know."

I like the confidence he has in his daughter.

"I do," I say.

He closes his eyes and deepens his smile.

"And my mom? Where did she fall into all that history with Martin?"

Mannie draws his legs back to his chest and drops his forehead against his knees. "I'm sure she's told you all this before."

"Actually, I only found out about who she was—a King, I mean—last week."

He makes a noise that suggests he is impressed by Mom's tenacity in lying. "Bethie was always good at secrets. Always tough." He draws the word out long, with a ton of respect in his voice. "You had to be if you sat opposite Rebecca King." His voice sours. "And Bethie was never quite who her mom wanted her to be." He smiles sideways at me. "I loved your mom then and that hasn't changed. She'll always be eighteen to me. Francis too. Or eleven, listening to my kid rattle on about whatever her obsession of the moment happened to be."

"Did Mom and Cora get along?"

"They slipped away from each other that last year after your mom found out what Cora did to Frankie. But you ain't gotta worry. If Bethie killed Cora, she'd have told me and she'd have gone away herself sooner than watch Francis go through what she has. You might not believe that, since she's lied to you, but her lies, that lie in particular, comes from a different place. Lies have good origins and bad origins."

"What do you believe happened to Cora?"

Mannie hauls me and the empty berry bucket to standing. Without a word, we cross the field and the hedgerow and the garden to another of the buildings in his yard. This one has a desk, lamp, and filing cabinets. He rolls open a drawer and removes a file labeled *Martin Jarvis*.

The file is slim. After a cursory glance, he hands me two pieces of paper. One is a bank statement from May of 2000. Five thousand dollars, paid to Martin Jarvis from an account labeled *Tatti*. I nearly swallow my tongue.

Another is a copy of a job application. In February of 1995, Martin applied to be a miner in Santiago, Chili, for De Beers. The diamond company. Attached to the résumé is a reference letter from none other than Senator Rebecca King. Her stamped signature has faded only a small amount.

"Where did you get these?" I ask.

"Pulled together some money to hire a private investigator. She turned up dead ends and these scraps. Left me with nothing but theories I can't prove."

"What theories?"

He begins, "Well, that glowing endorsement letter the senator wrote for De Beers. All BS. Ask anybody around here and they'd tell you Martin was up to his neck in things that you'd never put on a reference letter. So why'd Rebecca write all that unless he had something on her? Way I figure it, she spent time with him in that Leap program of hers and that must be where she realized he could handle an unsavory job or two and that worked fine until he developed a thing for Cora. I'd bet my life that woman paid Jarvis five thousand dollars to leave Nockabout. Maybe he said no, or took Cora hostage, hoping to get more money, and things went south. Then maybe Rebecca found out, killed him, and staged a suicide. And my baby being held responsible was icing on the cake. All the better to blame Frankie than for any of that stink to worm its way to the surface. Way it played out . . . Rebecca King rode sympathy straight into another term. Maybe she supports the ADPA, maybe she doesn't, but for her, she doesn't truly get away with her sins until my Frankie's dead."

I don't know what to say at first. I say, "Wow," but really I mean, *You sound a little crazy*. I'm also focused on the fact that Jarvis applied to De Beers. Who applies for a mining position in Chili? Why do diamonds keep cropping up? And could Senator Rebecca King be behind the jump drive video? The Tatti connection puts her close enough.

"My version's more truth than Frankie killing Cora."

"I know I said I wouldn't ask this, but would you shoot a short video saying you believe Cora's disappearance is connected to the death of Martin Jarvis?"

He's reluctant but agrees. At the very end of filming, he departs from the questions and says, "Frankie, baby, if you're watching this, I love you so much. If any of you out there remember my Frankie, tell Nyla your best Frankie stories in the comments."

I couldn't have planned that diversion any better myself.

CHAPTER 35

B ack in the car, Mom peppers me with questions about my time with Mannie in the strawberry field. There's no FOMO going on. Just nerves. Like he might have told me unsavory details, which of course makes me wonder what's left to tell.

"That's it?" she says after I give her a brief synopsis. She cranks the engine. "Strawberries and the pecan grove?"

We pause at the end of the driveway. Her fingers drum away in time to the music and her thoughts.

"Basically," I say. "Until the end. He had information he thought connected Jarvis to your mom." She starts to turn right and I send her left instead, to follow the same path Cora would have taken on June 2. "I think he feels like it's insensitive to hate your mom in front of you."

That makes sense to her.

"Do you think she killed Cora?" I ask.

"Mom?" She huffs. "No. She's a piece of work, but Cora's death ruined . . . There's no way."

"Same with your dad?"

"Baby, I didn't leave home because I was scared they'd hurt me physically. I was scared I might . . . without Cora or Frankie there to balance me . . . turn out like them. That felt like more of a betrayal of Cora than anything. And then there was you, and things with Ben, and I . . . couldn't."

That's the most she's said about her past.

Up the hill is the barn Mannie and I saw from the bottom of the pecan grove. Mom slows the car to a crawl in the middle of the road, her gaze transfixed on the leaning structure. She taps on the window, giddy to share. "Oh, Ny, we used to play there. The three of us. The loft is the closest we came to having a clubhouse and—"

Eyes feasting on the barn, I interrupt. "Mom, do you miss her?"

"Every day."

"Not Frankie. Your sister."

"Oh." She tightens her grip on the wheel. "Well, yes and no. She's my childhood, and when I think of memories, I can't believe there's no one left to ask about them, but I don't think of my childhood much. Maybe because she's gone. But maybe because it wasn't all that happy."

"Is *Death Daze* hard for you on that level? Like, does me talking about her death . . . hurt you?"

She sucks on the chain of her necklace. She is driving *and* somewhere else. Her eyes are blank and so full she looks like she can't cram another memory in if she tried. "I think I'm shocked, you know, and I'm afraid you're going to find out something you can't live with. Being back here, knowing I left my parents when I was your age . . . I'm honestly more scared I'll ruin us than of whoever shot out Richard's security light. That's silly. And now there are idiots out there taking pictures of you and making veiled threats online and who knows what else—"

"Mom, we're fine." I'm not as confident as I should be. "I know why you lied about Nockabout and Cora. I don't like it, but I get it. Let's do everything we can to save Frankie and then get out of here."

"What about Sam? You two seem to be peas and carrots."

My cheeks flush with heat. "Yeah, something like that. We can get rid of Nockabout and keep him, right?"

"If my last twenty years with Frankie are any indication, I'd say absolutely."

We both laugh and that feels good. The clots of stress and tension ease with every mile marker.

Beauty is the only thing out here.

Deer and bees and gravel roads with potholes you have to drive around. Turtles sunning on logs in the water ditches and drains. And all around us a sky that buzzes blue if you stare at it too long. Summer air rushes in and out the windows, blowing our hair into knots. I like this mental break from death and dying. We pause the car for a mother deer and fawn to cross. They bound into the trees, and I remember Mom talking about honking the horn at deer in this very park. A reminder she didn't lie about everything.

We exit the state park and encounter scattered houses on the landscape. They range from gorgeous wraparound porches with "Welcome, Y'all" signs to one yard with a collection of fifteen ambulances in various states of rust; Christmas bulbs stretch across the open air to connect them. I wonder about the people who live out here. Where they work and what they do. And how does an individual go about starting an ambulance collection?

I am about to mention the abundance of service vehicles when Mom points at the small house that accompanies the collection and says, "I'm pretty sure that's where Anna grew up."

I keep my response to a "Hmm," but secretly I'm impressed with Anna's trajectory—if she did indeed start here.

"We should get back," Mom says with a sigh of disappointment. "The ferry's leaving in twenty minutes."

I convince Mom we can call Sam and leave the car on the Lone Valley side. I don't mention that I'd like to do a special interest piece in the barn and maybe include a talk about Cora's childhood after I interview the senator. That barn has a gravity of its own. Plus, I'm excited to tell Sam about Mannie's revelation and see if he's learned anything that might link Martin to Senator King.

The ferry lot is slammed. We drive up the hill and behind Ned's to leave the car. Hopefully Ned won't mind. Mom and I stop under his shop's awning and wait for Sam.

Ned taps at the glass when he spots us and Mom waves. He holds up a Coke and hand signals that he can bring us one. She shakes him off and he deflates.

"He likes you," I say.

Mom nods. "But it was Cora he loved."

"Seriously?" How many people did she have wrapped around her finger?

"If we ever find who killed Cora, there'll likely be another homicide on Nockabout. Ned'll kill 'em."

Wow. Strong statement. "Sam said Ned stayed here because of his mother."

Mom shakes her head. "He's here because he can't let her go."

"He didn't blame Frankie?" When Sam and I were in the pawn shop, Ned felt like an ally, but I'd like to be sure.

Mom says, "Never."

"What about Martin?"

She wavers. "Ned and I had a bunch of conversations about Martin and Cora between the memorials and Frankie's trial and when I left Nockabout. Best I can say, he didn't know how to feel about Martin. Betrayed. Angry. He missed him and hated him. Martin was messed up. He'd be all flirty over here with Cora and then on the phone telling Ned he was gonna kill himself three hours later. Always wanting Ned to come rescue him. According to Ned, Martin tried before. Before he succeeded, I mean." She sighs. "Sad stuff no matter what he did to Cora."

"Did Ned know it was Cora who beat up Martin?"

"No, but he wasn't surprised when I told him during Frankie's trial."

"Who did he think killed Cora?"

Mom shakes her head. "He never came right out and said Ben, but that's what he thought back then."

I can't believe we're having this conversation.

"And you? Who did you think did it?"

Down the hill, a big crowd cheers and claps and distracts us. What I initially assumed was a busy day on the lake is more than it seems. These aren't merely fishermen and skiers; they're spectators and fans of *Death Daze*. They stand in clumps, recording various messages and stories on their phones. *Free Frankie* is on shirts and hats and bumper stickers. The opposition is here too. Pro-ADPA shirts are sprinkled among various clusters. A man with a megaphone tries to rally the crowd and get a chant going.

"Look at that," Mom says when she notices. "You're super famous." She puts her arm around my shoulder and I distract myself with the comments sections of the latest *Death Daze* posts. My request for information on Martin Jarvis has received numerous answers. Colorful answers. But most information I know or have already been able to infer.

I tell Mom what I'm doing and ask her opinion on Martin and Cora's relationship, which she boils down to a few short words. "Cora needed to save the world."

"Just like Rebecca?"

Mom giggles, enjoying that I've called her mother Rebecca. "Mom probably would have been first to throw the rice if Cor married Martin Jarvis. Talk about a tale she could spin—crazy big story about the transformational power of Leap. Although if I remember right, Daddy wanted to hire him and Rebecca said no. Maybe I'm being too hard on her." She sighs deeply.

That's interesting, given the senator's glowing letter to De Beers.

Ongoing comments below the post provide more context. Martin's childhood was lived in a blended family. There's a discrepancy on the number of siblings. Some say ten; others, nine. He graduated from Adair County High School. If the date listed is correct, he was five or six years older than Cora and Frankie. There are photos of him in football and basketball uniforms. Handsome and cocky. Cutoff shirts and washboard abs.

Plenty of photos have been uploaded. Most from the same source, probably from the same event. Him on the bow of a boat, cannonballing off the dock, shooting skeet. There's even one of him playing the piano with two beautiful girls seated on either side, their fingers resting on his. The captions all read *Jarvis on Nockabout Island* or *Leap*. None mention diamonds or De Beers. One shows a 1099-MISC income tax form establishing he worked for the King family in 1998—guess Creed won that battle. Very few people speak to his life in the five years leading up to his suicide. However, there are commenters berating my insensitivity to his mental health.

Abbi1999: Martin's depression and subsequent death

shouldn't make him a suspect in a murder that's already been solved.

JonandJen: Go dig elsewhere for your murderer. Martin's death was tragic.

Five comments down, **Tattihatesyou:** This time I'll shoot out more than the security lights.

I drop my phone.

"What is it?" Mom asks.

I don't want her to know I'm being threatened and I'm forced to disguise my reaction. "These comments are brutal," I say.

I switch to the video I uploaded at Mannie's, aware I promised the audience an interview with the senator. A few have noted this, saying I can't deliver. Others have responded to Mannie's request.

Facts, stories, pictures, and videos. Mom has me read them aloud to her. They're overwhelmingly positive and paint the picture of someone likable and kind. There's nothing juicy or helpful until we come to commenter JacieJay. JacieJay has uploaded a picture that must have been taken at Floyd. She and Frankie are sitting on a pair of bleachers, a basketball balanced on Jacie's index finger, the concrete court abandoned behind them. Frankie has her head thrown back laughing and her arms crossed over her very pregnant stomach. If I have any doubts about what I'm seeing, JacieJay puts them to bed.

Me and my girl Franks. 8 mons along and she can pump
and drain the 3.

Mom reads over my shoulder.

"You didn't tell me Frankie has a kid."

I enlarge the photo and confirm this isn't a joke and that's a basketball tucked under her shirt. Unless that basketball has a belly button, this is real. "Gosh. Do you know where he or she is? We could host them on *Death Daze*." My brain's spinning wicked fast, already foreseeing problems with the idea but too excited to keep it in. "The adoption was probably closed. I mean, her kid might not even know. But you do, right? Or you could find out?"

I hear Mom swallow. She chokes on the air and I pat her back.

"You did know, right?"

Mom's hair falls like a dark screen around her face. Her whole body trembles. "I knew."

"Oh my gosh." I lift up her hair, my adrenaline soaring. Her eyes are swimming with tears. The pieces fall into place. "It's Sam, isn't it? He knows and that's why he started the tours."

Mom grips my forearm and works to steady herself before saying, "It's not Sam, baby."

I exhale. My gratefulness is probably selfish. I'd rather the thing I have with Sam be between us rather than because of *Death Daze*. There's purity if he's not biologically involved.

"You know where to track them down? Or maybe you already have." She is gray and grave. "Oh." I raise my hand to my lips, horrified. "Mom, did the baby not make it?"

"She made it."

"She. Whew."

She starts not to cry exactly, but to almost cry.

There are moments we can't come back from, and most of the time we feel them approach. This one comes like a train.

"Nyla, you're that baby."

CHAPTER 36

There is no running away from history.

I never lived inside Beth Wagner. And she doesn't live inside me.

Francis Quick is a mother. My mother.

I am out in the gray.

Not thinking.

Not feeling.

Not capable of anything so rudimentary. Part of me is on the sidewalk, Mom's hand on my arm, and another part wanders away from my body. Like a lucid dream or that scene at the end of *Harry Potter* where Harry and Dumbledore are in a weird version of King's Cross station even though they are really in Harry's mind. Time passes, and Mom is there—squeezing me to her chest. When I return to conscious thought, I can't tell our heartbeats apart.

I search the planes of her face, the face I've never questioned and always known I came from, and for the first
time I can't see myself at all. I'm not in her brown eyes or
crooked nose or the curve of her jaw or the size of her ears.
I don't exist.

My fingers clench the fabric of my shorts. "How am I
supposed to feel?"

"I don't know. Just feel how you feel and we'll deal
with it."

How about like a rat is actively chewing on my brain.

Betrayed.

Confused.

Angry. So angry.

And oddly enough, so very, very loved.

This is what she has been terrified of my whole life.

I will never fully understand what this truth costs, but
I'm keenly and quickly aware it wasn't a debt she had to
pay. There would have been another family to have me,
if not Beth King. Instead, she abandoned her name and
relinquished any hope of coming home. All for me. I am too
shocked to say thank you or wield my emotions in a neat arc
that tells her I'm grateful she's the mom life gave. A very
big part of me wants to scream, *You should have told me!*

Though I already see both sides of that coin.

When would have been a good time for that conversation? First day of kindergarten? Middle school graduation?
Maybe my eighteenth birthday two weeks ago. *"Here's a red
velvet cake. By the way, your real mother is being executed."*

I choose, right then and there, not to hold the entirety of the lie against her. At least not until I find out if I should. And only later, when the larger problem isn't a blade against our necks.

Frankie Quick, my mother, will be put to death in twenty-three days for a crime she did not commit. I can want the circumstances of how and when I found out about my birth mother to be different, but I'll never change how they unfolded.

"Bless it all. Please don't hate me."

"I don't hate you."

There's no sign of relief from her. She looks worse.

In one way, this awful confession brings a new understanding of her relationship with Frankie. I can't say I feel better—there is far too much shock to call my state "better"—but I have a comfort I've never felt. Mom hasn't turned our world upside down for the last eighteen years because she loves her best friend more than her daughter. She turned her world upside down to love us both.

And even now, her decision to come home to Nockabout and face her family . . . she's doing that for me and Frankie.

"Who's my father?" I ask.

She bites her lip. "That's for Frankie to tell."

"Were you ever going to be honest with me?"

Her tears come fast now. "Yes. When you were older and could maybe forgive us. But then the ADPA and the appeal happened and we couldn't wait anymore. But neither of us knew how to tell you and then you went to see her on your own and started *Death Daze* and . . ." Mom exhales and wipes her right cheek with her shoulder; the tears keep coming.

"How did I . . . I mean . . . how did she decide you could, like, how did I end up with . . ."

"Me?" Delight blooms across her face and a memory takes her away. When she returns, she says, "I asked for you, and that was complicated because she didn't want anyone here to know."

"But she loved me?"

Mom belly laughs. "Enraptured, baby girl. Everyone has loved you your whole life."

I look out to the lake, a rippling blue-green buzz of activity. Families skiing and boating and fishing. A couple wheels a cooler toward the dock with a three-year-old riding on the lid. She holds a chihuahua and is singing the *Sesame Street* theme song at an octave that will make fishing difficult for a quarter mile down the lake.

A deep breath.

And then another.

Frankie couldn't have kept me. She's been in prison my entire life. She gave me to Mom, and Mom has loved me fiercely and chosen not to put me through Frankie's life— until the ADPA forced the issue. That kicks my thoughts back to Frankie.

Our visit.

That must have been excruciating. I think about how she exploded when the guard hit me. I hear her final words,

"Tell her I love you." Tell Beth I love Nyla. That's what she'd said. Not *Tell Beth I love Beth*, the way I heard and assumed.

Now I am crying. "How do we help her?"

Mom kisses my forehead and slicks the wisps of hair that escaped during our windy ride. She is heavier. She is lighter, too, now that we're on the same side. "Good girl," she says. "Good girl. Always practical."

"We aren't done with *this*," I tell her. "But we'll put it away for now."

I know her and because I do, I know she is scared of what will come after the dust settles. She's right to fear it. Everything is on the line: Our relationship with each other and her family. Our lives. Frankie's. This didn't start for Mom during the appeal. This narrative began the moment she carried me out of Floyd—a needy, hungry baby who smelled her impostership and probably wailed in protest.

We're both wailing now. And it is still for my mother.

CHAPTER 37

Sam: On my way. Tour went long. Much to tell you.

Nyla: Same.

Thirty minutes later, Sam appears at the dock and starts up the hill at a sprint. A pair of cutoff khakis hangs low on his hips. His camo shirt has *Leap* embroidered in the corner—a little reminder that no one escapes the senator's reach. A Cardinals ball cap covers his eyes and makes his hair curl around the rim. "Sorry. Sorry," he calls, readjusting the cap. "Nockabout's swarming with tourists or whatever you want to call them. I couldn't get to my boat. Did you ever in your wildest dreams anticipate *Death Daze* would draw a crowd with merch? I saw a girl wearing a *Nockabout, Home of Death Daze* hoodie. I didn't know whether to tell her, 'Girl, it's ninety-five degrees out here,' or ask if the shirt was copyrighted. We should have thought about other revenue streams."

Sam stands in front of us now, sucking air, hands on his knees. When he looks up, he grows quiet. The laughter in his tone and face flatten completely. It doesn't take an emotional genius to read the room. Sam's smart enough not to comment.

I say, "I'll tell you later."

Adaptation is in Sam's arsenal. "Let's get you ladies back to the pool house pronto. Richard has been hand-cranking vanilla ice cream for hours. Maybe that'll cheer you up."

Mom and I attempt smiles. Our efforts never reach our faces.

"You're going to want this, Lion," he says and lays his cap on my head and tugs it over my eyes. "And I brought this for you." He hands Mom a black scarf for her hair. We make it to the boat without being recognized. As we're pushing off, Sam eyes a rock at the shoreline and picks it up. After an examination, he tosses it to me. It's the size of a large marble, mostly smooth, with one sharp divot. He says, "Not exactly a diamond, but nice enough to be a tiny gift."

I bring the stone to my nose and smell the lake. "Thank you."

"You're very welcome."

No one talks again until we're at the pool house. Sam sees us all the way to Richard's ice cream and then pulls me aside as Mom collapses into Richard's arms. "Are you okay?" Sam asks.

"I will be," I tell him. "Will you go somewhere with me tomorrow?"

He understands I'm saying I'm done for the day. He squeezes my hand and says, "Go sleep," even though it's only three thirty. After Sam leaves, Mom and I settle on one bed and Richard takes the other. We watch *NCIS* reruns on Richard's computer. I suppose at some point Mom told him what happened on the way home from Mannie's. We don't mention the day or Mannie or Frankie or the Kings. We ignore the phones that ring and ping and the knocks at the door around 6:00 p.m.

No one speaks the word *YouTube*.

Or *Death Daze*.

Richard doesn't even sneak me to the side and give me one of his, "No, how are you *really*?" talks. Which is nice. We don't eat dinner. Don't brush our teeth. When Richard finally closes the laptop at eight forty-five, he leans over the bed where I'm lying and kisses right above my ear, deep into the recesses of my hair, all the way to the scalp. Then he turns off the light and we breathe together.

I don't remember falling asleep in Mom's bed. I blink myself awake in the night; down the hill, a coyote bays for a mate. I turn my head. Mom's curled into a tight C shape, her breath buried between my shoulder blades. I relax into her warmth and time my heartbeat to hers.

No matter how mad I feel, her body snuggled against mine, her warmth, the length of her fingers threaded through my hair like she's fallen asleep stroking it, reset the world. The love is always perfect, even when the living isn't.

I'm closing my eyes when the dim stream of light coming through the mini blinds shifts. Again. And then again. I strain my ears toward the window, fully awake, heart racing. *It's nothing*, I tell myself. There's a noise that accompanies the shifting shadows.

Something or someone is out there. Probably with a stupid camera.

Heart in my throat, I slide off the bed and onto the floor. The blinds tilt toward the ceiling. Whoever is out there only has the ability to look upward. I slink across the floor toward the window and talk myself into what has to be done next.

Raise the blind.

Look out.

Scare the crap out of a tourist.

Try to go back to sleep.

I pull the cord and register instant motion. A balaclava-covered face. Wide shoulders whip around to run. The uneven ground makes for odd strides as my Peeping Tom runs downhill into the woods. Height, race, clothing: there isn't a solid detail to anchor the encounter other than I feel sure I'm dealing with a male. He hadn't even made a sound when I yanked on the blinds. I hear Tattihatesyou's comment in my head: *I'll shoot out more than the security lights.*

Did he come and I caught him?

The logical thing to do is wake Mom and Richard and tell them what I've seen.

I don't. I worry this will be the thing that makes them

give up and take us home, and I don't want that. Not yet. I need a chance to figure this out, for myself, for Frankie, whether it's safe or not. And odds are, that guy is a crazy tourist trying to get an interview with a member of the King family. Heck, he might not even know someone is staying here and was simply looking for a souvenir to brag about online. It's four o'clock in the morning. I'm not claiming it makes sense.

When the adrenaline fades, I am out. Mom nudges me what feels like five minutes later but is in fact five hours later. "Up, up, up, baby. The senator is here for her interview."

CHAPTER 38

Mom left out an important fact.

The senator has arrived with Creed, Cassandra, Anna, and Ben. I can hear them out there on the patio, chatting about flattering angles and spatial depth. When I peek through the front window, Ben is working in the shadows, shining the wrought-iron chairs that will be used. Anna's role is appointed to her by Cassandra: she will arrange the family in a pose that's "not too staged and not too casual." They've orchestrated a photo shoot that's nothing remotely close to *Death Daze*'s style, if it's fair to say *Death Daze* has a style. I'm not sure who I have to thank for this, but I'm guessing Cassandra. There was no way she'd let Rebecca talk to me without her present.

Across the bedroom, Mom is freaking out because Granny has told her she has to join us. She rifles through clothes in her bag. "What am I supposed to wear, Ny? What am I supposed to say?"

I'm not present enough to answer.

The last twenty-four hours contain the largest emotional ambush in my life and I'm somehow supposed to put all that aside and shoot a video that will likely have a million watchers. I am the envy of every journalist in the world and I not only lack skills, I don't have a game plan. *Think. Think. Think.*

What do I know?

1. Cora, not Frankie, attacked Martin Jarvis.
2. Martin was dead before Cora disappeared.
3. Cora was searching the mines.
4. This whole mess, past and present, feels tied to diamonds. Which makes no sense.
5. I'm close enough to the truth to make me a threat.

What can I use?

None of that.

If I bring up those discoveries live, I'm likely cutting off the greatest sources of information on Cora King's life. I can't afford to isolate anyone, but I also can't go easy. Frankie's another day closer to dead.

I correct myself . . . My mother is another day closer to dead.

I don't know how to process Frankie being more to me. Under these circumstances, it's easier to make her a cause. Easier to make *Death Daze* about saving Mom's friend. And yeah, I want her to live and for justice to be served and to have the chance to know the person my mom loves so much, and yet a part of me knows that if Frankie dies, my life will be simpler.

Grief is a gas that takes the space and shape that's given to it. Therefore, I can give this nothing, giving her nothing of me and taking nothing from her, and she will float by as this thing that happened when I was younger. I imagine she'll be an event I chat about with a therapist or the person I'm forced to reveal if a doctor asks me a medical history question and there is no one to ask. The more I give, the more I will hurt. The reverse might also be true. The more I give, the less Mom will hurt.

Mom asks, "Baby, did you hear me?"

"What?"

"I don't know what to wear," she says.

I force myself to sit up in bed. "Go naked," I say. "Then I don't have to figure out what to ask Rebecca."

"Not funny." She throws a T-shirt at me that she has discarded as part of a possible outfit. "These all make me look like Hercules," she complains. "How is it that I have nothing that fits?"

This is not the conversation I imagined having today, and I have to admit, I'm grateful. She's her and I'm me. "Wear black," I say. "It's the most flattering on video."

Since I can't film in my underwear and cami, I slip into a pair of dark jeans and a soft Poetic Justice tee from Target. Big hoop earrings. Light pink gloss. I use a huge plastic claw to clip my hair back in a messy updo. When I see myself in the mirror I think, *Well, if there was ever a time to look like Emma Stone, today is the day.* She is my auburn hair and freckles goddess of inspiration.

Mom has found her way into a sleek black-on-black ensemble that tones down her more *WWE Raw* qualities. "You're not going to—"

"—tell them I'm Frankie's? Nope. No need to worry about that."

"What are you going to do?" she asks.

I exhale and accidentally spray spit on the mirror. "Ask me when it's over."

CHAPTER 39

While I prep the camera and tripod, the outdoor scene becomes movie poster worthy.

Creed Junior and Rebecca wedge themselves onto one side of a two-seater wrought-iron bench. They ask Mom if she wants to squeeze in and she politely declines, which means Ben has to shine another chair and Anna has to choose a place to add Mom where she doesn't appear tacked on.

Creed wants her seated near him. Rebecca says she should be off to the side. "We shouldn't force Bethie into the limelight, Creed."

Creed scoffs. "I'm not the one with the worldwide podcast."

Cassandra settles the ordeal. "Beth will lean here, on my armrest."

With that simple phrase, Cassandra confirms that she

alone has written the instruction manual for today. Three interviews. Not one.

Whether it's wise or not, I've decided to talk about the King legacy and hope it gives Creed room to puff up about the Center, allows Rebecca to talk up her beloved Leap program, and places Cassandra in the position she enjoys most: queen. It doesn't give much to Mom, but she was never going to get much out of this anyway. She has been asked to join as a punishment for her betrayal.

After we discuss an order, I say, "Ready," and they all echo, "Ready."

I begin, "Hi. I'm Nyla King, and you're watching *Death Daze*. I promised you an intimate investigation into the death of Aunt Cora, and nothing could be more intimate than time with her family. My family," I correct and then offer lavish introductions for Creed, Rebecca, and Cassandra that leave them nodding and proud.

Pump primed, I say, "Before we get the tea on the King family, let's review. In a previous episode, we examined one of the three original suspects, Martin Jarvis. I asked for stories and you answered." I hold my hand against my heart and pause to give them thanks. "One person came forward with a theory that Francis Quick erroneously pled guilty to assaulting Jarvis and that Francis was in bed with a migraine at the time of the assault. Another person claimed Mr. Jarvis was dead prior to Cora King's disappearance, which clearly removes him from the suspect pool. Yet another said that in the week prior to Cora's disappearance, Mr. Jarvis broke into the King house to search Cora's bedroom. The source didn't know what the search entailed; they did, however, express surprise that a former employee of the Kings would show disloyalty, as the Kings are known to have very good relations with any and all staff."

I will watch this episode later. I want to zoom in on the power couple behind me and dissect how Rebecca and Creed react to each piece of information I share. For now, I dive in headfirst.

Blood hums through my system. I need to know what to say next and I can't remember how to get from these theories to legacy and money. There's not time to decide or polish. I turn the camera around and address my family. "Thank you all for coming on *Death Daze* and discussing such an intimate and painful topic. The death of a child is the worst pain to endure, and in many cases families struggle to stick together. Divorce is a frequent response. Here, we saw not a divorce between husband and wife, but between parents and the surviving child. Before we talk about Cora's death, I'd like to ask the matriarch of our family to speak to the discord. Cassandra?"

Cassandra can't be more pleased to be addressed first.

"We're Kings. And the legacy of the King family is one that can close a mine and open a hospital and make millions"—a pause—"of strides for our community." That pause was a work of art. I've never seen anyone so effortlessly remind the world she's rich. "We build forward. And now, with our Beth at home and you, Nyla, our little lion cub, we look again to the future. No one can bring our Cora back to us, but you are carrying her memory forward and we thank you for that." She clicks her armrests to signal she's done.

No mention of Frankie. Hardly any mention of Cora. Quite a tour de force, as always. I thank Cassandra and then say, "Rebecca, will you tell me, when you look back on the months leading up to Cora's disappearance twenty years ago, what was it like to be a King?"

Rebecca stalls momentarily. "Honestly, we were busy. What family isn't?" She is a pro at this. Strong, charming, and relatable, a feat considering Cassandra built an eleven-mile-high pedestal. Rebecca continues, "Cora was getting ready to graduate. Elizabeth was immersed in college test prep. Creed was having daily breakthroughs at the Center, and I was readying myself to hit the campaign trail. We were ninety to nothing in different directions."

"Am I right in thinking that Francis Quick's arrest for the assault on Martin Jarvis caused your girls distress?"

Creed can't help himself. He rears back, a spooked horse. "It has been a closely kept secret until now, but we paid for Francis's defense in that case."

That is new information. I roll with it, asking, "What made you side with your daughters' friend over your employee?"

Rebecca answers, which is good because Cassandra is hiss-whispering at her son. "Martin was in the Leap program. And Francis had been our daughters' best friend since before they could talk. Originally, there was no question of sides."

"Let's come back to Francis's role in your family in a minute. Tell me first, how did you feel about Martin dating your daughter? He was older than her by, what, five years?"

Creed pops off, "He wasn't dating Cora."

To my right, Anna catches in my peripheral vision. She's signaling, which seems odd, but then I realize she's trying to get Cassandra to smooth her blouse. The attempt fails; Cassandra has her eyes on her son. I'm fairly sure it's his job to contain his wife, and he's not doing so to his mother's liking.

Mom takes her first turn to speak. "Daddy, yes, he was."

Creed gathers control and awareness. "I thought she was dating Ben." In a perfectly executed move, he turns to Mom. "Or am I getting the two of you confused?"

Mom rolls her eyes at the camera, dismissing her dad, like, *Of course he didn't know what was really going on.* And I'm guessing that plays well to the audience. This family. Whew. Layers and layers of pretense and illusion. Mom says, "Frankie was in and out of our house like a sibling for years. She probably ate Sunday dinner at our table more than I did. Maybe even more than Cor."

"Maybe even more than Tatti," I add, hoping for a reaction. "That's one of the family dogs," I tell the audience. Somewhere out there in listening land is my brick thrower and Peeping Tom. I hope this reference to Tatti gives him pause. I move on, aware I've got two seconds before I floun-der. Anna is back to signaling Granny about her blouse.

"Let's talk about what happened in the wake of the murder," I say. "There was a memorial, a trial, a conviction. Mom, you left home. Not only left. Changed your name. Let go of the amazing legacy and wealth of your family and set out on your own. This is the first time in our lives I've been to Nockabout. That's a pretty drastic decision."

Everyone nods, willing to acknowledge the elephant in the interview.

I push forward delicately. "You never believed that Francis Quick, a woman you consider your best friend, was capable of murdering Cora, but your mom did. Having a rift with a mother is hard and painful. Is that why you left?"

There's another nod.

"Senator King," I say. "This is the question that all *Death Daze* watchers want to know: What made you so sure Francis Quick killed your daughter? So sure that twenty years later you feel as though the ADPA is an appropriate punishment? So sure that you let your remaining daughter leave home and stay away for two decades?"

I know I'm hitting hard, but Rebecca has years of media training on difficult questions and I'll only get one chance to apply this sort of pressure. I need to do it with wisdom and empathy, but it can't be avoided or *Death Daze* will lose ground. Other interviewers have asked her similar questions and she's given plenty of long answers. The short answers equate to *Francis Quick had opportunity, motive, and means. All the evidence points to her, and I trust foren-sic science and the justice system.* I'm relying on the fact that I'm accessing emotional buttons no one else has had the ability to push.

Senator King creates the slightest gap between her body and Creed's. Maybe half an inch, but the wiggle is noteworthy. She looks directly into the camera and says, "I don't anymore."

I can't keep myself from gasping.

She continues, "And I'm taking this opportunity to announce that I sent a letter of resignation to the governor this morning. I'll be relinquishing my seat in the Senate, effective immediately. It has been my honor and privilege to serve the people of Kentucky over the last twenty-seven years, but the time has come for me to step down. Beth, I'm sorry I failed you. And, Francis, if you're watching, I don't know whether you killed my baby or not; I sincerely hope not. If you were a mother"—her fists tighten; her knuckles whiten; she is wholly believable as the ever-grieving mother—"you'd understand what I am going to say next. If you killed Cora, the ADPA is a pop on the wrist compared to the way she died. If you didn't, I'll work to find whoever did. The name Rebecca Creed has always represented the truth, and I will endeavor to make sure that remains true."

I turn the camera around and capture my own shock. This is huge. I don't have any idea why she has done this or if I've been outplayed. I manage to outro, "I'm Nyla King and this is *Death Daze*. We'll stream again soon."

CHAPTER 40

The patio erupts when the camera falls to my side. If you were on Sam's tour today, you'd hear the shouting from down at the cabins.

"What have you done, darling?"

"Rebecca?"

"Mom?"

Rebecca has surprised more than me; Creed didn't know her plan to resign. He heard it live, same as the rest of us.

"Why didn't you tell me?" he yells. He is in her face and his fists are clenched. "What about my work? You think this doesn't affect me?"

"You can trust me. I know exactly what I'm doing." She removes a piece of paper from her pocket, a photocopy of the 1099 tax form Mannie showed me at his farm. She dangles it in front of her husband's face. "Do you? You didn't tell me Martin worked for you. Not even during all the media swarms at the trial. What else are you hiding? I need to know everything in order to have a chance at a VP bid."

"He didn't *work* for us," Creed says, examining the photo. The doctor does nothing to conceal his fury. I watch Ben slide closer to the man, poised to intervene if he grows violent. "Ho-ney." His syllables patronize. His tone paralyzes. "Martin had a truck. We sent him to get supplies for your precious competition. You should have made me part of the decision before assuming I'm not on your side."

"Please!" She tsks. "You're on the side of your meal ticket. Is it me today? Or your mother?"

"And you're on Richard's. How convenient he's here." Creed's venom is undeniable. "You think he'll be suitable in the White House? Mr. Terry Cloth and Old Spice."

Creed's implication is clear: he believes Rebecca and Richard have engaged in inappropriate behavior. I bite my lip and try to locate Richard in the crowd behind me and can't. He slipped away earlier, which, under the circumstances, is probably for the best.

Cassandra has allowed for all the loose lips and sinking ships she's willing to put up with. Her voice booms. "If anyone other than Nyla speaks, you're disowned."

Mom, Creed, and Rebecca are obedient statues. No one is sure what's happening. Least of all me. I can only assume Cassandra will blame me for being the chemical dissolvent of the family legacy. She doesn't like her daughter-in-law, but Rebecca is a valuable political power. Maybe even more so in stepping down.

"Nyla!" Cassandra says.

I straighten my spine and lift my chin, hoping Cassandra doesn't eat me alive. "Ma'am."

"Please tell me that you monetized your channel."

I nod. The night the BBC signed on, Sam and I monetized.

"Good. You'll need to invest, and I'd like to help you with that. Would you agree to a financial chat later on this evening? Anna, ask Ned to come along as well. We'll use his expertise." She's not asking; she's telling, and therefore doesn't wait for anyone to agree.

"Mother?" Creed says, like this is a personal affront.

"Not a word," Cassandra warns. And then to her daughter-in-law she says, "All you did was make yourself look guilty, my dear. Go take a shower and wash the blood off the name we gave you."

She clicks her wrists, Anna moves behind her, and Cassandra is wheeled away.

CHAPTER 41

W hether Anna was instructed to walk slowly or chose to, the effect unhinges those of us who remain. Our eyes lock on the back of Cassandra's head, the perfect turned-under white bowl of hair, the metal of her chair gleaming like diamonds in the midday sun. Rebecca and Creed are beholden to their silence. Mom too. Mother, father, and daughter stand in various postures of shock.

Ben comes quietly behind them, removes the heavy patio furniture, and effortlessly returns it to the original placement around the pool. He disappears into a nearby outbuilding as though he was never there.

My phone pings.

Sam: What in holy hockey pucks just happened?

Nyla: I have no idea.

Sam: Did you know she was going to resign?

Nyla: I'm pretty sure no one but the governor knew.

Sam: Creed?

Nyla: Nope.

Sam: Dang. Your family is cray.

Sam: The internet thinks she's vying for a VP bid.

Sam: BTW. You did great.

Nyla: Did you find anything out about Martin yesterday?

Sam: ☺ Yep. Want to meet or you stuck with the fam?

Nyla: Pick me up at the Nockabout dock in an hour?

Sam: Absolutely.

Creed gives the women in his family a haughty shake of his head. Myself included. Halfway across the pathway his mother took, he changes his mind and comes back to me and says, "Nyla, I'll write you a check for fifty thousand dollars to delete every *Death Daze* video and never make another. If you want to be part of this family, protect it."

"From what, sir?"

He bows his head.

I do not let myself think about fifty thousand dollars. "What was Martin looking for when he broke into Cora's bedroom? What did he think she had taken from him?"

"Clearly I don't know anything that happened between those two."

Creed is weakening.

I remind myself that he is Cora's father; his daughter's body was dumped in the lake. I soften my tone and reapproach as an ally. "Dr. King, I think whatever she took got

247

her killed. That's what I'm trying to find out with *Death Daze.*"

He looks at me with intense sadness. "You should take the fifty thousand, Nancy Drew. You don't need the internet; a call to Floyd Penitentiary will give you everything you're looking for. Francis Quick killed my daughter, and I'll never forgive her. But you, you're killing her again, in front of me, and I'm going to ask you nicely to stop, and then I'll ask you not so nicely."

Mom hears every word he says and launches toward him to defend me. "Dad! What are you doing?"

Rebecca reaches out, takes Mom's arm, and stops her from approaching Creed. "Let him grieve his way, Bethie," she says. "We all have to."

"He can grieve all he wants, but he's not threatening my kid," Mom says.

"Or what, Bethie? You'll leave?" Creed gives a sad laugh and strolls away.

Rebecca makes an attempt to embrace my mom and the exchange is awkward; they are not women given to hugs of comfort.

CHAPTER 42

I find Richard, hands on his knobby knees, in a dead stare at the trodden ground beneath my bedroom window. "Print wasn't here yesterday, and no one came around this side of the house this morning." Richard compares his own shoe print to the impressions. "I'm six one. This person will likely be shorter, but not by much." That basically only removes Mannie from the suspect pool, and there is no way he is that agile anyway.

"I saw him," I admit.

Richard shakes his head in disbelief.

I offer a defense for what he has already deemed stupidity on my part. "Telling you last night would have only kept you up."

"You're wrong."

"Please. Were you going to Vietnam him down the hill?"

He flinches. "Did you use *Vietnam* as a verb?"

I shrug. "Am I wrong?"

"The point would have been for you not to be the only one who knows hard things." He raps my skull gently, like he's knocking on a door.

Everything that's happened in Nockabout has my life upside down. The stone façade of the pool house is rough against my back. Richard moves to stand beside me. "What's your history here? You've got to share or else I'll be the one shaking my head at your stupidity."

"Lion, you don't know what you're asking."

"What happened between you and Rebecca?"

Richard keeps his eyes on Cassandra's roof. Two birds sit atop the highest chimney, chirping and singing. We watch wordlessly until one flies and the other falls. They make me wonder who left Nockabout first: Richard or Mom, and if the leaving was connected or coincidental. Richard's silence feels like a wave gathering strength. "More than should have. And I tried to bring a lawsuit against the Center in the late '90s."

I exhale all the air in my lungs. That would do it. Given Creed's offer of fifty thousand dollars to keep a YouTube channel from bringing bad publicity, and the fact that he appears to be a man with more pride in his work than in his immediate family . . . The animosity must have calmed over the years, but it isn't hard to conjure a younger, less contained Creed.

"I thought he was either buying girls from foster homes or getting them hooked on meth and then swooping in to look like a hero to their families. Or maybe both. The girls on my caseload kept ending up in the Center. Like, a dispro-portional amount. Some OD'd. Some had intake files and no discharge files, but they weren't in the treatment wing."

That's crazy and awful. "You're sure?"

"No. But I had enough suspicion at the time to warrant an investigation. The Center didn't have the reputation it has now. It was underfunded, under-researched, under-staffed. Creed needed stats and those girls, no one would miss them. Or at least that's what I suspect he thought." Richard's hand looks like a clenched claw as he taps against his chest. "But I missed them."

"Is there any evidence of this?"

"What do you think, Lion? Look who left town. Wasn't Creed, was it?" He gestures at the comically big house on the other side of Cassandra's and then down the hill toward the multimillion-dollar facility. "And he made it impossible for me to work in the tri-county area. I was a laughingstock."

"How?"

Richard rolls his eyes and buries his hands in his pock-ets. "I paid an intern to bring me records. And later, when I got an audience with an investigator, the same intern said he falsified the records because he was scared of me."

"Should he have been? Scared of you, I mean."

"I had a temper back then."

"And now?"

He shrugs. "I repaint pink houses."

"Tell me about your relationship with Rebecca."

"Before the accusation, we worked together on Leap. Basically, all my kids were her kids. I'd get a new case; Rebecca was the first person I'd call and see if I could get them enrolled in Leap and set up rides and boats and scholarships."

"You liked her?"

"We were doing the same type of heart work."

I hadn't seen much heart out of her. Thirty minutes ago, when she stepped down from the Senate, I'd have bet every penny it was a politicking ploy and an ulterior motive would emerge. Women like her don't get played; they play for keeps before anyone else knows they've entered an arena.

"And what did you think about Rebecca's heart when Mom showed up at your door?"

"That people aren't perfect. That Becky was grieving."

I laugh outright at this. "She sure grieves funny."

He sighs in the way that makes me feel young to the world and then says, "You live long enough and you'll figure this out: everyone grieves funny. We lie, we love, we hate, we get married, we get divorced, we drink, we eat too much, we starve ourselves, we look for God so we can scream at Him. Don't ever go thinking you'll figure out grief. You won't until you've done it."

"And you've done it? Grieve, I mean."

"Yes." He doesn't elaborate. The walls he constructs are like concrete between our hearts. Whatever lives in this precious space is something he can't look at, much less share with me. I move on.

"So you're sympathetic toward Rebecca?"

He nods. "Creed too. Even though I can't stand him. He lost his kid. You don't get over that."

"It's been twenty years. Do you still believe he did something illegal or dangerous to boost the Center's research or reputation?" It's hard not to think about Houdini in this regard. Who is she? Who was she? Who loves and misses her?

Richard lifts his hands in question. "I don't know, Lion. It's awfully hard to hide anything that heinous in such a small place for that long."

Mom was able to hide a massive lie for eighteen years in the smallest of places. It's not that hard.

"What about Martin Jarvis? You work with him?"

"Only through Leap. I don't remember much about him." Deep trenches crease Richard's forehead as he thinks. His lack of memory is telling in itself. Martin didn't stand out to him, and I'd think Richard had a keen sense for troubled kids, given his work. "All I remember is he ran around with Ned."

"Ned wasn't in the program."

"He was. Money's not the only route to poverty, Lion. Ned had a complicated relationship with his dad. Never could get on his good side, no matter how or where he excelled. I'd bet you anything, he's trying to prove himself with his business. Kids like that, sensitive, who never get an attaboy from their father. Whew. Messes you up." Richard shares a fondness for Ned that makes me wonder if he kept an eye on him the way he did the rest of his caseload.

I picture Ned in the back room of his shop, working with delicate pieces of jewelry and learning Spanish, in hopes that his dad will accept him someday. Richard's assessment seems accurate.

He continues, "As boys, Ned and Martin were both rock hounds. In and out of these mines. Always asking Cassandra to give them her maps and share her dad's equipment. Ned was looking for a quartz or agate vein on Nockabout. Totally obsessed with rocks until his momma got sick. But what's a guy like Jarvis doing running around in a mine? Total lake kid. Ladies' man. Cocky little SOB. I figure if the dude needed a cave, it was for activities more suited to a hotel room. Never saw him as the type to check out the way he did, but then again, a lot of times it's the kids you don't expect."

"Was there an investigation into Martin's death?"

"Yeah, the coroner's report said death by suicide. Plus, Cora disappeared on the same day he died, and while I'm sure there are many who assume the events are connected, by and large, back then people were one-tracked to find Cora."

"Martin came from a big family, though," I say, according to what I've learned from the *Death Daze* comments. "Weren't they upset?"

"Yeah, I'm sure they were. Anyone who didn't believe he died by suicide came to the consensus that Frankie finished the job she started the year earlier."

Richard and I are so engrossed in the conversation that we haven't noticed Anna standing at the corner of the house, listening, waiting for a moment to interrupt. She's crying, not hard, but with what I assume is exhaustion.

"You okay?" I ask, hoping she's okay and that she hasn't overheard us.

"What?" Her face is a stage, her emotions visible, and then the curtain falls and you're not sure what is going on backstage. Whatever it is, she's composed when she meets my gaze. "I'm worried about Cassandra's health."

"Right now?" My heartbeat speeds up and I move into helper mode. "What do you need?"

Anna raises her collar over her eyes and from inside the shirt takes a deep, composing breath. When she reemerges, she says, "Not now. She's sick. Cancer, and she's refused treatment. She doesn't know."

"Know what? About cancer?" There's no way. Cassandra is sharp as a tack.

"No," Anna says. "She doesn't know the money's gone."

"What money?"

Anna waves her hand over the entirety of the King kingdom.

"Ned runs the books and doctors the reports so Creed can put additional money into the Center. I guess they're banking on her passing on and then being able to sell her house and assets to settle the estate."

I can't hide my surprise. "Why does Ned run the books? He's a jeweler."

"He's educated, and according to Cassandra, no one has better attention to detail," she says in Cassandra's voice.

Anna looks empty now that she has released this enormous secret. Richard stands statuesque, appraising the news. I can't tell what he's thinking. I can't even tell if he already knew or suspected these things might be true.

I'm bowled over and confused. "Why are you telling me?" I ask.

"Good question," she says, like she asked herself this very thing and isn't convinced of her decision. "I'm loyal to Cassandra, and she loves you. And because you should know if Creed tries to buy you off, as he's apt to do, he doesn't have it."

Fifteen minutes ago, when Creed was busy offering me fifty thousand dollars, Anna was inside with Cassandra, settling her boss for a nap. She couldn't have known. She only could have predicted, and that means she nailed his behavior with a precision that makes her psychic or correct.

"Have you been paid?" I ask.

Tears spill down Anna's cheeks. "Not in several months."

"Why stay?"

"Because Cassandra promised me the house."

I exhale sharply. "What about Ben?"

"Creed pays his salary from the Center. I don't think he knows."

I have to work hard to harness my emotions, to function as a reporter instead of a family member. "What's your take on Creed?"

"He's desperate to save the Center and his reputation. I've seen this before. If he gets desperate or feels threatened, it won't be good. You should be careful."

"What are you telling me?" I ask.

Anna clams up and looks over her shoulder. Richard steps in and touches her arm with practiced gentleness. "Anna, you're safe with us."

"I'm scared of them all." Her eyes linger on the two houses up the hill and then float across the lake toward Lone Valley. "They'll get rid of anyone in their way. Be careful, Nyla. You don't have to finish this story."

I grasp her hands in mine, grateful she has chosen to trust me. "And you don't have to stay."

She looks lovingly at Cassandra's house. "Yes, I do. Not for the house. She's been like my mother. I don't like what Creed and the senator are doing."

Anna hands me two pieces of folded paper. I unfold them and see identical copies of an intake form for the Center. *Patient: Laylah Williams . . . Methamphetamine addiction . . . Entered treatment: June 6 . . .* Signed into treatment by Creed King.

"What's this?" I ask, unsure what I'm looking at or its significance.

Medical records are private, and despite Anna's connections with Cassandra, I doubt she has complete access to the Center's internal paperwork. Especially given the tensions between her and Creed.

"I nicked them from Creed's home office when I was dropping off financials from Ned."

I scan each line of both pages, comparing the two documents, searching for differences that might clue me in to what Anna is trying to tell me. Richard reads over my shoulder; he's quiet, perhaps drawing the same blank as I am, until he points to the date. One form has Laylah Williams entering treatment on September 6, nine months prior to the first form.

"One of these is fake," I conclude.

The slightest nod of Anna's head and then a whispered, "I have to go." Then Anna's running, a Houdini herself.

"Who did this?" I call after Anna.

"Ask that girl."

Richard swears and swears again. "I failed her, and he's still hurting women."

CHAPTER 43

Thirty minutes later, I have worn a hole in the dock waiting on Sam to arrive. My adrenaline reaches unparalleled levels—I haven't jittered this much since I drank a six-pack of Red Bull on a dare. So much has happened and none of it has a vocabulary.

There's no casual way to say Frankie's my mom.

Yo, Frankie's my birth mom.

I found out I'm not a King.

So . . . my mom's not my actual mom.

I'm not sure I'm ready to tell myself about Frankie, let alone Sam, which is dumb on many, many levels. You can bury a secret in a shallow grave. A deep grave might make you crazy, but a shallow grave is a survival tool. Dig a few inches, toss in the pain, and shovel the dirt over the top. Go on living and deal with the weeds as they emerge. Which makes me and *Death Daze* . . . Beth Wagner's weed.

I trust Sam. I could tell him. I already want to tell him.

This is the rub.

I want to be known without having to change. If Sam knows about Frankie, he'll grab his own shovel and unearth my pain. I am not ready for that.

And there are other things to tell. Facts. Suspicions. Fears.

Like someone tried to open my window in the night.

And Cassandra has cancer.

And the Kings are broke.

And Richard thought Creed was trafficking girls for medical trials twenty years ago. Did Cora find out and Creed killed her?

Whatever's going on, there's a very good chance Houdini wasn't a patient at the Center before Sam rescued her.

Sam runs into the sandbar at a speed that can't be great for the boat and is on land and by my side saying, "I have a lot to tell you," before I've had time to decide which thing to tell him first. I laugh, relieved to momentarily be out of the hot seat. He must have had some luck digging up Martin's belongings. "Oh, wait, I need the bag." Sam retrieves a vintage screen-printed, red-and-blue Adair County High School basketball duffel. "Feast your eyes, my dear. I have procured a rockhounding relic. And tell me how you managed to unseat a senator on 'your little YouTube channel.'" He mimics Cassandra's elderly voice.

Watching him so full of himself, snapping and dancing around, makes it easy to forget the stress of the day. Even more when he leans over and kisses me on the cheek.

"What are you on today?" I ask.

"Just feeling hopeful. And . . . maybe Dad came home with a check for five thousand dollars last night and paid off my boat loan and now I can probably get a car . . ."

"That's great."

"You don't look like it's great."

"Where'd he get the money?"

"Bonus from Creed and our former senator."

"Huh?"

"Oh, come on. You've seen Dad work. It has nothing to do with all this. Let a guy be happy about having a generous dad and a boat in his name."

I kiss Sam on the cheek. "I'm delighted to ride in your fancy boat."

"Yeah, you are."

Although we could talk about a thousand things, we let ourselves enjoy the wind and sun as we cross the narrow channel and dock in Lone Valley. When the boat is tied off, I toss Sam the keys to the Pilot. Sam shoulders the pack and we hold hands on the way up the hill.

Ned's standing at his back door, smoking a cigarette. He eats the cloud of dust when he spots us. Every other encounter with Ned frames him in a docile light, not a puppy exactly, but a kind breed. A poodle or a pug. Now I see the muscles in his calves, fit enough to run down the hill. He's, what, five eleven? I remember he was in Leap and learned to shoot skeet. I lean over to Sam and ask, "What gun do you use for skeet?"

In the spirit of my whisper, he whispers back, "A 12 gauge or a 20."

Ned drops his cigarette, grounds it out, and retrieves the butt. He's agile for his size. He calls out, "*Amigo, amiga,* where are you two off to? Picnic?" He points at the bag Sam has slung over his shoulder.

Thankfully, the screen printing faces Sam's body. Ned would have to be very astute to recognize the bag of his old rockhounding buddy. I'm not sure the idea I'm having is smart, but I run with it. "*Hola,* Ned!" I say cheerfully, and then lower my voice and make sure to wear my submission. "Can I tell you something?"

He flaps his hand at a nonexistent cloud of smoke, coughs, and says, "Of course."

"I wanted to apologize. I didn't know Martin Jarvis was your friend. You might not have seen *Death Daze,* but I—"

Ned isn't curt so much as quick to respond. "We weren't really friends."

"Oh." I cover my face like I'm embarrassed. "I thought you guys mined or rockhounded or whatever that's called together." I use how little I know to my advantage. If Ned feels like he's in control, he might say more.

The jeweler doesn't dispute the implication, but his nonverbals ping: shaking head, skeptical expression in the eyes, tightened jaw. He doesn't like me bringing up Martin.

"Anyway, I was hoping that you might be willing to work on my ring. It was Mom's. I broke it one day and haven't told her." I take the little envelope out of my purse and hand it over.

Very carefully, he shakes the contents into the palm of his hand. "I can fix this," he says. "There are diamonds missing."

"What would it cost to replace them?"

"I'd have to check," he says. "But I can let you know. How's your mom?"

"Rattled."

"You should stop *Death Daze* if it's hurting her," he says. "She's been through a lot."

I try one more avenue to see if he flinches and say a silent prayer that he won't. "You're probably right. Oh hey, you're in and out of the Center visiting your mom, yes?"

"Every day." This is a point of pride.

"Do you happen to know Laylah Williams? The girl who—"

"Mr. Man here rescued?" Ned finishes and beams at Sam. "Sure. All the nurses up there call her Houdini."

"Do you know how long she was in the Center before she jumped ship and ended up in the cave?"

Sam stays quiet, uncertain of what I'm doing. With every question, he drifts closer into my side. Intentional or an involuntary reaction? Whatever it is, I'm grateful. Ned pouts his lips, considering the question, and shakes another cigarette loose from the pack. When he lowers his chin to light the end, he says, "I don't know."

"But you're sure she was there previously? That she was a patient prior to Sam rescuing her?"

Ned takes a long draw. "I'd say she was there maybe six or seven months before the Houdini trick, but it's easy to lose track of time. I can't believe Mom and Ms. Rey have been in there all these years." He falls against the metal building and takes another long drag.

"Thanks. Sam and I wanted to check on her. We were thinking of bringing her a few things to remind her she isn't alone, but if she's been there that long, she probably has plenty of stuff. We might visit."

"Yeah," Sam says agreeably. "I'd love to see her."

"They might not let you in," Ned warns.

"But could you get us in?" I ask.

He uses his cigarette to jab the air and laugh, like he's on to me. "You, my dear, are even more clever than your channel. I'll get you in. If you promise to stop *Death Daze*."

"I'll think about it," I say.

"Meet me tomorrow morning," he says. "And now, I've got a ring to repair."

I say, "*Continúa con el buen trabajo*," and we all laugh at my mangled Spanish.

Ned says, "Or we can stay home and have our own Spanish for Dummies class." He gives us a mock salute, repeats the environmental care of pocketing the cigarette, and disappears into his workshop.

When Sam and I are in the Pilot, air-conditioning on, windows rolled up, he says, "You're not going to give up *Death Daze* to meet Houdini, are you?"

"Nope. I'm not taking bribes or threats these days." I

laugh uncomfortably and tell him about the figure outside my window in the middle of the night.

Sam straightens at the notion, his handsome face framed with confusion. He lets me talk and I tell him what happened from the moment I caught Peeping Tom at the window of the pool house until Sam docked at Nockabout this morning.

"Well, I don't know that I can top all that, but . . ." He unzips the bag and shows me what he found in an old cabin behind the Center. Sam lays a five-by-seven framed photo of Martin Jarvis, Cora King, and an elementary-aged girl on my thigh. The threesome pose like a family, with the child standing between the couple and Cora's arm stretched in a loving way over her Jonas Brothers T-shirt. Sam turns the photo over.

A typed message is taped across the center.

Do it or she dies.

CHAPTER 44

T hat's a proper threat on Cora's life," I say.

There was no tangible motive for Frankie wanting to kill Cora back then. It was like everyone lived in a state of climax following Cora's death and they immediately accepted the denouement of Frankie's guilt from that one drop of blood and forgot to ask about the rest of the story. Twenty years later, Sam and I could probably put together a better timeline than the original detectives. It makes me wonder how often I skip to the end with people and make assumptions. "Where'd you find that picture?"

"In a frame, buried three photos down, in a box, buried more than three boxes down." There's no doubt he has undergone a search and been rewarded for his perseverance.

The photo, printed at Walmart, is glossy and has the blur of being enlarged from a four-by-six. "I wish there was a way to know when this picture was taken."

"Well, since the three of them appear happy, we can safely eliminate Frankie and Dad as the person who took it. And probably Ned, too, for that matter."

"Why Ned?"

"'Cause he was bat balls in love with Cora."

"Sam." I almost tell him about who my real mother is. I try to take a deep breath and can't. "Can we drive around? I need the air."

He drives, and as he gets to Mannie's side of Lone Valley, I give him directions to the old barn. He cruises past Mannie's house and drives up the hill, where the old clubhouse waits. "You want to go in?" he asks, already understanding that I do.

I've heard it said that most mysteries hang on little details. Little nudges that push us this direction or that. A low, quiet question in your gut that gets louder and louder until you need, rather than want, an answer. Since Mom paused at the barn, I've been having that sensation.

Of course, it's less likely there's something significant inside the barn and more likely there's something significant that happened inside me, right here, on this road. After all, this is the last place Mom and I stopped before she told me about Frankie. We were us and we were unbreakable: that's a nice mythos. Fifty years from now, if this barn stands, I'll feel the deepest truths inside me squirm and think, *This is where I was before I learned Frankie was my mother.*

Sam doesn't interrupt my thoughts. Whether he understands I'm battling private enemies or he has his own to trifle with, we give each other the respect of silence; our only interruption is Brandi Carlile's indomitable voice in the Pilot's rusty sound system. In the break from one song to the next, I say, "Let's check it out."

The ancient remains of two narrow tire tracks cut through a field. Honeysuckle grows in force and there are patches of Queen Anne's lace. The air is sweet and alive. The barn is missing more paint than it has, giving the impression of a bad sunburn. The front loft door is nailed shut. Every visible nail is rusted and loose. At the gable, the roof has been peeled by the wind like an orange.

"What are we looking for?" Sam asks.

Using guesswork, I make a four-by-six square with my fingers. "Mannie said Cora showed up that day with a purse. Mom claimed Cora never carried a purse. Just that backpack your dad has in his cave. I know a lot could have happened to that bag between here and her disappearance, but she intentionally drove the longest way to the ferry, and that route takes her by this barn. The barn my mom said was their childhood clubhouse."

The barn is padlocked. That would be a problem if the lower portions of the doors weren't dry-rotted and an animal hadn't already burrowed out the space below, creating a tunnel wide enough for us to wiggle through. We stand in the empty space, smelling the perfume: the rot of wood, the tinge of long-ago sprayed insecticide, the musk of death. Light pierces the numerous cracks and pinholes in the wall. There's a tarped window to the left. Sam rips away the plastic and gray daylight spreads across the hay-filled floor. An aged tractor collects cobwebs in the far-right corner, and behind the tractor, a ladder leads to the loft. That's where I'm guessing we'll find whatever there is to be found.

Up top are treasures aplenty. The perfect clubhouse for curious little girls. Shiny glass crocks, dust-covered furniture from generations before, piles of wood, crates, tools, army hats. There is more, far more, but our destination is set from the first casting of phone light. Under the eaves, in the opposite corner, three chairs are arranged around a table. The remains of a card game in front of each seat, as if the players were called away without a chance to finish.

I start to reach out and drag my hand through the dust and think better of disturbing the time capsule. There's no way those girls could have known what lay ahead. Sam points to the corner of the table and a faint scribbling, layers down in the dust.

"Is that an arrow?"

I nod.

The arrow couldn't have been drawn on the day of the card game, and I'm not too excited about where it suggests we go. A place where the metal roof meets the wide plank floor. A place that requires us to duck and then partially crawl through the dirt and dead bugs to get there. Sam bites the bullet and feels around in places I would never put my hands before prying up a loose board.

"Ny, light," he says, followed by, "Ugh."

Suspended in the beam of my flashlight is a gray, hollow

animal. Sharp fangs protrude from the skull. Its tail curls like a rat or a whip. The juicy muscles and organs are long gone; the remnants mirror a leather baby shoe rather than something that was once alive. I lean closer to Sam; the rivulets of sweat on his arms mix with my dirty hands as I brace to peer into the hollow skull of a possum.

I've never seen a thing so very, very dead. Other than when I saw the picture of Cora.

Sam lays the animal to rest out of reach and inches closer to the hole. There's no way to see inside; the space is too tight. I can't see his hand, but I imagine him patting the air cautiously, nervous to touch anything after the possum. "There's something else," he says and lifts a small dark heap of fabric from the hole.

Heart racing, I shine my light into his hands. The black velvet is matted gray with dust and no longer pliable or soft. Its folds are as rigid as the possum, but there is little doubt that this is the black "purse" Mannie recalled. This is what Cora had with her on that last day before she disappeared.

Sam drops the bag into my hand. Whatever's inside is heavyish. Marbles? I wonder. Maybe rocks. Sam and I reverse crawl until we reach the table. This time we feel less compelled to preserve the scene.

I can't speak for him, but I'm barely breathing.

Objects hold power. Especially when you know you're getting ready to look at an object hidden by a girl murdered twenty years ago. Sam works the aged zipper until he's able to pry open a two-and-a-half-inch hole.

"You ready?" he asks, suspending the bag in midair. I nod and he pours the contents on the table. Sparkles cascade and land in a loose pile of crystal clarity.

Sam says, "I'm not an expert, but—" He lifts one to the phone light and examines the stone. "These are diamonds. Ned would know for sure. They've already been cut. These are rounds. These are princess. If the caret and clarity are good, they could be worth a million dollars. Or they could be lab grown and worth hardly anything. Diamonds are weird."

There are maybe a hundred stones on the table. Some dime-size. Others the circumference of a bobby pin's point. I don't know enough to have an opinion on anything beyond their beauty. They're striking. Even sitting in a pile of dust and playing cards.

Sam finds a wedged piece of paper at the bottom of the bag.

Together we read:

Frankie,

If you find these diamonds, don't say a word until you talk to me, and whatever you do, keep them here. I'm in serious trouble and I don't know what to do.

I need to tell you what happened the night I attacked Martin and explain why I kept going back after he hit me in September.

It all began with the girl in the woods. After that Labor Day party Martin and I started messing around and we were supposed to meet at the body tunnel entrance after I finished school, but I skipped last period to get there early. Martin was carrying a girl toward the tunnel like a freakin' Neanderthal, so I called out and asked if he needed help. He told me he had found this chick passed out in the woods and was trying to get her to the Center. He knew my dad would help and figured the body tunnel was the fastest route up the hill. I offered to go with him, but he didn't want Daddy to see us together—and I was supposed to be at school—so we planned to meet at his cabin later.

When I got to the cabin, he wasn't there yet. I let myself in; I figured he wouldn't mind. I couldn't help myself; I poked around a little and looked through his mail and found one of Daddy's envelopes on the counter. It was full of cash. Like a thousand bucks and there was a note that said "For #3."

When Martin got there, he saw me with the cash and flipped out. We got into a fight about me respecting his privacy and he shoved me backward and I hit the corner of the fridge with my face. I was outraged, obviously, and told him Daddy wouldn't ever pay him for #4, whatever that means, and he said, "You ever tell anyone about that envelope and I'll kill you."

It was pure evil. So evil.

I didn't know what to do, but I took him at his word. You would have too. I let you think I was protecting Mom, but I didn't even know what I was protecting. I thought he'd kill me. But I couldn't get that story and that cash out of my head. I started thinking, what if that girl was #3 and I caught him and Daddy in the act of something far worse than him shoving me into the fridge and bruising my cheek? I didn't know what to do, and I thought that anyone I told would be in danger.

Plus, he brought my dad into this. And the drama around Mom's career is real. And the Center helps so many people . . . Anyway, I came up with a plan to get back in Martin's graces to keep investigating. This plan, as you saw, involved a lot of flirting, playing dumb, and hurting Ben. It took months, but it worked. Every time I was at Martin's, I'd snoop around, looking for something that might help me understand what was going on between Martin and my dad.

The night I attacked Martin, I found this bag, Dad's jeweler's bag, in his cabin. Martin caught me and flipped. He had this war with himself about whether he should kill me or "make me one of the girls." He kept looking me over and saying things like, "You're strong enough to mine," and then "But you're a King. Everyone will look for you and then the operation . . . I've got to kill you. I don't have a choice."

Frankie, he implied that this mining operation he was involved in was done with patients from the clinic or from Mom's program or were women, girls basically, that Mom and Dad hired him to kidnap. I don't know.

He was too crazy to understand. He let go of me for a split second and I squirmed away and got his bat. I hit him until he stopped moving. And then he was there on the floor with so much blood. I hid the jeweler's bag in the woods and woke you up. That's where everything went even more wrong. I told you Martin was abusive, and I let you think it was sexual.

You never should forgive me for letting you take the fall. I will tell the truth. I promise you. While you've been in juvie, I've been trying to find answers.

I know there's a diamond mining operation somewhere in the Valley.

I know we're talking about serious money.

I know Martin was willing to kill over it.

And more than likely, a family member is doling out the cash for operational costs. Which likely includes kidnapping young women.

But who? Dad? My mom? Grandpa Creed? Ned works with jewelry, but he wouldn't do this.

I've been searching the caves for evidence of mining and started moving the jeweler's bag around once Martin got out of the hospital. And I've been using Daddy's map of the old shafts. You remember those caves we used for hide-and-seek. I'm thinking there could be more.

I'm writing this note now because I'm terrified. Martin's memory is coming back. He broke into my parents' house and tossed my room, and then yesterday

I found tiny holes drilled through the kayak I take out every morning. I think it was him.

I'd go to the police, but (a) I don't think they'll believe me after I tell them I lied about attacking Martin and sending you to juvie; and (b) there's a risk they'll get bought off, given how much money is involved; and (c) it would be a huge political scandal so I need to be right about who did what; and (d) if no one believes me, whoever is doing this might hurt those women in the mines.

You and Ben and Bethie hate me because of what happened with Martin, but please, Frank, trust me about this. Whatever's going on is bad, really bad. For now, I'm putting the diamonds here, where Martin will never find them. If something happens to me, it's Martin.

I love you, friend. You are the kindest soul I've ever met.

Cora

CHAPTER 45

U p until now Cora's murder was tragic because murder
is always tragic. If I'm being honest, I didn't like her.
I hadn't been able to get over the fact she beat a man and
let her best friend go to jail. Unforgivable. Especially given
how that action set the trajectory for her best friend's death.

This letter makes her more.

She is a girl.

She is scared.

She is regretful.

She is stuck.

She is brave.

She is a deliverer of freedom.

She is fire.

She is.

She comes alive, only to die again, and this time her
dying hurts. I don't realize I'm crying until Sam speaks and

the lump in my throat is a boulder. Instead of words, I lean toward him. He wraps his strong and wiry arms around me, and I sob into his chest and tell Cora I am sorry for every second I made her less-than. Sam tilts me backward, holds me at arm's length to look at me, and cups my face.

When I find my voice, I say, "This proves so many things."

"Except who killed her, because it certainly wasn't Martin."

"Say we go live right now," I suggest. "We put the photo threat, this letter, and the diamond discovery out there. You can't kill us in front of the world, right?" Even as I make the suggestion, fear idles in the pit of my stomach. "And the authorities would have to investigate and let Frankie go."

Sam resituates one of the chairs and eases onto its dusty seat. He wears the worried look of someone much older, someone tasked with telling a child there's no Santa. "This letter isn't exactly proof. It definitely won't help Frankie in time."

Another terrible thought occurs. "What if Houdini isn't a patient and never was? What if she's a girl the Kings kidnapped and there are others down there?"

Sam squeezes my hand. "But Anna said the family's broke, right? If they're running a diamond mine, where's the money?"

"That's true. And Anna would know."

The noon sun burns through the metal roof and creates a veil of heat. I slump into the opposite chair; the diamonds

277

and abandoned game lay between us. I spin a pair of aces on the table as I consider what he's saying. I reread the first paragraph to make sure I've read correctly. When I speak, I am measured and more in control of my emotions. "Cora says right here she's the one who attacked Martin."

Sam stops my fidgeting hands. "Agree. And that would be great if Frankie had pled innocent to that crime. I'm not a lawyer, but with time running out, I don't think you'll get that overturned in time. And even if you do, you have a woman on death row with a history of lying to the authorities. If she had years of appeals left in the system, I'd agree with you, but we have twenty-two days. This isn't enough for twenty-two."

Fair point. "But doesn't this change the motive?"

Sam leans and nearly tips the chair. "I don't think so. You could argue Frankie never saw this and the chain of events leading to Cora's death wasn't influenced by this letter."

"You're saying we don't tell anyone?"

"No."

"Good," I say. "We're not making the same mistake as Cora. We have a bag of diamonds and a letter from a dead woman and we're going to tell the world if we have to."

The seriousness of the matter tempers his laugh to a huff. "Okay. Who do we tell?"

I'm ready for him. "Your dad, maybe."

Sam cocks his head to the side and considers the suggestion. "No. Not after the five thousand dollars. If the Kings are broke . . ."

He stops. The rest of the sentence hangs in the pause: *You don't give bonuses like that for no reason.* I move on, understanding the hesitation. "Ned? He could at least confirm the value of the stones, and we know he helps Creed cover up the true state of Cassandra's finances."

Sam taps a king of spades and an ace of diamonds against each other. "Feels like a risk when there is a strong possibility Ned cut these. Diamonds aren't worth as much raw. You need a master cutter to make them truly valuable."

"And that's Ned."

When I think criminal, Ned isn't who comes to mind. He's a momma's boy to the core with his bouquets of flowers and thousands of visits to a hospital. I ask, "Richard? We can at least trust him to be on our side."

"No one believed Richard last time. How about your mom?"

Valid suggestion. Mom would have been too young to be involved with the mining operation. "We could tell her, should tell her, but there's more to know before we do. If we go to her with this, I don't think she'll be able to think straight. She'll blow it up, and I don't think that's best yet."

Sam stands, pushes in his chair, and rakes all but one diamond into their velvet home. The loose stone, midsized and polished, he hands to me.

What's this worth? A thousand dollars? Nothing? A woman's life?

"I can't think in the heat," he says. "I'm going to put these back and let's get out of here." Sam army crawls the velvet bag to its previous position, complete with its possum carcass lid. I agree that it's far better to leave the diamonds in the place they have gone undiscovered for twenty years.

Sam guides me toward the middle of the barn and tosses the card table and chairs and surrounding objects. They clatter and land; dust motes suspend in a beam of light created by the loft door. When everything settles, he scuffs out our footprints and appraises the work. You mostly can't tell anyone has been here. He lifts the ace of hearts from the floor and hands it to me. "For luck," he says, and I trail him through the barn to the car.

Sam reverses down the driveway in a burst of speed and a rush of wind. We sigh with relief when he turns onto the empty road. "Who does that leave to tell?" he asks after we've driven five miles and are no longer sweltering like pigs. "The cops?"

I'm not sold. This could be my bias and the Lone Valley cops are phenomenal, but I'm having a hard time believing there hasn't been some "looking the other way" treatment if Cora's letter is true. Add the fact Houdini wasn't transported to a hospital—that bugged me the moment Sam told me—to Anna's doctored intake forms and there's no doubt in my mind we should be careful who we trust. Plus, if we go to the authorities with the same tale Richard took years ago, in the midst of *Death Daze*, we're a slander lawsuit waiting to happen. I wouldn't put that past a desperate Creed, and Sam agrees.

"That doesn't leave us many options," Sam says.

"Cassandra's sick and could yield her power unpredictably. Anna would have insight on the photo and perhaps the threat, but I'd rather not give her another reason to leave, considering she isn't being paid and she's Granny's only comfort. That leaves us with Houdini."

"Yep," Sam says. "There's nothing like banking your investigation on a meth addict." He's thinking of his mother without understanding I'm also thinking of mine.

CHAPTER 46

We drive through the state park, eat gas station pizza, then stop at a mostly empty swimming beach marked with bobbing red and white ropes. Behind the buoys, the lake hops with fishermen and speedboats. The sun slides along its daily track. Neither of us want to go back to Nockabout until we have our heads around a next step. Off and on, we check *Death Daze*. The internet can't stop talking about Senator Rebecca King's resignation.

The for and against camps are running their mouths.

Relief. Disgust. Hope.

She's brave for prizing healing over politics. She's weak and this is why women shouldn't be politicians.

She's a victim of Death Daze. *She's a murderer about to be caught.*

She's who the country-at-large needs. Politicians like her make me sad to be an American.

No gray. Only polarized opinions.

On the whole, I'm glad they're wound up. They're moving the story and sustaining the *Death Daze* audience without me creating new content. That stasis can't last long, but the reprieve is a gift. Sam pulls over at a trailhead. We leave the Pilot and hike into the cool of the woods. It's a mile-and-a-half loop to the waterfront, and it feels good to be moving. Our words are looser. Our ideas less cramped.

I say, "So, Martin has diamonds from the operation that he is likely supposed to fence. Cora finds the diamonds; he flips out and tries to kill her. During the fight, he shares information about the illegal mining operation. Cora injures Martin, escapes with the diamonds, and sets off a series of problems: one, whoever owns the diamonds knows they're missing; two, there's no one to run the day-to-day job with the miners in captivity; and three, Martin's life is subsequently threatened."

"The timing is funky," Sam says. "If you have a sack of diamonds missing, why the lag? Why the lack of urgency? Martin gets attacked in October, Frankie goes to juvie for six months in late November, but Cora doesn't disappear until six months later when Frankie comes back from juvie in June. That's almost nine months those diamonds were MIA and Cora has them."

My answers are all questions. "Maybe Martin hid the fact they were missing. Maybe his employer gave him time to heal. Maybe something else happened that was bigger than the diamonds. Maybe they shut down the mining operation or moved it. There's no way to know."

A fallen limb lays across the trail and Sam and I move it sideways. Sam says, "Let's go back to the money angle. We should look around for any financial stuff from 2000."

"That seems like a long shot." I pick up my pace. "What about the photo you found? 'Do it or she dies.' Do we feel like it's safe to assume that Martin's employer sent that to Martin postattack, believing that a threat on Cora's life would be leverage enough to motivate Martin to get the diamonds back? Meaning, this adult sees the two of them together and thinks they're tight."

"No. I don't think it's safe to assume anything. There's no date on the photo. And that threat could have been what got Martin into the trafficking business to begin with. But why didn't she tell my dad or your mom?" asks Sam. "Why not come clean and explain the whole thing?"

That one isn't hard for me at all. Shame is a powerful silencer.

Sam turns midtrail and puts a finger to his lips. Ahead of us, two girls walk hand in hand up from the lake. When the shorter of the two sees us, she untangles their hands, her cheeks flushed with embarrassment. I give them a huge smile, hoping to ease their minds.

"Are you Nyla King? You are. Dang. I can't believe this is freaking happening." The girl asking has short jet-black hair with teal streaks and a bubbly confidence to match. "You're gonna get Francis Quick out of jail. Gretch, this is epic. That's Nyla King," she repeats, as if there were a way Gretchen missed the first pronouncement.

"Hi," I say, feeling suddenly old and strange.

Gretch unscrews a water bottle and takes a long drink. She lifts an awkward hand and says, "Hi, Sam," without looking up. Her cheeks have more shades of red than any sunburn could give her.

"Hey, Gretchen," Sam says. He doesn't appear to know her friend and Gretchen doesn't make introductions.

"I'm Sue," the friend says. "And we're fans. Huge fans. Like, my dad's pro-ADPA and he says I'm not supposed to watch." She rolls her eyes at the suggestion. "But we do. We totally do. I mean, he says lots of things I don't pay attention to. This is happening here. Like, in our backyard. How can we not watch or have an opinion?"

"And what is your opinion?" I ask, curious to hear a local point of view.

For a moment, Sue falters and then says, "Gretch, tell her your theory."

Gretchen shakes her head. "It's dumb."

Sam tries to intervene. "It's okay. We won't tell anyone." He's as interested as I am.

Sue realizes Gretchen isn't going to share and says, "Gretchen loves politics." Clearly not a mutual love for Sue. "She says the senator spoke to her fifth-grade class years ago and *opposed* the death penalty. So her stance on the ADPA doesn't make sense unless she has another reason to support it. Like she killed her kid or wants to run for president or is writing a tell-all book about the Kings. And I said that's brilliant—the tell-all book part—because my dad is on the council for Leap, and he says the finances are in the toilet. He swears the Kings are broke and the senator blames her husband's hospital. Anyway, a mom-murder is too obvious. I'll bet it's someone no one expects. Are we right? Do you, like, already know who did it and are saving it for a big reveal?"

Sue's staring at me with crazy eyes and I don't feel like a true-crime streamer; I feel like she thinks I'm George Lucas, and locked inside me are all the secrets of the Star Wars universe. While I can't blame her disconnect and envy her distance, it curls my stomach.

"I don't," I answer honestly.

"Right," Sue says with a wink and squeezes Gretchen's arm with delight.

Sam rescues us. "Ny, we should keep at it if we want to finish the trail and not be late."

As we part, Gretchen looks briefly at Sam. "Don't tell my dad, okay?" Her head rocks slightly toward Sue, her eyes wide with fear. Sam nods that he won't, and Sue immediately looks wounded. The two leave us, walking at different paces toward their car at the trailhead, Sue in front, Gretchen a little behind.

We wait until they're out of earshot. "That was crazy," he says. "I keep forgetting you're a celebrity."

No, I'm a daughter, I think. "Where were we?"

Sam says, "We have an employer with missing diamonds

and a girl snooping around the mines who has to be gotten rid of. The question is pretty simple: Who in the King family is ruthless enough to kill Cora?"

Thinking about the answer disgusts me. "Creed? Rebecca? Or both of them together? They both have huge motives. Creed has the hospital. Rebecca had her senate seat. Cassandra all but accused Rebecca outright. And it sounds like locals are leaning that way too. They're at least suspicious of Rebecca's motives."

Sam asks the question I'm thinking. "But a mother killing her daughter?"

You get equal DNA from a father and a mother, but the womb breaks biology's tie. No matter how much we know about the female psyche, it is easier to peg a father for a crime this heinous. That could be my bias given I don't have a relationship with my father. "What I can't really see is Rebecca killing Cora over money. I haven't spent much time with her, but she's not as beholden to that King legacy stuff."

"Maybe she's beholden to what that money means to Leap," he says.

"But why save teenagers only to lose your own? Leap predates Cora's death."

We arrive on a bluff no more than ten feet off the water. It would be a great place to cliff jump based on the way the rocks cut away beneath us. We sit together and watch the lake ripple with movement. He asks, "Opinions on what would make the senator snap?"

"Disappointment?" I shrug and pull at a patch of wild onions. The root balls release sweet fumes as they leave the soil. I chuck them into the lake and switch to hacking at crabgrass. "What if the senator found out Cora attacked Martin instead of Frankie and she insisted Cora confess and when Cora refused, they fought and Rebecca accidentally . . ."

Sam agrees an accident is more believable than a premeditated act. "Again, why have an inspirational program for teens while you're secretly trafficking teenagers? Unless one program is to aid the other. But that's . . . that's savage."

"Creed is more savage than she is," I say. "But he's a doctor who has made crazy strides to stop meth. That doesn't make any sense either. They both have empathy systems that don't match the mining operation and certainly don't match killing your own kid."

Given the limitations of what we know, I'm forced to admit the truth. "There's a chance it's neither of them. A number of people have worked for the family over the years. I mean, Anna swiped those intake records off Creed's desk without batting an eye. Other people would have access to family envelopes and who knows what else."

Sam says, "If we're not telling the cops because we suspect a payoff, it opens up a cluster of unknown suspects."

He throws a handful of rocks into the water. We watch them sink into the bedrock. The truth is, whoever we're up against has outmaneuvered everyone for twenty years.

I hate questions. I hate the sheer number of times I've wondered, *What if?*

I stand and pull Sam up. "I think we focus on the diamond-mining story and try to get details out of Houdini. We do that and hopefully it'll lead us to the murderer."

"Or get us killed," he says.

CHAPTER 47

The day has come and gone.

Sam's discouraged. I'm gross. My hair is knotted and gnarly, an auburn rope that I've thickened by braiding. I smell us and rotten pumpkins come to mind. We barely speak on the way to the Pilot. Thankfully, when we emerge from the woods, ours is the only vehicle in the gravel pull-off. We're likely a mile off the water, but we can hear country music blaring. The houseboats must be docking in their coves, the parties starting. Their barbecues burn and my stomach reminds me it has been too long since we stopped for pizza.

Sam unlocks the vehicle and we receive simultaneous texts. His from Ben. Mine from Mom. Both messages translate into expectation rather than invitation. They're eating dinner together and we're joining them. I remind Mom about Granny.

Nyla: But I'm supposed to meet Cassandra.

Mom: Delayed. Anna says Cassandra's not well tonight.

Nyla: When do we come to Ben's?

Mom: Now is good.

Sam sighs when I show him. There's a hesitation I don't understand. He says, "Our house isn't like yours," in an apologetic voice. I am not sure what he means, but he doesn't want to talk about it.

The heaviness of the day steals our words and we make our way through the park and into Lone Valley. The townlet is three blocks in length, five churches in total, one walk-up restaurant called Flav-o-isle, and a Dollar General at the far end. Behind an old high school turned daycare sits a maintenance garage with shells of empty buses from bygone eras.

His house is a three-tone tan manufactured home with no underpinning, landscaping, or driveway. The yard is a bare dirt patch with an old Ford F-150. The metal frame and wheels beneath the trailer are surrounded by scrub brush and weeds. We park and a kitten pokes its head around the concrete blocks doubling as front porch steps. The tiny feline slinks toward Sam. Lucy barks her welcome by jumping against the screen door.

Sam tucks the cat into the crook of his arm and says, "Butterbean, say hi to Nyla. Nyla, this is Butterbean."

I nuzzle the cat's chin. "Hello, Butterbean." She is adorable.

But not adorable enough to distract Sam. He appears to have lost two inches of height. "Meth sucks," he says with his back to me.

"Hey, it's okay," I say.

"Easy for you to say."

Wow. How quickly I became a King to him. Like the day we spent together was a dream and now we've returned to reality. This reaction throws me. I wouldn't have a home if it weren't for Richard, and Sam knows that. Why would I hold his home to the King standard? Injustice spikes my anger. I don't like being judged, and I particularly don't like when the judgment assumes I'm shallow.

Ben opens the trailer. His height takes up the entirety of the frame. My mother stands in his shadow. They each wear wry smiles that worry me. Wordlessly, Ben steps aside and takes Butterbean from Sam. He holds the trembling creature against his chest and strokes her fur until she purrs. Lucy's huge paws land on my legs and Sam bats her down, like she, too, is a disgrace.

The trailer smells of Pine Sol and lemons. Sam toes off his shoes at the door and I do the same. I survey my clothes. The thick coat of barn scum. The cobwebs in the crooks of my clothes. Mom is giving me the up-down *Where have you two been all day?* look. She's wearing a sundress that makes her look ripped and cloggy heels that add three inches to her height. Ben's got on a short-sleeved plaid shirt and what I'd guess are his Sunday jeans. His mustache and beard are freshly trimmed.

When Sam and Ben turn their backs, I mouth to Mom, "Is this a date?"

"No." She's practically hissing and bright red.

The eat-in kitchen isn't made for four people. Ben has set the table with clear glass plates and bowls. "Vegetable beef soup," he announces and points out the kitchen window at a PVC pipe greenhouse. "Meat's venison. I hope you don't mind."

Mom says, "Not at all," and Sam whispers to me, "It's okay if you don't like it."

"Thank you for inviting us," I say directly to Ben. I've never eaten venison and silently pray my tolerance holds up to my politeness.

Ben dishes soup, doles out soda crackers, and fills four glasses with Kool-Aid from a pitcher in the fridge. Sam and I alternate turns at the kitchen sink; as we scrub, the water turns brown. Before we even sit, there's a pretense. I feel like I'm strapping into an indoor, complete-darkness roller coaster.

Mom says, "You two seem to have had a day."

Sam answers, "We went hiking."

Before Mom asks a follow-up, Ben lifts his spoon to tell us all we are to eat before supper gets cold. He digs in and Mom does the same. I take a bite and find out I'm not a fan of venison, but I'm not about to show even the slightest look of distaste. I keep my head down and eat, wondering when they're going to explain why we have been summoned. Five minutes into the meal, Mom sets down her spoon and reaches for my and Sam's wrists. "We've decided you should stop."

Sam and I throw them quizzical looks. Ben takes

another sip of his Kool-Aid and then drains the cup as Mom says, "*Death Daze*. All of it. Everything."

Sam fidgets as if he's considering the request and then says, "No."

Mom fires back, "We watched Cor do this twenty years ago and we're not watching our kids do the same."

I don't even know what to say. "Watched Cor do what?" I ask at the same time Sam says, "*Death Daze* is bigger than us, and we won't stop."

It's nice to be on the same page.

"It's not safe," Ben says.

"Since when has that mattered?" Sam asks. "Considering this thing started with a broken window and tear gas, we're well aware there are risks."

That earns more sideways glances. More cryptic gestures. Something else has happened. Sam picks up on it, same as me. "Tell us," he demands and then puts his foot down. "Dad. Tell us."

Mom's fingers dance on the tabletop. "Another threat."

"What threat?" I ask.

"Ben, show them."

Ben stands, walks to the fridge, and reaches up to the cabinet above. He retrieves a bulky manila envelope. There don't seem to be any markings on either side. Ben opens the clasps and shakes the contents onto his placemat. A red zip-up sweatshirt lands in a heap. Mom turns the worn fabric to where the left breast pocket is visible. *CJK* is monogrammed in dirty white thread. Ben slides a note in front of Sam. Five words.

Leave now or Nyla's next.

Even without knowing the origin of the sweatshirt, I understand the chilling implication.

Ben provides an explanation. "That's what she was wearing the day she disappeared." He does not need to say Cora's name. We understand.

I paw at the sleeve, feel the threadbare fabric, trace the monogrammed letters. A surprising triumphant feeling fills me up. "Unless you think Frankie has someone on the outside, this is evidence Frankie didn't kill Cora—who else but her killer would have this sweatshirt, right?—and you want to pack up here and be done?"

"I want my daughter alive, and that's what Frankie wants too."

I ignore her desperation, ignore the sound of her fist jarring the glasses on the table when she strikes it. I say, "Ben, you know the mines. We need to know what's going on down there." Under the table, Sam clenches my thigh. The adults stare at me, curious as to what I'll say next. I'm almost curious myself. I'm not sure how to make my argument, but I barrel on. "Something bad was going on twenty years ago, and that's what Cora discovered and it got her killed. Right, Ben? Right, Mom?"

"Nyla," Sam says quietly. He's trying to let me know we need to stick to the plan and keep the discovery of diamonds to ourselves. I plow on.

"But you want us to stop because . . . what? You got a five-thousand-dollar bonus?" I dig into Ben. "And you." I look at Mom. "How much did Rebecca offer you this morning? Because Creed offered me fifty thousand dollars to stop *Death Daze* and I turned him down." Not to mention Ned bargaining with me to meet Laylah.

"Ny, stop," Sam says.

Mom and Ben give each other an unreadable side-eye. This is not how they expected their warning to go.

Mom says, "This isn't your ticket to YouTube fame. You're in real danger."

My fists are on the table. It's my turn to rattle the glasses. "What about Frankie? What's she in?"

Mom's sadness is visible and profound. "Baby girl," she says.

"Don't baby girl me. You've spent your life loving Frankie and you know this doesn't add up. Sam pulled a girl out of a cave. The same cave where your dead sister washed up on the beach. Someone shot at the house, gassed us, is making threats. Why? I wonder what they'd do if they knew we found their precious diamonds."

Mom stands now, her sadness eclipsed by a horrific curiosity. "What do you mean? Diamonds?"

I skip straight to the point. "Twenty years ago your family was mining diamonds with a workforce of trafficked girls. That's what Cora figured out and that's what got her killed. And if we stop investigating, like you're suggesting, not only will Frankie die but so will anyone else they have locked away in those caves."

"Are you high?" Mom asks. She turns to Ben. "Are they high?"

I laugh. "I wish. We're going to talk to Laylah Williams tomorrow. You wait. I'll bet she tells us one heck of a story."

It's Ben's turn to smash the table like Hulk. When he brings his fists down, the silverware skitters over the edge and pings on the floor. "I don't care what Laylah tells you," he says. "I've been everywhere in those caves and there's no way."

"And yet . . ." I hold out the diamond for him to take. "Proof is in the sparkle."

Mom ignores Ben's assessment. "What are you saying?" she asks me.

"I'm saying your family is broke and corrupt, and if the senator offered you money today, she doesn't have any."

Mom stares out the sink window in the direction of Nockabout. We hear her swallow.

I redirect the conversation to Ben, who is busy examining the stone. "Think about where the Kings could have hidden the operation. A place you haven't been."

Ben's shaking his head. "There's nowhere."

"Dad," Sam pleads and gestures to the diamond.

"Why? So you can put it on your show and make a buck? Or are you adding to your tour, son? You think I don't know

297

what you're doing? Or how far you'd go with this hoax?" Every sentence is louder than the one before, but none are as angry as the last. "Don't you realize what I do to keep you safe and fed?"

"Ben. Calm down."

"Beth!" Ben repeats her precise tone, which is downright startling to everyone in the kitchen. "Y'all don't live here," he says. "Stop your channel and your tours. I can't handle someone else getting hurt."

This plea ignites Mom. Her temper gathers and amasses energy. Everything about her looks ready to snap. She has her soup spoon in her hand, her knuckles completely white. "Ben, what is it you know? I swear if I find out you're involved with trafficking girls or killing Cora . . . I'll . . ." Her voice dissolves.

Sam has retreated to the corner. I can't tell what's going on inside his head. I think he's not sure which side to be on, and he knows whatever he says or does will hurt someone. For my part, I am the eye of the hurricane. Listening. Watching. I've decided to feel later.

Ben holds up his index finger to the three of us, urging us to stay quiet as he collects his thoughts. With painful conviction, he says, "I've walked every tunnel in the mines. Same as my dad. Same as my granddad. Cora told me her diamond mining theory, too, and I took her seriously. There was nothing in the hills then and nothing in the hills now. You're tracking shiny ghosts. All of you. There comes a time to let the dead be dead and the nearly dead die gracefully.

That time has come." He sighs, knowing he likely hasn't convinced us.

"Wait. Cora told *you* about diamonds?" Mom walks toward Ben, the spoon in her hand, every muscle flexed. "And you kept it to yourself for twenty years?"

She is in his face.

He has six inches of height on her and she has fifty pounds of muscle on him.

He answers, "She was wrong, Bethie. Why make you miserable all these years?"

I walk over to stand between them, take the diamond from Ben, and hold the stone at eye level. "No," I say. "You were wrong."

"That's not possible. I don't even care if your stone is real because the situation is still bogus," Ben says. Again, he asks us to wait. He abandons the kitchen for the bedroom at the end of the hall and returns with three sets of maps, which he spreads across an empty counter. The first map is dated 1889; the second, 1935; the third is from 1959—the year the mine closed. That's the map he focuses on. It's well used and highlighted with penciled-in dates. All from 2000. This is his personal search for Cora King.

I can see him on that final day with her.

Martin Jarvis swings from the bridge outside.

Cora's in his cave. The shoeboxes are four or five feet high, a small stack in the corner. Cora stands in front of him, telling him about diamonds in Kentucky that can't possibly exist. He doesn't let himself believe her harebrained ideas; he sees how she has betrayed them all. He even lets himself wonder if Cora killed Martin in a lover's rage and then found a way to dodge his death the way she dodged his beating.

I can hear him cut those final cords between them.

"Go on," he says.

Cora is taken aback. Ben has always forgiven her. But not this time. This time she has hurt him too badly to reconcile. He listens to the echo of her walking away, deeper into the mine. He doesn't know this is the last time he'll see her alive.

She doesn't come home that night, or the next, or the next.

He goes a bit crazy.

There's madness on this map, in his markings, the notes and dates. Every tunnel in this kingdom has been explored. Every stone upturned. Over twenty years, his conviction has hardened to the confidence in his voice. "You can't hide the operation Cora thought existed. Drills. Footprints. Supplies. They weren't in the mines then and they aren't now. Ask Cassandra. I went straight to her after Cora didn't come home. She gave me these maps. She hired a team to work with me. If there was a diamond operation in that mine, we'd have found it when we were looking for Cora. Whoever killed Cora put her body in the lake, not the mines."

Mom deflates. She's already convinced by his conclusion.

I'm discouraged. What if Ben's right and Cora was wrong about the jewels in the velvet bag? I feel like I've sent myself out to the offensive line with no pads or helmet and been gut-rushed and smashed into the ground. I do not like to reckon with failure and wonder if anyone feels equipped to be wrong. Detectives. Investigators. Cops. I bet all the training in the world feels inadequate when you're fundamentally wrong and someone else will pay for your mistake.

Ben has won this round and decides against a victory lap. Instead, he lifts the lid off the cookie jar on the counter and removes a set of car keys, which he pitches in my direction. They bounce across the table and land on my placemat. He says, "That's your mom's Camaro, kid. All yours. If I were you, I'd drive it up to Floyd and see her before she's gone. You want to film, film that."

Sam whips in my direction. "Your mom?"

"Frankie," Ben says, like everyone knows. His mistake hits him. "I figured you would have told him."

From the fresh hurt on Sam's face, he figured I would have too.

CHAPTER 48

The Camaro keys.

Keys to my mother's car.

The ratio of keys to keychains is one to two. Frankie, at eighteen, sported a metal cross, a Harry Potter Lego figurine, an Adair County library fob, and a hand-painted wooden tab that reads, *"Wonder" Off Path*. The quotes indicate the spelling is intentional.

Mom traces the edges of the tab and says, "I made that at Camp Loucon when I was, like, twelve." It's clear she had forgotten Frankie kept the keepsake on her keychain. My eyes are on Sam; when I can't get him to look at me, I let myself engage with Ben and Mom. "Frankie liked to read?"

Ben and Mom say, "Yeah," and Mom adds, "She kept a book in her bag. I didn't like to read, but I would go to the library with her in the summers." Mom looks at Ben. "What was it she read all the time?"

Ben says, *"Jurassic Park?"* like he's conjuring her fingers holding an old paperback.

"Not that one." Mom is smiling now, the happy memory a medicine.

"Night Shift," Ben says. "I took her beat-up copy to Floyd that first year."

They're satisfied they've remembered and appear to be on the verge of telling more Frankie stories. I am torn between wanting to know everything about her and explaining to Sam why I hadn't told him yet. He stands at the front door, his back to us, hand on the knob. He doesn't care that Frankie was a fan of Stephen King short stories; he cares that we created global interest in Francis Quick and his partner left out the most important detail: she is the daughter of a famous murderer.

Sam is Sam, his father's son; therefore, my betrayal equals silence and questions rather than anger and demands. He tells Mom he'll meet her at the dock for her ride across the lake and doesn't look over his shoulder as he leaves. Ben says to me, "Give him time."

I say, "How much?"

Ben shrugs. He's used all his words already.

There's no more talk of threats or pleading to stop *Death Daze*. The purpose of the dinner has been lost in the mix. Five minutes later, Sam ferries Mom and me to Nockabout. The lake is gorgeous; the wind, warm and glorious. Under different circumstances, Nockabout by night with Sam is romantic. Rope lights line the personal docks along the shoreline. The stars are an epic movie of twin-kling heavenly hosts. When you listen closely, the hum of tomorrow's Jet Skis and fishing boat motors plays like a DJ's remix. And high on the hill, Cassandra's cathedral winks at the sky.

Tonight should have been different.

I am hoping when we dock Sam'll ask me to hang back. I want him to check on me and focus on the real issue rather than my unwillingness to share. But he's just a boy, not the perfect human I want him to be. Whatever is in his head right now doesn't have an emotional vocabulary.

In bed at the pool house, I wait for a text.

I lay my phone on my chest, wanting it to buzz and feeling stupid and girlish and angry and exhausted. There are bigger things to talk about, bigger things to feel. But they're too big and inaccessible so I think about Sam. To Mom's credit, when she must have a million questions about the diamond and the mines and her family's finances, she lies beside me, stroking my hair and soothing my heart-ache. "He'll come around," she says.

"He shouldn't have to come around," I say bitterly. "It's my life; why does he get to be angry about it?"

"I don't know, baby."

Hot tears hit the corners of my eyes. "Why is he making this about him when I'm the one losing Frankie?"

Mom doesn't bring up the fact that I was doing the same to her a week ago.

She thinks for a long time, curls in closer to me, and

says, "You kept your truth private. And that's okay and fair. If you value the relationship, give him that same gift of privacy without penalizing him for it."

I think on that for a long time. How maybe that's her way of asking for forgiveness too, and maybe I should give it to her.

Long after she has fallen asleep with her fingers in my hair and her breath on our pillow, I reach for my phone. Waiting on Sam to come to me is only satisfying if I want to fight about how long it took him to reach out, and I don't. I want help. We need to put our heads together on what Ben said, because even though Ben's account makes sense, there's more to the story.

I worry the light from my phone will wake Mom, but she doesn't stir as I start to type Sam a message.

Nyla: Tonight made me lonely.

Nyla: I probably made you feel lonely by not telling you about Frankie. I found out the other day and I've been processing. I don't think either of us did anything wrong. Even if you disagree, I hope you'll keep helping me.

Nyla: Your dad has to be wrong about the mines.

Nyla: See you tomorrow.

CHAPTER 49

In my dreams, a girl in a red hoodie slips beneath the surface of Green River Lake, sinking into the reeds and below the muck. No matter how deep I dive, she is unreachable. Sometimes she is Frankie. Or Mom. She is even Sam. I wake up frustrated and tired.

My mood doesn't improve when I check my phone and discover no return text from Sam. Hopefully he'll show up at the Center to meet Ned. He's bound to be a source of comfort for Houdini.

On the table that's doubling as a kitchen counter, Mom has left a Pop-Tart, a scribbled note—*Working out*—and a new invitation to dinner at Cassandra's. Anna's handwriting is on the latter. Granny has extended beyond Ned and me; the family *WILL ATTEND*, she wrote in all caps. That explains why Linkin Park blares from the open garage.

Outside, Richard has parked himself in a fancy

Barcalounger, coffee in one hand, phone in the other. The scrunches across his forehead say he's thinking too hard, hard enough he doesn't notice me. I let myself spy for a moment as he scrolls through baby pictures on an app. Given the age and odd sizes of the photos, they're scans from a long time ago. No one I recognize.

"Hey," he says, startled, and sets his phone on the armrest, screen down.

"Hey," I say. "I'm headed out to meet Sam."

He nods and lifts his hand in the air for a high five. I grip his fingers and he squeezes longer than normal. "No videos," he says and I nod. "Be careful, please," he says in a tone that reminds me I'm lucky to have him in my life. I kiss the scruff on his cheek. This makes him smile and I smile too. He's not my dad, but he's a really good dad-guy.

I turn up at the Center before nine; Ned's alone at the gazebo and pleased to see that I've shown up. "Good decision," he says. I'm sure he's assuming I will discontinue *Death Daze* since I'm here. Cora's red sweatshirt flashes through my head. Her monogram. *Nyla's next*, I think, and pray I'm safe.

We give Sam five minutes. Ten. Fifteen. While we wait, Ned and I are both on our phones or at least pretending to be on our phones to avoid having to small-talk this early. I don't let myself text Sam, but I keep our message thread open and check for dots to see if he's typing. At twenty after and no new messages, I'm not sure whether to be worried or mad. I tell Ned we should go on in.

Ned closes his phone, rubs at his eyes, and says, "All right. Let's do this," like we're attempting to summit Everest. And in some ways, we are. This is Creed's territory, and he doesn't like me all that much.

We pass right through the check-in process without a hiccup and are given access to the same elevators I rode with Anna on my tour. The difference being everyone we encounter says, "Morning, Ned," and no one spoke to Anna. Ned knows names, that one man has a new grandbaby and another has a janky motor in her boat. He stops at a coffee station and makes a cup that is more sugar than liquid. He says, "I usually take Georgia a cup."

Georgia's working at the fourth-floor reception area. She's bleary-eyed and has purple rings deep enough to make you wonder if she was recently punched. When she looks up from her computer and spots Ned, she taps her watch face. "If I fall over from dehydration, I'm blaming you, Ned Damron."

Ned says, "Girl, blame me for insulin levels, not dehydration. There's enough sugar in that thing to cube every horse in the Derby."

Georgia grins, sips the coffee, and breathes deep with satisfaction. "Two cups in one shift. Mmm, mmm, mmm. You're my favorite."

Repartee satisfied, Ned asks, "How was Mom's night?"

"Ah, you saw . . . Long, long, long. Your momma brings the feisty."

"You come at night too?" I ask.

He nods and Georgia turns toward her computer with renewed energy. The hallway is empty, same as on our tour. Framed inspirational quotes from nurses and doctors decorate the walls. I imagine you need all the happy thoughts to work here. At his mother's door, Ned says, "Don't go wandering off on your own. We'll check on Houdini during the shift change," and then he pushes open the door and disappears into the room. I hear him call, "*Hola*, Mom. Dad sends his love. *Hola*, Ms. Rey. You ladies look beautiful today."

I don't know if Ned says these things because he believes them or to make the women happy, but one coos in response. I have a sliver of a view. The foot of both beds. Fuzzy blankets. Painted toenails. A dresser with no accoutrements or photos. The emptiness makes me think about Frankie and what's in her room at Floyd. Does she have a room—a hotel-like cell? A roommate? Has Mom sent photos of me, of us, of them, of her and Cora? What, if any, are the little things she has kept?

Would she want a photo of me in her Camaro? Or would that hurt?

I can't think too long thanks to Ms. Rey. She starts belting out a Prince mash-up, starting with "Thieves in the Temple" and ending with "Diamonds and Pearls." Her volume sends Ned running toward me. He leans into the hallway, looks both ways, and says, "I'll try to calm her down. If you need anything, knock." The door clicks closed.

I'm alone again. Ms. Rey moves on to the Beatles. The volume peaks uncomfortably during "Yellow Submarine." Ned takes a page from their book and begins to sings with them. He has a decent voice, the best of the three. The women join him for "Peace Train" and then "Scarborough Fair." Judging from the quietness that follows, they've fallen asleep before the canticle ends. I'm struck by the gentle magic required to perform such a feat of love and patience.

I can't help myself.

I open the door and peek in. Ned is on his knees between the beds, holding the hands of both women, his head bent toward the floor. Whatever circumstances led these ladies, with mops of stringy hair and pale copy paper–colored skin, to these beds, their lives would be far worse without Ned.

I check my phone. Nothing from Sam. Death Dazers are asking for a private interview with Rebecca King. There are fifty thousand new followers and a direct message from a woman claiming to be a producer of NBC's *Dateline*. I stuff the phone in my front pocket; the noise coming from the internet is ten times louder than Ms. Rey.

I'm restless and decide to walk toward the elevators and give Ned privacy. Georgia's not alone at her station. A male doctor, Dr. DivJak according to his badge, leans against her counter, updating her on the condition of a patient. Georgia types furiously as he talks and spots me when she looks up at him to repeat a medicine dosage. "You look familiar." She's wagging her finger in my direction.

"I was here with Anna on a tour."

Georgia curls her lip. "Oh, you're Dr. King's grand-daughter. The one on the other side."

"Other side of what?" I ask.

"Of us," Dr. DivJak says.

"Who told you that?" I wonder if Creed made me the subject of an all-staff email.

Georgia and Dr. DivJak shrug, unwilling to out whoever has given them this idea. I decide to be straightforward. "I'm curious about Houdini," I say.

Georgia's eyes roll back. Dr. DivJak stares at her like she needs to be careful. "What?" she snaps. In return, he holds up his hands, like he's not getting involved any further. Georgia's offended and defends herself. "She came in here with Ned. He'll tell her about Houdini if we don't."

"What about Houdini?" I ask.

The doctor, nonplussed, lowers his voice and harnesses his superiority. "Georgia, your shift's over."

I'm uncomfortable now and know I haven't made friends. Before they kick me out, I say, "I'll go wait for Ned," and leave the two of them in a tense argument.

Ned is still with his mother. Even though he's promised to take me to Laylah's room, I'd rather take myself before Georgia and Dr. DivJak decide to make me leave. I make my way along the corridor and find *L. Williams* on the door of a room in an offshoot hallway. Knowing I won't have long before Georgia realizes I'm not standing post near Ned, I take a deep breath and open the door.

The room is small and empty. One bed instead of two. The sheets, stripped. The recliner in the corner looks like it has been vacuumed recently. The bedside table has a telephone, a remote, and a sippy cup with the Center logo. Similar to the dresser in Ms. Rey and Ned's mom's room, there's an emptiness that goes beyond the bed. The dry-erase board with Laylah's name and vitals is the only evidence this was ever her room.

She's done it again. Escaped. They must know already and that's what Dr. DivJak didn't want Georgia to tell. No patient would strip her bed before she snuck out of her hospital room. I close the door behind me and walk to the dresser. All the drawers are empty. Even the ones in the bedside table. I check under the bed. A singular earring is up against the molding on the wall. It could be from anyone, but it looks like a diamond and I'm not leaving that here. I lie down and scooch under the bed. The mechanics catch my hair as I wiggle. As I blindly detach my hair from the coil, the room door opens. With no way to explain my presence, I tuck my feet closer and hope no part of me is exposed. Two pairs of legs stand near the door. One in Crocs. One in expensive loafers. I hold my breath and listen.

"I emptied the room before the coroner came."

"Where will they take her?"

"Adkins's, I'm sure. That's where Dr. Creed sends the fatalities without families."

There's no way to tell which voice belongs to which shoes. Not that it matters. Houdini is dead.

"I checked on her at three. Ned Damron was asleep in the chair and her vitals were fine."

A sad giggle. "He's such a freak. Do you think he killed her?"

"Yeah." There's more laughter from both men. "Actually, no. She threw a clot."

"Like, for real?"

That question chills me. There's no way to know if it's a hyperbolic reaction. There are no clues in the answer either: "I saw the chart." Followed by, "You know the drill?"

A dry-eraser scratches. I imagine the nurse removing Laylah's name from the board before he answers, "Of course."

I am stunned. My brain is in total whiteout. I've nearly forgotten why I climbed under the bed to begin with, but the earring is now within reach. It's a single stud. Diamond or cubic zirconia. Tiny little stone, like something you see on an infant with pierced ears. I don't reach for it until the shoes move on. When I'm sure they're gone, I slide from beneath the bed, then wait a full count of sixty seconds before slipping into the empty hallway. As fast as I can, I return to Ned's mother's room and gently knock.

Ned pokes his head out, a chorus of snores behind him. "You okay?" Then he looks at his watch. "Gosh. Sorry, it's after ten."

"Houdini is dead," I announce, wanting to see his response to this.

Ned tilts his head all the way back and stares into the fluorescent lights. His hands find his hips, elbows out like he's about to start flapping. By the time his spine returns to normal length, he's wiped his mouth with the back of his hand and arranged his face into something reminiscent of sadness. "That's awful. Did they say of what?"

I have no choice but to push here, given what I know. "They said you were maybe one of the last people to see her alive."

Ned shakes a cigarette from the pack in his front pocket and places it behind his ear, his itch to smoke almost audible.

He says, "I visit everyone on the wing. The ones without families. They shouldn't be alone."

"Do you know them all?" I glance down the hallway of doors and think of all the stories in this building.

"Laylah's is a sad one."

Before I ask why, he says, "I need a cigarette," and heads to the elevator. I'm forced to follow. On the way down, I take the earring from my pocket. "Is this a diamond?"

Ned's chunky fingers lift the stud to eye level and then higher toward the light fixture. "That's an eighth of a carat. Cloudy. Not worth much by diamond standards."

The elevator dings and Ned already has the cigarette shoved in the corner of his mouth, his lighter out. We cross the lobby floor and he strikes the flint the moment the door opens. After a deep inhale, he says, "Be careful, Nyla."

"How careful?"

His face twitches. "Very." And then he's gone, the cloud of smoke following him down the hill to the dock.

CHAPTER 50

A lanky figure watches me from the gazebo.

Sam. I recognize his shadow before he steps into the sunlight and walks in my direction. Without a word, he offers his hand. The gesture is simple and thoughtful, an ointment applied to the rawness of last night. I accept and he leads me off the property of the Center. Every few seconds he checks over his shoulder like we're being followed. Given the noise coming from the docks, that's wise. The ferry has arrived with a fresh horde of *Death Daze* enthusiasts.

I start to speak and he shakes his head. *Not yet.*

Not until we are nearly to the King driveway does he take out his phone and lead me into the woods. He stops when we can no longer see Circle Drive. I wait while he locates a picture, wait longer as he holds the phone against his chest and considers his words.

Sam says, "Before you look at this, I need to tell you where I've been and why I didn't answer your messages last night." He's shaking and I reach for his elbow, unsure of how or if I should comfort him. "I was frustrated last night." He gives me a pointed and apologetic look. "And a lot of times when I'm like that, I go diving. I have lamps and equipment and it's not a big deal. Except I decided to redive the cave where I rescued Houdini. That way when we talked to her this morning, I might be able to ask for specifics."

I try to interrupt and tell him the girl is dead. He won't give me an inch. "Please, let me get this off my chest." He continues, "First, I didn't get your message until after three in the morning because I used the flashlight on my phone and killed the batt—"

"Sam—" I want to tell him my time at the Center has dulled the strong emotions of last night and even of this morning when he didn't show up.

"And second, I found something in the cave."

Oh my gosh. "You found the girls?"

"No." He's trembling again.

What could be worse than finding the girls? I take his hands and massage my thumbs into his palms. "Hey, you're okay. Breathe."

He takes a breath. "It was this." He turns the phone around for me.

The image is of a stone wall. Nothing stands out. "I don't see . . ."

He slides to the next image, a zoomed-in view. There, in very small letters, scratched next to a rupestrian-like horse, are eleven chilling words.

If I die in here, it's Ned and my sister's fault.

316

CHAPTER 51

T hat can't be right," I say. *If I die in here, it's Ned and my sister's fault.* There's another explanation. There has to be. "Mom was taking the ACT when Cora went missing. And even if she weren't, she wouldn't do this. Not to her sister. Not to Frankie."

Sam's expression is cruel, forceful. "Nyla," he says without removing the belligerence he clearly feels. He's thinking, *Once a liar always a liar.* But that's not true. People have codes about the way they lie, and Mom's lies are protective, not vicious. I think about her lying in bed with me last night, the kindness of her love. Her fear when she and Ben demanded that we stop *Death Daze.*

"She'd have access to Cora's red sweatshirt," Sam says.

"No."

"Yes, and she wouldn't want you to keep investigating."

"No. No." I'm adamant.

"You said she basically apparated into the living room when the brick crashed through the window of Richard's house. What if she knew it was coming?"

"No way. She was in the garage at the back of the house. Plus, why send us that video of herself?"

I've scored a point, but Sam's not backing down. "Nyla. Read this again." He puts his phone in my hands, the photo blown up.

If I die in here, it's Ned and my sister's fault.

"But why? She's her sister and Ned was in love with Cora." I am defensive and nearly screaming. Sam pats the air. Whether he's patronizing me or not, I snap, "Don't tell me to calm down."

He asks the question pecking at my heart. "What if it's guilt, not love? By their own admissions, they weren't really friends until after Cora disappeared."

"She loves *me*. She wouldn't do this to *me*."

"You didn't exist when she did this—"

"She didn't do this."

"She can love you and kill her sister. Put all the pieces together, Ny. She left. She changed her name. She wasn't coming back here ever again until you made it impossible for her to stay away. She didn't tell you about Frankie. Not even after the ADPA announcement. Maybe that's why she was so against the ADPA. It's hard to vote for death if you've done some killing."

"She was going to tell me."

Sam's gaining certainty. "Someone has been plotting against us since the beginning. Someone close to this."

"Yes, but it's not her. She was in bed with me last night when Houdini died. She was holding me because you didn't text back."

Sam's eyes narrow. "Wait, what? Houdini what?"

I exhale. "Laylah Williams is dead. That's what I found out this morning when I was with Ned. But . . ." Oh gosh. "Ned *was* with her last night. Fell asleep in her room."

"She died while he was there?"

"Maybe. I don't know. I couldn't tell."

Sam drops down to a crouch. "You don't think . . ."

"What?"

"Who knew we were seeing Houdini this morning?" Sam asks.

I say, as measured as I can, "We did not get Houdini killed. We did not."

"Ny, what if we did? Think it through. Ned and Beth knew we'd be there questioning her this morning. Now think about what Cora wrote. *It's Ned and my sister's fault.* Same cave. It could be the same killers. They could have done all this together."

"But the timeline—"

"—wasn't precise. The lake damaged the body. They never pinpointed the time of death. If Ned and your mom were working together, your mom could have taken the ACT and met up with him afterward."

"There was no reason for her to hurt Cora."

This stumps him momentarily. "What if Cora was running diamonds with Martin Jarvis? Or your mom and Ned were running diamonds for Martin?"

"Come on, Sam. You're stretching."

"We need to talk to someone from back then. Someone who has no reason to lie," Sam says.

I harrumph at that notion. "We seem to be losing people we can trust by the second."

"Your mom," he says.

"I will not ask my mom if she killed her sister. I won't do it."

"Your real mom," Sam corrects.

My chest feels heavy. I bend, put my hands on my knees, and try to swallow the bowling ball in my throat.

Sam continues, "We drive to Floyd and show Frankie the picture and the letter and tell her everything."

I am not ready for that, but I'm ready for the truth.

"Okay," I say.

CHAPTER 52

We tell no one our plan. We cross the lake in Sam's boat and take the Pilot.

We encounter the first demonstrators a mile from Floyd. Small groups on either side of the road with pop-up tents and wooden signs. By the first *Floyd Prison* sign, protesters line both sides in picketing clumps so thick they spill onto the asphalt. They are like politicians on Election Day. Vote for him. No, vote for her. Except in the case of Francis Quick, the debate isn't regarding leadership. The right side screams, "Death for Francis Quick. Death for Francis Quick." The left: "Free Francis. Free Francis."

It's difficult to understand how strangers, whole families, and church groups—people who don't know Frankie or Cora and never will—have come to care so deeply they'll risk a heat stroke and scream themselves hoarse.

I've always tamped extreme emotions—never been a

kid who hated my mom or couldn't stand a classmate. I feel things deeply, but I'm pragmatic. And the pragmatism is a bumper for unhelpful feelings. I've never wanted to go where anger takes me. Never really understood why people get so worked up over something adjacent to their lives. But as a cluster of protesters scream, "Free Frankie! Free Frankie!" and overtake the volume of "Death to Francis Quick," I understand the value of anger.

There are more *Death Daze* folks than pro-ADPA.

"Is there enough traffic moving in and out of Floyd to warrant a protest this large?" Sam asks.

The mobs are close enough to see inside the Pilot. "It's her! Nyla King is here." The girl bangs on the window, inches from my face, and continues to scream at her mates, "It's her! Nyla King. She's here!" There are more bangs then. Hands rock the car side to side.

Phones are out, recording, documenting, and probably already uploading for newshounds around the world. So much for slipping into Floyd without Mom finding out. I bury my face under the dash until Sam reaches the guard shack. The crowd's chants and cheers are unbearable with his window down. Sam asks the guard to lean down close enough to mouth, "Visitor for Frankie Quick."

"No visitors except family. Quick's rule," the guard says.

I lean across Sam's space where the guard can also see me. I say, "Please. Tell her that her daughter is here."

We wait. Five agonizing minutes. I'm sure they'll come back and say we aren't allowed to see her, and I've never wanted to see someone this badly in all my life. "Ma'am," the guard finally says. "You're good to enter."

To put distance between us and the protesters, Sam floors the Pilot through the gate. The lane to Floyd's is a winding half-mile trek over open fields. The chorus "Free Frankie" remains audible when we park. "Man." Sam stares in their direction. "That's insane."

He takes the keys from the ignition.

I ask, "Would you maybe let me talk to her alone?" I'm tired of masking emotions for the sake of others. "This might be my last chance and she's my—"

"She's your mom and I'm your best friend"—he takes my hand—"and I'll be here when you get back."

My mom.

This will be our first and maybe our only conversation where we know who we are to each other.

CHAPTER 53

Precisely an hour. That's how long I have with her. According to the guard we'll be under strict surveillance. "They'll have a gun on her," he tells me and points to the watchtower, where an officer sights us through a scope.

"Will our conversation be private?" I ask.

The guard gives me an abrupt, "Well, it won't be recorded, if that's what you mean. You're in a freakin' yard and with all that poppycock going on over there. They haven't shut up in days." He waves dismissively toward the front gate. "Out here at night too." He yells at them, "Go home. Go to bed. We're gonna fry her no matter how much you chant."

Don't react. Don't react, I tell myself. And somehow I don't.

"She'll be here," he says. It takes another twenty minutes for her to exit the building. She first acknowledges the protesters. That same dimpled smile from the photo in Ben's shoebox. I hold this smile like it's a photograph, and the next one too. Because that smile is for me.

Her face is love. Only love. And I give it back like I'm an open hydrant.

My birth mom.

I behold Frankie with a fixed and curious gaze, wondering how our lives would have been if they weren't what they are. Would she have baked cookies or given me a curfew? Would we have fought over the fact I haven't applied to a college yet? And Sam. Would she like Sam?

I can't tell, and it's likely I'll never know.

We have an hour. Not long enough for anything, much less what I've come here to do. And I've made a mistake. I didn't ask my security guard if I am allowed to touch her. I brave the question to her escorts and am drowned out by the chanting crowds and clanking chains. One guard takes up his position by the door. The other informs me he'll lock Frankie to the fencing and I am to stay in my corner. "Don't want a repeat of last time."

"I'm not allowed to touch her?" I ask.

The stodgier of the two answers, "Sure, kid. Save the state the money if you do. Bullet's cheaper than an injection cocktail." He laughs, flaunting power over her. Even though she's still bruised from their batons.

As Frankie and I wait for privacy, "Free Frankie" rings out like an anthem. With affection, she says, "Your handiwork."

"Maybe a little."

We're alone now. She wastes no time. "They said my daughter was here. You know you're mine." She's not asking. She's braced for my rejection or anger; for the response she has feared if this moment ever came. We are mother to daughter. For the first and last time. That thought brings the tears. "I have all these questions."

"Anything."

I scoot closer. We face each other, little cages of knees and elbows. I reach across the concrete between us, stopping before I touch her knee, eyes never leaving the tower guard. I want her to hold my hand or kiss my palms the way Mom did when I was scared of the bogeyman. She barely shakes her head no. A subtle reminder that's not in the cards for us.

"My father?" I ask.

"There's a rabbit hole." Frankie twirls a lock of blonde hair around her finger. "For the sake of timing, I'll give you the five-minute version here and a much longer one in writing." She begins. "Early on, at the beginning of my sentence, they had me in PeeWee Valley. That was before my hope broke. Before I understood I wasn't getting out of here. I was obsessed with my case. Ten months before you were born, I had my sights set on the Kings. They'd been adamant and outspoken in the media regarding my guilt and I couldn't reconcile their judgment with life experience. They'd always loved me. Anyway, I started questioning the Center and the campaign . . ." She lowers her voice. "Your father was one of the men 'helping' me look for answers."

Frankie looks grim and ashamed. "Your dad doesn't know about you. Richard pulled strings with some old friends and got me moved to Floyd before the prison infir-mary did a pregnancy test. I knew right away." Her arms stretch across her narrow stomach, the memory lucid on her face. "My whole body was off. And maybe he was a good guy, but I didn't want him raising you. He died a couple of years later, when you were almost four. Boating accident. Beth let me know."

"Free Frankie! Free Frankie!"

"Death for Francis Quick!"

The crowd cranks their volume. Nothing drowns out the bombshell about my father.

"Did he help you find anything useful?" I ask.

"Not really. Creed leveraged the house and property to cover the Center's debts. Rebecca's political career carried them in the late '90s. Every penny they inherited or made went into keeping the Center afloat or to Leap. But being broke isn't illegal, and it certainly wasn't a motive for murder."

"Who did you trust back then to ask for help?"

She reels off names like they are items on a grocery list. "Richard. Ben. Bethie. Ned would have helped, if I'd asked. His mom was in the Center. He needed Creed, but he was always loyal."

He'd said as much to me. But now I didn't know what to think. "How did you know to trust them?"

Frankie gathers her mouth and nose in her hand and exhales through her fingers. "Because they believed me. Plus, when you have a senator telling the world you killed her daughter, you take what you can get."

"You never wondered if the reason they believed you might be because one of them killed her?"

Frankie stands, metabolizes the question. She twists each knuckle until it pops and I know she has considered everyone over the last twenty years—even the people she trusts. "Why are you asking?"

A million reasons. Starting with I need to be able to sleep. Rather than show her the photo Sam took in the cave, I start slowly. "We should eliminate everyone. Even the people you love. Husbands kills wives. Wives kill husbands. It happens. Especially when there are secrets. Here's what I know: You never attacked Martin Jarvis. Cora did. Mom and Ben knew, and they were ticked off about what she did to you."

"Sure. But they wouldn't kill Cora."

For now, I accept her conclusion and move along the list. "How is Richard caught up in this?"

"Not how you think." She shakes her head, like she almost can't believe what she's about to say. "Richard is Cora's dad."

I'm floored to the point I can't breathe. Talk about a skeleton in the closet. Rebecca King had an affair with the man who tried to ruin the Center. No wonder Creed hates Richard being here now, and if Cassandra knows, her animosity toward Rebecca and Richard makes sense. That type of betrayal would need to be kept in check. "Whoa. When did Creed find out?"

"Not back then. Maybe never."

"You're sure?"

"Reasonably. Creed and Cora were tight in their own way. I doubt he could have faked their bond if he'd known."

"When did Cora find out Creed wasn't her father?"

"She didn't. Bethie did. Years later."

That's a twist I didn't expect. And another lie from Mom. "And Ned? Why did you trust him?"

"Because of his tenderness toward—"

"Cora."

"Well, yeah, but I was going to say toward everything and everyone. He started working for Cassandra, learning finance and entrepreneurship, when he was like twelve. Gave every penny away. Guy like that . . . He didn't hurt Cora."

Guy like that. Has money from somewhere else? Frankie's opinion of Ned jives with my experience. He's the dog sitter, the diamond mentor, the man who brings fresh flowers to his mother, the one who sings "Peace Train" to calm her roommate's meth angst.

"He was in love with her, right?"

"So head over heels he rolled instead of walked."

"But she wasn't into him?"

Given the slight huff, the narrowing of her eyes, Frankie has given this question consideration over the last twenty years. She rocks back on her heels and then forward, thinking. "Cor loved his attention. Marinated in it. Ned was earnest and I think . . . I think he was too easy for her. He didn't require any thought, and she liked to think. Loved a challenge. That makes her sound shallow and that's not what I mean. Ned was the guy you married, not the kind you dated at sixteen, and she wanted both experiences."

"It must have torn Ned up for her to mess around with Martin."

"Tore everyone up. No one understood. But Martin and Ned stayed friends. Right through all that initial flirting. They were Ferris and Cameron even after the attack—"

"Who?"

Frankie's eyes are cartoon-wide. *"Ferris Bueller's Day Off.* John Hughes."

"I've seen that title on Netflix, I think."

Frankie is more animated now than I've seen—a devilish smile, that wicked dimple. "I'm gonna kill your mother for gaps in your education. Anyway, you know, they were a cool kid plus sidekick combo. Sidekicks don't have much power in those relationships."

"Was literally everyone in love with Cora?" She was Ben's girlfriend, Ned's crush, and Martin's cheat.

"Basically."

"Who were you in love with?"

"None of them. All of them. I was there."

"And Mom?"

"Ben. Always Ben. Which is why Cora dated him."

"That's pretty evil for a sibling."

"Not as evil as you'd think. Cassandra never would have allowed Bethie to marry Ben. He was the help. Kings didn't date below them, and Cora knew it would be Bethie choosing between love and family. Ironically, Cora dating Ben was the most protective thing she did for Bethie. Or at least in her mind."

There's much more to this story. More than I have time to hear. How many pages of this book could I piece together in Ben's cave of shoeboxes? First crushes and loves. Rejection. Weird motives. Twisted family relationships. There's an absence, too, when you examine the scope with a twenty-year lens. My mother has never dated, and I always assumed that was because my father broke her heart. If Frankie's right, she's been alone since she left Nockabout. And alone when she was here.

I check my watch. We have thirty minutes left. Being careful not to get too close, I lay Cora's letter on the concrete for Frankie. "She left this for you in the barn at your dad's. On the day she disappeared."

Frankie reads quickly. When she finishes, she holds the note against her chest and emits the softest, saddest laugh I've ever heard. "Unbelievable."

"Which part? The bag of diamonds or her apology?"

"All of it. All of this. You." She almost smiles.

Don't smile yet, I think. "That's not everything." My heart races. We're on the brink of finding out if the woman she gave her child to is also the reason she's in prison. Is it fair to ask Frankie to tell my future by reading her past?

"You can tell me," she prompts.

I can and I have to.

Frankie braces herself as I open my phone and show her the picture Sam took in the cave. *If I die in here, it's Ned and my sister's fault.*

"Please explain this."

CHAPTER 54

Frankie's initial reaction is difficult to gauge. She reads once, twice, a third time.

I release a sharp breath, afraid of the worst. "Oh no," I say, blood draining from my face.

Frankie exhales so hard she nearly bends in half. "You had me scared, kid. This is okay. This is o-kay. Cora would have done this way earlier. When we were kids."

She blows up the photo and waves me close enough so we can both see the screen.

Relief sends me to the ground. Frankie follows me and says, "We used to play this game, a spin on hide-and-seek. Rather than you picking a hiding place, your opponent picks one for you. One team hides the other team's teammate somewhere on Nockabout. The goal is to be found. The non-hidden teammate gets to ask ten yes-or-no questions to narrow down their partner's location. We played island-wide, and Cora drew these stupid horses everywhere. She figured if she marked all the great hiding places, people would stop using them or she could ask fewer questions. *Is he or she near one of my horses?* She was also impatient. I'm sure she wrote this when it took your mom and Ned too long to find her. Where was this one?"

"Inside the cave. On the beach where she was found. Sam says you have to dive thirty feet to get to that access point. That's pretty intense for hide-and-seek."

Frankie huffs through her nose. "Not if you go through the body tunnel. I mean, it could be closed up now, but back then . . . Shoot, ask your mom. She and Cora were down there all the time. Two rats in a tunnel pod from the first time Cassandra told them mine stories."

"This was a game." The cogs turn at something else she said. "Wait. Did those tunnels link up to the mine?"

"Not that I know of. They linked up to the Center. That's how we'd sneak into the kitchen and steal potato chips." She laughs at the memory.

That explains Houdini's escape. My mind works overtime, processing everything. There are other tunnels, separate from the mines, that connect the Center to the cave. Perhaps that explains how Ben and Cassandra's team searched the mines and found nothing. All the tunnels aren't on Cassandra's maps.

Frankie says, "Rest easy, kid. Your mom didn't do anything to Cora except underestimate her character. Same as me."

"I think that's fair given juvie," I say.

Together we talk through the remaining players.

Ben didn't do this.

Richard would never kill his daughter.

Martin Jarvis was dead.

Ned probably didn't kill Cora, but he has to be involved. How likely is it that a world-renowned jeweler isn't connected to an illegal diamond operation on the private island where he lives? He knows about the tunnels off the body cave and had Cora's trust.

I needle a theory for Frankie. "Maybe Cora went to Ned with her discovery first, not knowing he was connected to the mining operation. Maybe even running it. Martin might have worked for him."

"Yeah, but why?"

"Health care?" It must be astronomical to pay for around-the-clock care for his mother, and I don't get the idea his father is all that involved. That money's coming from somewhere. Add that to his connection with Houdini and we've got him in place in both timelines with a lot to lose if Cora blows open the operation.

Frankie concedes the possibility, adds a challenge. "Ned wouldn't have the stomach to traffic women as diamond miners. That's not his style."

"But Martin would?"

"Martin's dead, and according to you, part of the operation is ongoing."

"Frankie, doesn't that mean it's gotta be Creed or Rebecca who killed Cora? There's no one else."

Frankie is relieved by my conclusion that the Kings are behind this. The power couple have been her number one suspects her entire sentence, and finally someone other than my mother believes her.

"Ah, but proof?" she says with a sigh.

The best evidence we have is unusable. I show Frankie the threat on the back side of the photo of Cora, Martin, and the girl that Sam found in Martin's stuff. There's no handwriting to match. No way to prove Creed or Rebecca typed those words. It, like everything else, brings more questions than answers.

"Hmm," she says as she stares at the note. "Gosh. Anna Gapper. I'd forgotten all about that kid. I don't know how. She was Cora's little shadow." Frankie wears a far-off look.

I point to the young girl again. "Who did you say this is?"

Frankie lifts the photo closer. "Anna."

Cassandra's Anna? I'm not sure Frankie would know the answer to that, given her time at Floyd, and she has moved on to another thought. "You sure this photo was a threat for Martin?"

"Who else?"

Frankie leans against the fence, thinking. "There's a chance it was given to Cora and the 'she' is Anna. Maybe 'do it' meant give back the diamonds or cover up the mining operation, and if you don't, Anna dies. Cora never would have let anything happen to that kid, and we already know Martin knew Cora was willing to risk her life to take him down. No. I don't know. That's complicating an already impossible situation."

She's right. We don't have time for another rabbit hole.

I say, "Okay, here's what we've got for sure. The Kings are basically broke and the Center is sucking them dry. There would have been immense pressure to keep their do-good projects going, for both Creed and Rebecca. Meanwhile, Rebecca's carrying the family finances with her political career. Her illegitimate child discovers an illegal venture that is not only keeping the Kings afloat but keeping them in teak-lined boats and glowing newspaper headlines." I let myself breathe before I continue. "One of them . . . both of them . . . realize Cora's searching for proof and isn't far from it. She has to go."

Frankie's nodding vigorously. "That's conjecture, but sounds true."

"Say Creed found out Cora wasn't his."

"Doesn't prove he killed her."

"What about Rebecca? She probably wouldn't get her hands dirty. We could dive deeper into her finances and look for a payoff. And if the diamond operation is ongoing, where's the money now?"

Frankie's laughter is loose and easy. "You need them all in one room after I'm dead. They'll talk then. Probably brag. When there's nothing to lose."

She speaks casually and conclusively about her own death. I'm not ready for that. "They did this to you." I stumble over my words. I feel my body trembling before I see my hand quiver.

"They did much worse to Cora."

"I hate this," I say.

Frankie smiles, and the smile travels deep into us both. Her eyes swim with tears. "Bethie says you're like me. That Richard calls you Lion." A deeper smile than the first. "And you are. Never in my wildest dreams did I imagine my daughter fighting for me the way you have. That's enough."

"I'm not done."

"Baby." She says *baby* the exact way Mom does. "You can't save me, and that's okay. Not even with all your grand diamond theories and your brilliant brain."

The guard racks his baton along the fencing and we jump. "Five minutes, Quick."

"No," I argue. "We need more time." I don't know how to spend these last minutes with her. Talking about the case or being with her? There are so many things I want to say. Things I'll never get to ask or do.

"Baby girl, it doesn't matter now. It's over and I'm at peace."

An idea hits. Wild and crazy. And it might not work, but it'll matter to *Death Daze* and I'll have something to remember her. "I need you to do me a favor," I say. When I explain, she tells me I'm clutching at straws; when we're done shooting the video I'll edit later, she makes me promise I'll be safe.

"You owe me a favor too," she says.

"Anything."

"I don't want you there when they . . ." She mimes placing a needle into her arm. Her voice trails off. "Remember me here. This." She scoots toward me again. Close enough I'm scared they will shoot her in front of me. The guard

337

yells from the tower; the other storms toward us with his baton. Time slows down. I start screaming.

"She's my mom! She's my mom!"

The baton is raised and I cover Frankie's body with mine, crying out, "Don't shoot! She's my mom. She's my mom," and praying they won't risk hurting me to get to her. Frankie is beneath me, sobbing into my chest.

The shot doesn't come.

The baton doesn't either.

When I check over my shoulder, the guard is standing in the sight line of the gun and waving off his partner in the tower. "I didn't know, kid," he says.

"I'm going to help her up and hug her," I say.

He gives a fast upward nod that says I should act before he changes his mind.

I fall into her. "I love you."

Her chains come around me, with their rattles and clinks, and her heartbeat, hard as a drummer banging his sticks against my chest. "I love you too, baby," she says.

I am imprisoned.

One of the things I love about love is you don't have to be perfect for it to exist. Frankie is a human I love automatically. Innate love. I feel close to a God I barely know, because you can't have all these feelings without understanding they're bigger than you; they're bigger than the entire universe.

Off in the distance, the crowd chants, "Free Frankie! Free Frankie!" and I find myself whispering the same words as a prayer.

338

PART III

PART III

CHAPTER 55

The guard peels Frankie away.

My grief is undignified and sloppy. I love someone I don't really know, and it occurs to me that Frankie has felt this way my whole life. My love for her is new; what I'm receiving is old. Older than my breath, the very age of my heartbeat. Which means she's hurting now, even more than I am. I hurt for my hurt and hers and all the hurts to come.

But I stand and I wave as she's guided back inside. She walks backward between the guards, drinking me in, waving like a kindergartener waves at a parent on the first day of school. She smiles bravely, for me, and then she's gone.

I am left with a video and wounds of injustice.

Back in the car, I am all tears and no talk. "Get me out of here," I plead to Sam. Before we reach Floyd's outer gate, a guard steps into the road and puts up his hand. We have no choice but to stop. Here, this close to the protesters, it's hard to think, much less have a conversation.

The guard yells, "Turn right out of here. Take the back way to the interstate. Longer, but it'll keep you away from the crazies."

"Thank you," I say.

He gives a formal nod and an empathetic sigh. Sam takes his suggestion, and after a mile we're able to roll down the windows and hear tires on the asphalt and wind rattling the trash in the back seat. The air smells fresh and I gulp it down in heaps. Sam holds my hand and then my leg when I wipe the tears away and tell him everything. He's floored about Richard and as intrigued as I am about my idea to show Frankie's video at the family dinner.

"Do you think it would work?" I ask. "Showing them?"

He's not sure. "I don't like you going in there and goading a killer. You need protection."

"No one can protect me for sure."

"What if I record it?" he asks.

"The Kings will never talk if I'm recording them."

"No," Sam says. "What if they don't know they are being filmed? I'll film it with my phone. You'll have yours there, always visible, and they won't think a thing about it."

I laugh him off.

"Stop," Sam says. "I'm serious. Dad has a key. I can get into Cassandra's."

"Yeah, and Cassandra probably has alarms out the wazoo."

"I'll sneak in tonight before Anna leaves and sets the alarm."

"And what? Stay hidden until tomorrow for a dinner that Cassandra might cancel? No way. What about food? What if you have to pee?"

He lifts an empty bottle from the cupholder. "I'll make do."

"Ugh."

"Come on. I need the night to prep a hiding place in the dining room and I'll sleep in a closet."

"Sam. I hate this idea."

"Lion, this is our best choice to save Frankie. You said it yourself. There is no evidence that exonerates her. We can follow the money, but not fast enough for a retrial. The only hope we have is a confession. Let's put the guilty parties in a room, amp them up, show them Frankie's video, and get them to spill their guts."

"The video isn't very convincing. We didn't have much time to get the point across."

"Send it to me and I'll take care of that."

"I thought you were breaking into Cassandra's tonight."

He grins. "I'm a multitasker, *and* I know who to ask for help."

CHAPTER 56

I dress for dinner—fitted silk tank top under an off-white baggy crocheted summer sweater that falls off my shoulders and wide-leg yellow jeans. They're a style I never wear and only brought because Mom packed them in her suitcase for me. I was supposed to wear this outfit to a graduation party that never happened and she's determined to see me in it once. Since Cassandra's the type who will appreciate the extra effort, it's the right time to please them both.

Mom whistles at me. "I love when you wear your hair down."

"You've mentioned that a time or two," I tease. She doesn't look bad herself in a fitted blue dress and Michelle Obama arms, totally fierce, totally beautiful. There's a mirror hanging on the back of the door. One of those skinny, flattering kinds that takes off ten pounds. In tandem, we half spin to smooth the fabric on our backsides. The sameness of the motion snags my heart. A fast jerk, like a baby tooth coming out.

"You should wear your ring." She's already across the room and digging in her suitcase for her own earrings. I am forced to come clean and tell her how and why I broke the ring. "Ned's working on it," I say. "I'll give it back when he's done."

She exchanges her hoops for the diamond studs. "Daddy gave me the set before I left Nockabout," she says. "He had these and another piece for Mom made out of a bracelet he gave Cora. After she died, he said we should have something to remember her by and thought diamonds were the most appropriate."

I'm sure he did. I keep that thought to myself.

I check my phone. Nothing from Sam.

Not wanting to waste phone battery or risk a vibration during daylight hours, we've limited our texts. Last night he let me know he was settled in the closet, had succeeded in making a camera-size hole in the wall, and his friend had Frankie's video and would send it to me to play for the family. Other than an "Okay" text at noon, I haven't heard a peep.

That's good and nerve-wracking. I try not to think about what happens if Cassandra discovers his hiding place or the seed of our plan, not to mention the danger we're in when tonight's conversation gets out of hand. The livestream is my only ammunition: I'm banking that whoever killed Cora isn't dumb enough to hurt anyone else once I tell them their confession has been broadcasted to the world and that her killer is in the room tonight. If not, someone's getting away with murder. And I'll be slayed online. I can't make an accusation without receipts. Especially not against a family that has a trajectory toward the White House.

Pretty much by the time tonight is over, I'll be canceled and labeled an entitled brat who preyed on a grieving family in exchange for YouTube fame or I'll be a hero or I'll be dead.

Richard comes out of the bathroom wearing the ankle holster he bought in Lexington. The bulge is ridiculous and he's no longer stepping like a normal human being. "No," I say immediately. "If I can see your gun, so can everyone else. We're having family dinner, not meeting with the mob."

"It goes," he says.

"Well, put it somewhere else."

I can't have him escalating Creed or the night will get messy in the wrong direction.

I want to tell Richard that I understand the gun and why he scrolls through baby pictures and that I'm sorry he lost his daughter. I don't. We're already late to being fifteen minutes early.

"You're carrying a purse," he says, eyebrows up.

I want his mind off the purse. I say, "You want me to take the gun?"

He laughs and moves the gun from his ankle to the back of his pants. Not much of an improvement, but you don't spot the pistol when you glance.

We walk the stone path between the pool house and Cassandra's cathedral with our eyes on the horizon. The sinking sun lays a pinkish-orange glaze on Nockabout and Lone Valley. There's a doubling of the sky and shoreline on the surface of Green River Lake; the reflection of rocks and pines glimmers with impressionistic imitation. Monet would never run out of things to paint if he were to sit on Granny's balcony at sunset.

Anna greets us at the front door. A waft of yeast, oregano, and garlic knocks us over. Mom's nose is up, eyes closed with delight. "Mmm. Is that Granny's bread?" Anna grins and nods. She's dressed in black-and-white service attire and there's a small smudge of flour on her collar. Before she escorts us forward, she removes a folded check from the interior of her coat pocket.

"The second half. As Cassandra promised," Anna says.

Mom is taken slightly aback. "Is Granny done with me?" she asks.

Anna checks the hallway behind us, her face sallow, her whisper bleak. "She's afraid she'll forget. Tonight will be hard."

You have no idea.

"They're in the formal dining room," she says. "Excuse me while I pull the bread out of the oven."

She hustles away and I experience a brief moment of panic. Are there two dining rooms? Is Sam in the right one? Will he risk texting me to confirm? No matter, Ned waits at the entrance with a woven basket extended. "Phones," he says, leaning in my direction, smelling of cigarette smoke and mouthwash. Mom, Richard, and I add our cells, each with our own eyeroll over this new policy the Kings have adopted. Four of the five attendees have already done the same. Who does that leave? Anna, maybe. Or Cassandra.

There are two potential doors for Sam to be behind. One over Cassandra's shoulder, the other to my immediate right. Either will give a wide perspective for the audience. The room is large, the ceilings high, the décor a minimalist mixture of antiques and modern art. The space is Cassandra to the hilt, consumed by a cherry table with service for eight and her welcoming presence. "There's the star of the evening," she calls to me. She's parked by the window, a position she likely chose for its view of the pool house pathway and easy access to the head of the table.

Creed's on her hip. At her greeting, he raises his wineglass, a triumphant look on his face, most likely regarding the phones. "No *Death Daze* tonight," he says, confirming my guess.

"No, sir." I lift empty hands into the air and acknowledge he has beaten me.

Rebecca is tucked into the opposite corner, nearest the entrance, and leeches immediately to Mom and Richard.

Anna arrives with a drink tray. I lift a water glass from her service and she gives me an encouraging nod; something in the *Don't back down* category. Knowing she's right, I force myself to cross the room and kiss Cassandra's cheek. Much like the first time we met, Cassandra's pale blue eyes capture me. I see pain in the irises, feel pain as she squeezes my hand. "You look marvelous, darling."

I deliver my line flawlessly, "Not as marvelous as you," and am rewarded with a wink.

Creed and Rebecca watch our exchange with confusion. Cassandra's affinity for me doesn't jive for them. Even Ned seems shocked that the girl behind an exposé on the King family could win over its matriarch. I have a feeling Cassandra likes me in spite of herself, or Anna has worked miracles that I'm likely to undo in the next five minutes. Either way, I'm grateful for the favor and I intend to use it.

When we're three sips into awkward small talk, I clink my glass with a fork from the table. Seven heads turn in my direction. I flush with embarrassment. "I've always wanted to do that," I say, hoping Sam heard our agreed-upon cue and has started the stream.

"I have the perfect toast." I offer my water goblet to Mom and remove the velvet bag Sam retrieved from the barn just hours ago and flash it around. There's a spark of recognition from Creed and Cassandra, while Ned, Anna, and Rebecca hold an unreadable expression.

The electricity in the air sends Mom and Richard closer to me. I lift one of the larger stones out of the bag toward Ned. "Make sure it's real," I say, but he's already gawking and nodding.

I take my glass back and raise it high. "Let's toast to the King family fortune."

No one lifts a glass.

The sheer lack of reaction from the elder Kings speaks volumes. Maybe they're all in on this together, like a *Murder on the Orient Express* type thing. That would be far more dangerous than I previously imagined. Mom is staring at the basket of phones on the credenza, subconsciously asking the question for the room at large—*Is this rigged?*

I smile. "Nope, Mom. Just us Kings," I say. "Let's sit for this one."

Cassandra rolls toward the table and assumes the head, and everyone else moves in sequence. I'm opposite Cassandra. Rebecca, Richard, and Mom take seats on my right; Anna, Ned, and Creed the left. When they're settled and silent, Cassandra sweeps a hand over the table. "Lion, I believe you have our full attention."

"We'll get to the diamonds in a minute. Let's start with who at this table knew Cora attacked Martin Jarvis, not Frankie."

There's a sharp intake of breath from Anna. I'll take that as a no from her. Cassandra pats the young woman's hand in a consoling way. Anna must have loved Cora, given how she has laid her forehead against the table and started to cry.

Rebecca's expression remains unreadable.

Creed says, "Water under the bridge, Nancy Drew," which makes Anna stare daggers.

"Thank you, Junior," I say, trying to stay on top.

Mom flinches at my defiance and Anna clenches her

fist. *At least I have one ally in the room*, I think before I say, "Okay, next question. Who at this table knew Cora stole these diamonds"—I give a flourish toward the bag, heart pounding—"from Martin, who stole them from the King family business? I mean, someone has been missing these babies for a long time."

Rebecca slides her chair away from the table and knocks into the wall, making the paintings dance on their nails. She's looking incredulous. "There's no *family* business involving those."

One point of innocence in her column.

"Where did you find that?" Creed asks, ignoring his wife's reaction to stare at his daughter. "Did you leave because . . ." The question fades.

I don't know what to make of that.

"Careful, Lion," Cassandra says to me before her son can say anything else.

Richard is inching forward on his chair with his hands behind his back, no doubt reaching for his gun. I glare at him, hoping he won't amp this up. He returns both hands to the tabletop.

I ask Ned, "What's a diamond like that worth?"

"Hundred thousand."

I reach forward and rattle the bag. Let them digest the dollars clanking against each other.

"Next question is a biggie," I say. "Who at this table killed Cora and Martin for taking these diamonds? Because we all know it wasn't Francis Quick." I land on Creed and stare through him. It takes everything in my power to keep my knees from knocking against the table. "Junior? Was it you?" I ask to gauge how the room reacts.

Creed throws his napkin. "She was my daughter."

I suspect this part will have Richard reaching for his gun, but I proceed. "No, Cora was Richard's daughter, which is probably why Granny hates"—I turn to Rebecca with a stone-cold face—"you, Senator, or are you already going by Ms. Vice President now?" I leave a pause for the room to catch up and then say, "If you're going to have an affair on a King, at least make sure you don't get pregnant." I wink at Cassandra, knowing it's a risk to walk this line.

Cassandra hides a grin with her napkin after she takes a drink. But even through the fabric I see she's pleased as punch that I understand what it means to be a King.

Creed falls into his chair. His face is the color of the cherries in his old-fashioned. He's staring at his wife in bewilderment, and then Richard, and then his wife again. If he knew, he fakes horror and contempt better than most. And now there's a point of innocence in his column.

"You didn't tell him." I reach across our corner and pat the arm of Rebecca's empty chair. She's backed against the wall, breathing like she might have another baby any minute. I say to her, in a very nonconsoling way, "Like he didn't tell you that when the Center didn't have patients, he made some. Nothing like a little human trafficking to keep his family afloat."

She lurches forward and bangs both hands against the

table. Water spills out of her glass. "Creed. You promised every dollar was clean."

I add to the dogpile. "Did you tell her every dollar is gone? That the family is broke?"

From the head of the table, Cassandra speaks. "You're good, Lion, but you got that one wrong."

"Granny." I show her my sympathy. "They're waiting on you to die to sell off your assets. Right, Anna? Ned? I'm guessing you're the one who doctors the financials and that you provide that and other services for Creed and he lets your mom stay at the Center for a reduced rate."

Ned wants to bolt from the room. Anna too. I need them to stay, and I'm not sure how to keep them here. Lucky for me, Cassandra has their rapt attention. She is butter and bread and knife to them. She slides her hand off the table and into her lap. Composed and controlled. Her anger is polite as it lands on Anna and then Ned—their betrayal of paperwork and numbers won't be forgiven. The hatred she levels at Creed is anything but polite.

"Mom?" Creed says defensively.

I laugh. "Don't 'Mom' her. You spent every penny in the pot on the Center, believing all those hammers in the caves would cover your butt. Then Cora took your diamond stash and you got behind and scared and threatened Martin. When he didn't get them back, you either went after them yourself or you had someone get their hands bloody." From across the room, Anna gives an audible sob, but I keep going. "Trouble was, that meant investigators were all over the island looking for Cora and you had to shut down your operation for, what, a year? Two? Five? Longer if your lovely, ambitious wife hadn't gotten on the Frankie bandwagon."

Creed's laugh is sharp and short. "You're crazy. I don't even know what you're talking about."

"Ned, tell on him," I coax. "Look at all those diamonds. They'll more than cover your mother's treatment somewhere else."

Ned is stoic and yet the planes of his face reveal a man I've never seen before. Or maybe I have. Except under a balaclava at the pool house window in the middle of the night.

Creed asks, "Mother, what do we do with these diamonds?"

"We?" Cassandra asks.

"Good question, Cassandra. I'd check your bank account before I'd go into business with your son."

"Get the paperwork," Cassandra orders Anna.

"Mother!" Creed says, pleading for her to ignore me.

"Not the paperwork," I suggest. "The online accounts."

"Anna, do what she says."

Anna is visibly shaking. "Martin?" she mouths to her boss. Cassandra's eyes bulge. "Not. Now," she tells Anna, a single finger waved in warning that sends Anna running into the next room for her laptop. For a brief moment Anna stands beside me, deciding which path to take to Cassandra: the left, Ned and Creed, or the right, Rebecca, Richard, and Mom. She takes the right, lays the laptop on the table's corner, and we wait for Cassandra to see the numbers.

Creed must know what she'll see, but he makes no move to leave. I hope I'm right. If I am, I won't even have to play Frankie's video for them. They'll all eat each other.

Cassandra lifts bifocals from the chain on her neck to the end of her nose and stares at the screen. She bangs her pearls against her chair and we all jump. "Creed." She's livid. "What have you done with my money?"

Creed looks to his wife. "Tell her what we've done with the family money, darling."

Rebecca recognizes she's being played. I see her summon control and then smile. "We're done with dinner, *darling*. No one else is saying a word. We're leaving."

Ned looks relieved for a path forward and jumps up to offers his arm to Rebecca, the way he would his own mother. Creed sees the wisdom in her suggestion and smooths the front of his shirt. Cassandra says, "Don't you dare."

Creed laughs. "Or what? You'll cut me off?" He laughs again. "If you're out of money, you're out of power, Mother."

It's Cassandra's turn to laugh. She gestures to the velvet bag on the table. "I have the diamonds."

Creed looks gut punched and then says, "And I have Ned on my side. The man who turns rocks into money. Right, Ned? You like your mother's standard of care, right?"

Creed stands triumphantly.

My stomach drops. They're going to leave and I don't have any answers.

The basket on the buffet rattles and rings. Eight heads turn. Eyes narrow.

Cassandra slips a phone from her pocket. A perk of being the homeowner who did not have to surrender her cell to the basket.

Anna is closest to the basket and retrieves her phone first.

Anna gasps and braces her body against her chair.

"Anna, what is it?" I ask slowly as I make my way to my own phone.

"It's from Ben." There's no color left in her face. "Francis Quick was just murdered at Floyd by another inmate."

CHAPTER 57

My mother screams. And then something I can't explain or couldn't have expected happens: Rebecca screams too. All around the room, phones are gathered and the link Ben sent is clicked on. We absorb the headline in a collective fog.

FRANCIS QUICK MURDERED TWENTY DAYS BEFORE ADPA EXECUTION.

My mother is sobbing and it breaks me. Her mother and Richard hover, trying to console her. Mom pushes away from Rebecca. "Don't comfort me now. You got her killed. You did this."

"I didn't," Rebecca says.

"I doubt your constituents will agree." I'm crying too.

I say, "It's not like it matters now. She's dead. You won. Whoever you are, you got away with murder." I hope we've come to the moment of the true confession.

Rebecca turns, not to Creed, but to Ned. "Was it you who got paid to do it? Did you kill our daughter?" She reaches for Richard's back, for comfort, to show him allegiance, and discovers his gun. I alone see her face light with hope. Without warning, and with the practiced gunmanship of someone who has an annual shooting competition, she levels the gun at Ned's face. "Nyla's right. Doesn't matter anymore. Tell me if you killed my daughter."

Ned is frozen against the wall. Urine spreads across his crotch, down his pant leg. "I loved Cora," he says and points at Creed.

Creed, a good Kentucky boy, carries a Glock and shows he's as adept as his wife with a gun. He fires his Glock through the closet door as a warning that silences the room. Terror rips up my spine and tears spring out. Sam could be behind that door. I take a deep breath and pray, *Oh God, Sam, please protect Sam. Protect us all.*

All eyes on Creed, he takes aim at his wife. "If anyone did this to Cora, it was you. You're the one who brought Martin into your program. You're the one who got Cora tied up in the family business." He uses air quotes and glances over his shoulder in his mother's direction and then back to his wife. "Oh, and you slept with Richard. We almost lost the Center because of him. And why did I stay all these years? Because you promised me the White House. You promised we wouldn't rely on her money anymore." He jabs in Cassandra's direction.

Rebecca takes the gun off Ned and shifts to Creed.

There is no way to step between the couple. The table is too wide. I stretch my hands in either direction, hoping to calm the wave of approaching violence. "Easy," I say.

I am a mouse squeaking at tigers.

"Your precious Center. That's all that's ever mattered to you. What did you do, Creed? Tell me about the diamonds on the table. Tell me you didn't get my daughter killed to save your addicts."

"My father was an addict, witch." Creed's writhing with anger, his trigger finger dancing dangerously close to a lethal solution. "And you . . . you never loved me. Never understood the Center." Snot falls from his nose and coats his lip. "We are the hope people need. Doctors. Not cheating politicians."

Creed is way off any script I would have guessed. He hasn't so much as glanced at the velvet bag. Instead, he has a gun on his wife and her former lover, like their affair is the true injury to the King family. I'm a little stunned. Whoever ran this operation cares about money. But if it wasn't him, that leaves Rebecca, and Rebecca didn't kill her daughter. She seems to be catching that thread at the same time as me; she's jockeying between Creed and Ned, thinking.

Ned must be the one behind this. He's the only one capable.

The jeweler shakes violently and does his best to inch

toward the hallway. He's thinking about running. If he does, Rebecca might shoot him in the back.

I hold my rage in the palm of my hand. In this room is the person who chose to take twenty years of freedom from my mother. It takes everything I have to stay focused and calm enough to think. "Ned, who paid you to kill Cora and Martin?"

"No," Ned says.

Creed glances at his mother, no doubt awaiting rescue, and Cassandra seems wholly unconcerned that her son has her daughter-in-law at gunpoint. You can see her thinking, *Maybe they'll all shoot each other and we can put this behind us.*

Anna, who has been bawling into her place setting, says to Ned, "You wouldn't kill Martin. You just wouldn't. We . . . You told me this would go away, that if we laid low, we'd be set. And all that time . . . you're the one who killed Martin."

That's a turn.

Cassandra says, "You'd be surprised what people will do for money. Now, please, Anna, fetch my diamonds and show our guests to the door before they get blood on my Persian rug. Except for Nyla. She can stay. She's the only real King left of use to me."

What will she say when I tell her I'm not a King and never was?

Anna's almost to Cassandra, diamonds retrieved, the handoff inevitable, when she hisses, "Did you call the hit on Cora and Martin? Was it you, or did Ned play us all?"

"My diamonds," Cassandra says again, exasperated, the way she might say, "The rolls," or "The carrots."

"Your diamonds," Anna repeats. All traces of the gentle caregiver are gone. She pockets the velvet bag on the table and snatches Cassandra's perfectly permed hair in her fist. Her lips are against Cassandra's ear. "You haven't been in the mines in years. Ned and I do all the work. And for what? The vein's dry, Cassandra. You hear me? There are no more diamonds down there and there haven't been any in the last five years. Right, Ned?"

Oh my gosh. The five-thousand-dollar checks that Cassandra wrote. One to Ben for a bonus. Another to Mom for coming home. And . . . one to Martin to kill her granddaughter? Maybe so. Tatti was her dog. That was the name of the account that paid Martin Jarvis. Maybe Creed wasn't lying to Rebecca about employing Martin for more than odd jobs; he didn't. Cassandra did.

The vein in Cassandra's neck strains as she lifts upward in her chair, trying to alleviate the pressure of Anna tearing out her hair. Anna's screaming, "We traffic for you! We mine for you! We throw bricks for you! Threaten people . . . We even kill for you. For what? The family experience? Health care? A promise to leave it all to us? You're going to tell me right now, did my brother kill himself, or was that you?"

Brother. Anna's brother is Martin Jarvis. That blended family Richard talked about. *Little Anna Gapper* found a way to fight back

Cassandra looks like she's seconds away from a heart attack. I need to back them down, lower all the guns in the room. "Cora came to you, didn't she, Cassandra? She told you about the diamonds, not realizing you and Creed have the same initials. The bag was yours, not his. Cora told you what happened with Martin. That she knew about the girls in the mine. And she wasn't going to stop until she found them. So you decided to cut your losses. Clean things up and lay low. You couldn't kill Ned; he's your diamond man. Far too valuable. But Martin was a loose cannon, and you had another young soul primed to take his place in a few years. Right, Anna? Cassandra, what did you pay Ned? Five thousand dollars for Martin and another five for Cora? That's your going rate for payoffs, right?"

Anna is speechless. She clenches Cassandra's hair tighter as she tries to catch her breath. "Is that right? Did Ned kill Martin?"

Mom cuts her off, staring at her father. "Did you pay Ned to kill Cora?" The grief is palpable, searing.

Creed lifts his non–gun hand in an *It wasn't me* gesture. "I turned down participating in this whole trafficking thing years ago. I was convinced the stress got Dad hooked on drugs; I wasn't about to go down that path."

Rebecca is horrified. "But you knew your mother was kidnapping girls and you were okay with it?"

Creed says, "Somewhere in your little Ivy League head you had to know Mother's money wasn't clean—the mine shut down in the fifties, Rebecca—but you just kept spending. Pulling all your little darlings through the grand Leap program. Anna, this is who you should be pissed at right here. Our great senator is the one who introduced your brother to the infamous Cassandra King."

Anna's eyes are crazy, but her hand doesn't shake as she lifts her own gun and clicks off the safety. "Who. Is. Responsible. For. Martin's. Death?"

Cassandra has had enough hair pulling and childish behavior. All this gun pulling doesn't faze her. "Oh, for crying out loud, Ned, tell all these people what they want to hear," she says. "No one will know. Frankie's dead. Let those three tear each other apart in the press or kill them, I don't care"—she thumbs toward Rebecca, Creed, and Richard— "and the rest of us can set about refilling the coffers. They'll all be yours and Ned's," she says to Anna. "I'll bet if you get the Lion going, she'll make more money for this family than all of us combined. Ned, tell Anna you're sorry for killing her brother and we'll all make nice and rich."

Ned doesn't get a chance to confess. Anna fires four shots in rapid succession.

Cassandra first. Her head is right there and then gone. Then Ned.

Creed drops his own gun before he staggers backward and crashes into the buffet.

Rebecca has time to lift her hands up and utter a single syllable before Anna hits her in the chest with the .45.

It happens fast.

The fifth shot takes a beat longer. The gun she fires

through her own chin drops her tiny body before Ned's husky frame topples onto me and tackles us both to the ground. Blood spreads over his chest and drips through the holes in my sweater. The last breath he takes is gargled Spanish. *"No muerta."*

He's wrong again. He's very, very dead.

CHAPTER 58

My name is being screamed.

By Sam. By Mom.

Richard hauls Ned off me like he's a rag doll. "Lion," he says, practically standing me up by my shirt.

"I'm okay. I'm okay," I say.

With me safely in Mom's arms, Richard kneels over Rebecca's body and cradles her neck as he feels for a pulse. Her pink shirt is soaked through. "Becky, sweetie." Her eyes are closed. Richard looks up at Sam. "What do we do?" he asks.

Mom sweeps the room. "Are they all dea—" She can't finish.

All the Kings are on the floor. What's left of Anna's face is spread up the wall and ceiling. The tiny diamond she wore around her neck dangles in her blood. At my feet, Ned's draining into the threads of the Persian rug.

"No one will believe this," Mom says.

She's going to faint from the horror. I slide my own wobbling arm around her waist to steady her and find I'm not any more stable. The blood. There's so much blood.

Sam says, "They will. It was all live." He holds up his phone for her to see. *"Death Daze* saw it all. The police are on their way."

Mom lets herself break. It isn't her father's, mother's, or grandmother's name she howls; it's Frankie's. "I can't. I can't. I can't breathe." She's ripping at her shirt, clutching her chest. Hyperventilating.

"Mom. Mom. Look at me." She can't focus. Both eyes glass over. I take her chin in my hand and apply pressure until she is cognizant and tracking. "Frankie's okay."

"No. No. The headline." Her breathing is erratic.

"Mom, we faked it. Frankie laid down on the ground and I shot a video of her, and then Sam fixed the footage to look convincing." It was a smart play to send it from Ben. Far more believable that he would text them all. "I'm sorry I couldn't tell you."

"Frankie's alive?"

I nod.

And then Sam says exactly what I'm afraid of. "Ny, we didn't get a confession. Anna killed Ned before he said he did it. It might not be enough to save her."

All this death.

My poor mothers.

CHAPTER 59

T he police come and do what police do. We're questioned
at the scene, but it's more a debriefing since the whole
thing was live. They find my mother's repaired sapphire
and diamond ring in Ned's pocket. Neither of us claims it
or even admit we recognize the heirloom.

Sam stands by me the entire time. I know he feels
responsible for not getting a confession. Which is crazy. I'm
the one who failed Frankie. Thanks to me, my mother has
to bury her entire family and go through Frankie's death
twice. I can't quit crying. They should all hate me.

"We'll need to bag your clothes as evidence, ma'am."

I don't even hear the officer's request. "I'll take care of
it, Stan," Sam says. He leads me out of Cassandra's cathedral to the pool house, chooses jeans and a T-shirt, and puts
me in the shower. "Hand your clothes out to me," he says,
then, "I'll be right back."

"Sam, don't leave." I don't want to be alone.

"Okay," he says from the other side of the curtain. "I'll stay right here. You take as long as you need."

I strip. The blood on the yellow pants looks almost purple. The white yarn of my sweater is crimson. Ned's blood. Although it feels like the room itself bled all over me. The crime that began twenty years ago is far more than one drop of blood in a Camaro now.

It's Cora. Martin. Houdini. Ned. The Kings. Anna. Frankie's to come.

And there might be more. The search for the girls in the mines begins tonight. Houdini might have been the last of them, but we have to know for sure.

"Not dead." I repeat Ned's final words. The audacity.

I wonder what his father thinks of him now. I slide along the wall of the tub until I'm sitting on my feet in the scalding water.

"You okay?" Sam asks.

"No."

"What do you need?"

"Them not to be dead. Her not to die for something she didn't do." I reach my hand outside the curtain and paw for connection. He puts his jaw and chin in my hand. I feel his tears slide onto my fingers. "I'm sorry, Lion. I'm so sorry."

CHAPTER 60

annie, Sam, and Ben come with us to Elizabethtown. They book adjoining rooms. Mom and I take the middle room; Sam and Ben are to the right, Richard and Mannie to the left. Our reservations run through Saturday. Frankie is to be executed on Friday at 3:00 p.m. Eastern time.

There's no talk of where we will go after. Only an understanding that we will go together. No more running.

We see Frankie every day.

Whether it's the imminent timeline or the Floyd administration hopped to the "Free Frankie" side, her guards allow us long visits in the yard. During those hours, our potential love turns fully kinetic. Frankie and I have the same birthmark on our lower backs. We both pronounce *spider* "*spy*-der," and that makes Mom laugh so we say it frequently. Ben, Sam, Richard, and Mannie visit too. Ben brings the summer of '99 photo box. The adults laugh and tell us stupid stories.

The real gift is I have time to see myself in her *and* in Mom.

I made a high-enough grade in human biology to understand DNA and chromosomes. I took detailed notes on nurture versus nature to pass a quiz, but nothing I learned helped me understand why Mom and I spin on our heels rather than our toes if we're not related and why Frankie and I say "spy-der" identically even though we didn't grow up in the same house.

I guess you get all the chromosomes you're going to get in nine months, but the umbilical cord doesn't stop there. Eighteen years with Mom is its own transfer of DNA. I am more than hers; I am theirs.

We cry together when the mine operation is finally found. Ned and Anna's records indicated seventeen women, including Laylah Williams, were used as slave labor. Remarkably, fifteen women are found alive and are being treated at a hospital in Bowling Green. They were recovering meth addicts. The body tunnel gave them perfect access to come and go without being noticed. Ned by night, Anna in the afternoon. Only one of the seventeen is unaccounted for, a woman named Megan Rafferty.

Fifteen women identify Ned and Anna as captors and Frankie still isn't exonerated. There's global weight on the ADPA, the world is watching, the riots are increasing—on both sides—and no one acts.

Every day Frankie is dying and every day she is more alive.

The crowds surrounding Floyd cry louder now. The press tries to corner Mom and me once they discover our hotel. "What will you do with the money?" and "What will you do with the Center?" Those are questions we'll have to figure out—Mom is the final remaining King and therefore the heir—but unwinding everything else takes precedence over how she will give the money away.

In the fallout of the King family, the Center's reputation has been scrutinized by a federal team. Turns out, Creed had everything on the up-and-up and Ned paid for his mother and Ms. Rey's bills.

Houdini's death and paperwork were all fabricated by Ned, with Cassandra's help. Who better to understand the loopholes of the Center than the wife of the man who began it? From the surrounding evidence, the police tracked the jump drive video to Anna, and Cora's sweatshirt to Ned. Why Anna gave me Houdini's intake form and whether it was her or Ned who shot at Richard's house or killed Houdini, there's no way to know for sure. Both Ned and Anna had guns registered to their names and both appeared on the Center's cameras the night Houdini died.

The intake form gets me. Did Anna give me the intake form as a means of self-preservation—a means to tip my investigation in another direction? I don't know. There's plenty we don't know. And only so much we can assume. Whatever motives that bound Ned and Anna and

Cassandra into their twisted relationship were sinister and ruined lives.

Including mine.

All the money and fame in the world won't save Frankie.

On the day before the last day, she asks me about what happened in the dining room.

"I've watched it. You lived it. Now, what can I do to ease that trauma before I go?"

We speak of her execution in these terms. Go. Going. Never gone. Like she might end up in Bangladesh or Mozambique. I lie not five inches away from where we bled on the concrete the day we met, with my head in her lap. She braids my hair and I tell her the things that niggle, the things the camera couldn't catch.

Like the way each hair on Cassandra's scalp made a tiny hill when Anna pulled.

Mom's howl when she believed Frankie was dead.

The sound of diamonds clanking in a velvet bag.

The smell of bread burning in the kitchen.

Not knowing if the stray bullet Creed fired hit Sam.

My embarrassment when Ned wet himself.

Later, his weight taking me to the ground. The heat of his blood on my chest and face. The smoke in his collar.

"*No muerta,*" I repeat.

"What?"

I haven't told anyone of the nightmarish way Ned gurgled those words onto my face. That I rubbed my cheeks raw removing the blood of *"No muerta."*

372

"Oh, baby. That's awful." Frankie unbraids my hair and rakes her fingers like a brush along my scalp and down my shoulders. "He must have been telling Anna not to do what she did. He knew better than anyone she was losing it."

"I guess," I say and curl toward her stomach where I once lived. I'd crawl back inside her if I could and let them put the needle in our body.

CHAPTER 61

She'll be dead tomorrow. My mother.
I can't reconcile this.

Sam and I walk in circles around the motel, up one staircase and down the next, moving, always moving. I can't catch my breath. I tell Sam everything I told Frankie this afternoon. He says, "She's right. *Muerta* is the feminine."

Ned was a complicated man. Rejected by his father, the dentist. Beloved by his mother, the meth addict.

"I wonder who'll sing 'Peace Train' to his mother and Ms. Rey now that he's gone."

"It's funny. Well, not funny-funny. Funny-strange," he corrects and shrugs. "*Rey* is 'king' in Spanish. Everywhere he went he was surrounded by kings." Sam doesn't laugh so much as sigh at the irony.

"I'll bet the nurses on the fourth floor have their hands full." I'm thinking of Georgia, wondering if there's a strange moment at the end of her night shift when she heaps her own sugar into a Styrofoam cup and realizes her favorite barista was the freak who killed Houdini and no one thought much about it because he loved his mother.

Sam runs his hand along the railing. "How old is Ms. Rey? His mother's age?"

"Old, I think."

"There are loose ends everywhere," he says.

"Yeah, there's no way those women understand where Ned went or why no one brings them flowers. Hey, Sam?" I ask.

"Yeah."

"How's your mom?"

"Well, she hasn't gotten enough flowers from her son; that's for sure."

"We could fix that," I say. Before he can respond, I say, "Wanna go for a run?"

"I'd like that. Helps me breathe," he says.

"Me too."

We sprint, we walk, we hold our sides, then repeat. We go until we can barely lift the keycards to our rooms. This is how I will sleep, I think. In exhaustion. With my heart in a knot that will never untangle.

When it's almost daybreak, I slide out of bed and dress quietly. Mom's awake. I can tell by her cadence she's faking sleep. The screen glow burns my eyes in the dark room as I text Sam.

Nyla: Meet me outside if you're awake.

Sam: Putting on pants.

I have the Pilot running when Sam climbs in the passenger seat. "Where we going, Lion?"

"To Nockabout."

It's almost five. Frankie's last day starts at seven. I'll bet she didn't sleep either.

"You aren't going to Floyd?" he says.

"I promised her I wouldn't."

"What are we doing in Nockabout?" he asks.

I take the Camaro keys out of my pocket. "Switching cars." We're too tired to talk. The interstate is empty; the parkway's a desert. I want to be here and I don't know why. We pull into the ferry parking lot to a crowd. They're Death Dazers; they've lit candles along the dock and in the parking lot. Printed posters of Frankie bob up and down on the wooden poles. "Are you going to tell them who you are?" Sam asks.

"Nah. I'd rather be a daughter today," I say.

I've been live once since the dining room finale. Took my best jab at a rally cry to save Frankie. To no avail on the legal end, but as for the illegal, I'd lay money that one of the Death Dazers in this crowd spray-painted *Murderer* on the window of Ned's pawn shop.

"Who ends up with the shop? His dad?" I ask.

"Who knows?"

I'll bet his dad doesn't touch it with a ten-foot pole. Staring at the front window, I see the table where Sam and I sat on my first trip to Nockabout. I think about the man who brought me a Coke and dog sat for Sam. I hear him singing to his mother and Ms. Rey. I'm supposed to hate him, and sometimes I can get up the energy, but mostly I am sad. What's the opposite of the Midas touch? Whatever it was, Ned Damron had it. "I can't believe he killed Cora and Martin and Houdini and probably Megan Rafferty too."

"Me either. I've raked through every minute we spent together in the shop. He talked about Cora all the time and he never sounded guilty. Never talked like she was dead."

"Maybe he had to convince himself to live with what he did to her."

"I guess," Sam says. "You can't argue with evidence. Especially dental."

"Oh my gosh, Sam. He could."

"He could what?"

"Argue with dental evidence."

"I don't follow." My wheels turn fast. "Nyla, the car's rolling." I barely hear Sam.

"Ms. Rey," I say. Sam places his hand on top of mine and manually moves us to Park. "You said *Rey* is 'king' in Spanish." Something's ticking like a bomb. *"No muerta,"* I repeat.

"She's not dead," Sam translates.

"Sam, he didn't kill her. He killed Megan Rafferty and swapped the dental records in his father's files. Ms. Rey is Cora King. He visits her every day to re-drug her."

"No way."

"Call the Center. If I'm right, we can save her."

CHAPTER 62

I t takes more than a call to the Center. We reach out
to the governor's office and it takes an hour for him to
return my call. I explain my theory and out of the goodness
of his heart, or his guilt regarding the ADPA, he requests
Hope Rey's chart. His team compares her fingerprints to
the prints of Cora King lifted twenty years ago from her
bedside table.

A match.

Another hour.

Sam has to physically hold me to keep me from going
crazy while the DA subpoenas Dr. Damron's records. Dr.
Damron, the only dentist in the county. He was the Kings'
dentist—he was everyone's dentist. It takes another hour
to confirm Megan Rafferty's records were swapped with
Cora King's.

It's 1:00 Central time, 2:00 Eastern, when my phone

rings. The governor says, "We've got proof Hope Rey is Cora King. Midnight hour, kid. Frankie's already started her last meal."

The governor lets me stay on the phone while he calls Floyd Penitentiary and formally stays the execution of Francis Quick. We hear cheers from the guards and I swear the warden says, "Amen," under his breath before he says, "You wanna tell her?"

The governor says, "I've got someone here who will."

Thirty seconds later, Frankie's on the line with us.

"Mom," I say. "You're free."

ENDING

The complete exoneration and paperwork takes three days.

A crowd is gathered outside Floyd Penitentiary. They do not scream or shout. They sing a hymn I don't recognize. Sam says it's a contemporary chorus for "Amazing Grace." That works; this day is a grace.

My mother stands next to the governor on a raised platform. They're joined by Frankie, pushing my aunt, Cora King, in a wheelchair. *No muerta*, I think as Frankie raises their fists in triumph. She's wearing ripped jeans and her prison shirt, which she strips off to reveal a *Death Daze* T-shirt. She throws the orange V-neck into the crowd and they go nuts. I laugh; I bet her ten dollars she wouldn't throw the shirt. She smiles at me, and I point and snap at her like she's a rock star.

The governor calms the crowd and places a microphone

in Cora's hand. This is her first appearance, her first public statement, and she's shaking too violently to hold the notecards with her speech. Her sister kneels. Working with Beth, Cora finds the courage to speak.

"My name is Cora King. Ned Damron held me captive in a cave for ten months and forced meth into my veins until I lost all sense of reality." She reads like this is another woman's story. I have to remind myself it's not.

"When I was hooked and unrecognizable, Ned checked me into my father's clinic under the name Hope Rey and kept me sedated for nineteen years on drugs he stole from his father. The victory of Frankie's innocence belongs to me too. We are both free."

Cora's voice dissolves. Unable to go on, she passes the microphone and paper to Mom.

With a clear voice, Mom reads, "I speak today for the seventeen women Ned Damron and Anna Gapper enslaved in a diamond mine and also for those struggling with addictions. I am one of you, and we will work together to create a new reality. I cannot repay what has been taken from us all, but I can honor what has been stolen. My niece, Nyla King, co-creator of the *Death Daze* YouTube channel, has donated her earnings to fund the Rafferty Williams Methamphetamine Recovery Fund. Nyla, thank you for making this dream possible by believing in forgotten voices. You set us all free. And thank you to everyone here and online for your support."

Mom folds the paper and returns it to Cora's hand. Cora

rolls backward and the sea behind me erupts. They are an earthquake of jubilance.

Tears fall. We could use buckets to catch them.

No one on the platform speaks and the singing starts again.

Finally, the governor steps forward. After the catcalls, hoots, and whistles, a wave of silence works itself row by row to the back. He announces to the media and everyone present that Francis Quick has been pardoned of all crimes and will be paid restitution for what she has lost—as if there is a precise amount that can be determined—and he and all Kentuckians are here to welcome Francis Quick back to society.

He offers the stage to Frankie; she waves him off. I knew she would.

She's tired of the spotlight. Tired of the interviews. She wants to go home. She wants to play me in ping-pong and take me cliff jumping. She wants to stand in her father's fields and sprinkle whacks of sugar over strawberries and shell pecans in the fall. She's insisting I teach her how to use her new cell phone and pick a new hairstyle. She wants to take Sam and me out for a real dinner and then snuggle on a couch with my mother. She wants to help Cora recover and for the four of us to watch the entirety of John Hughes's films, starting with *Ferris Bueller*. These are her plans. These, and a thousand more.

But today it'll be me and her in a yellow Camaro, with the windows down, the radio on, totally free. Not Kings, queens.

"Tense and haunting, *The June Boys* is not only a terrifying story of the missing, but a heartbreaking, hopeful journey through the darkness. Beautifully written and sharply plotted, this is a story that lingers long after you turn the final page."
—MEGAN MIRANDA, *NEW YORK TIMES* BESTSELLING AUTHOR

Available in print, e-book, and audio!

THOMAS NELSON
Since 1798

ACKNOWLEDGMENTS

We *Were Kings* came to life during the Covid-19 pandemic. What a strange and difficult time to create; there was so much to do in my day job as an outreach librarian and so little interaction with my creative writing family. With that said, I want to begin by thanking my editor, Becky Monds. Every time I said, "I'm behind," or "I'm discouraged," she came back with waves of encouragement and love. Everyone at HarperCollins Christian has my deep appreciation for the grace and support they showed during *We Were Kings*. Amanda Bostic, Jodi Hughes, Julie Breihan, KP, and the entire sales and marketing force: thank you all so much.

Kelly Sonnack, my rock of an agent, thank you for lending your wisdom to my career and projects; for supporting me when I'm up and down; for helping me forge a path that is suited to me. I love working with you.

Parnassus Books, Sarah Arnold, Rae Ann Parker,

teachers, librarians, booksellers—thank you for always supporting my work and me.

Special thanks to my coworkers at the Warren County Public Library. The entire managerial team came to my rescue—sending me home to write and covering for me and continuing to see me as an author. Heaps and heaps of thanks to Lisa Rice, Jennifer Bailey, Veronica Rainwater, Laura Beth Fox-Ezell, and Chris Jackson—I think you guys worried over *We Were Kings* like I did.

David Arnold and Ruta Sepetys—I couldn't publish a book without you. You're the ones who hear and see the mumbled, fumbled ideas through to the end with me. I love you both to the moon and back.

Goonies and Gnomies, you make me the luckiest friend in the world. To this wonderful bangarang framily, I love you all so much. Carla and Christa Lafontaine and the puppies—thank you for all the games of darts, new Chacos, cheffin' ribs, leading worship, and helping me look for Bigfoot. Leah Spurlin, you have the heart of a champion and are one of my greatest inspirations for hope. I am so glad we get to work together to love on our community. Katie and Matt, thank you for showing me how to love family in the fiercest of ways. Jeremy, Laura, and Louis—you are the pastors and friends I needed long before we actually met. I love you all.

Mom, Dad, and Matt—thank you for the prayers, love, reading time, gas money, and support. You are my backbone and I love you.

Emma Kate and Christopher—I love loving you and watching you grow into amazing people who love generosity, Jesus, politics, roller coasters, soccer, and all things made of sugar, caffeine, ketchup, and ramen.

G. Knight—you're my favorite lizard. Thank you for letting me do life with you and the chickens. Here's to a thousand more watermelons and a few less bowls in the dishwasher. Oh, and thank you for reading and making me sit at my desk and work. ☺

And as always, thanks for my readers. You will always be my better half.

DISCUSSION QUESTIONS

1. Talk about a time when you held an unpopular belief that cost you something socially, mentally, emotionally, and/or physically.
2. If or when someone else reveals a fact about you or a family member that you weren't previously privy to, how would (and should) you respond?
3. Sam has an unusual approach to making money. Is his business disrespectful or legitimate and why?
4. *Death Daze* is an instant success. How would you feel running a popular podcast or streaming service? What are the advantages/disadvantages?
5. Would you want to live on a small island like Nockabout? Why or why not?
6. Beth King did her best to put the past behind her. If you were Beth, how might you have responded to Cora's murder and the King family's feelings about Frankie? Would family money influence your decision?

7. There's paradox in the moral fiber of the adult characters in *We Were Kings*. Cassandra. Creed. Rebecca. Ned. Richard. Beth. Identify and discuss those paradoxes specific to each character.

8. What are pros and cons of an accelerated death penalty? Look at it from the side of the condemned, the government, the families of the victim, and the families of the condemned.

9. Is it ever okay to lie or "hide the truth" about who a biological parent is?

10. If you had a private room for shoe box memories like Ben, which boxes would be your favorite to visit/revisit?

ABOUT THE AUTHOR

Photo by Carla Lafontaine

C ourt Stevens grew up among rivers, cornfields, churches, and gossip in the small-town South. She is a former adjunct professor, youth minister, and Olympic torchbearer. These days she writes coming-of-truth fiction and is the community outreach manager for Warren County Public Library in Kentucky. She has a pet whale named Herman, a band saw named Rex, and several novels with her name on the spine: *Faking Normal*, *The Lies About Truth*, the e-novella *The Blue-Haired Boy*, *Dress Codes for Small Towns*, *Four Three Two One*, and *The June Boys*.

CourtneyCStevens.com
Instagram: @quartland
Facebook: @CourtneyCStevens
Twitter: @quartland